Reviews for the first two Milagro Mystery novels

THE QUALITY OF MERCY

WINNER OF THE 2016 LEAPFROG GLOBAL FICTION AWARD

"Tony Hillerman fans will welcome Medhat's excellent debut and series launch, a refreshing take on Navajo country's crime, culture and history..."
Publishers Weekly, starred review

"Move over Walt Longmire. Make room for Franz Kafka, aka 'K'... This book is a high-wire act and the author shines a bright, steady beam on the dark stage where clashing cultures meet."
Sara Pritchard, author of *Crackpots*

"In K, Medhat has created a unique character"
Durango Herald

"...a buddy novel, a work of history and collective and inter-generational trauma, a play with genre, from noir(...) to road movie...It deals with the pragmatics and compromises of daily living in a land that is far less than promised, its institutions deeply flawed. It is nevertheless a novel of kindness, depth and generosity, and it is under no illusions both to the best as well as the worst of what we can be."
European Journal of Psychotherapy & Counselling

LACANDON DREAMS

"*Lacandon Dreams* is a gem of a novel — one that engages the reader's brain, heart, and soul and establishes Katayoun Medhat as a rising star of the mystery genre. It's only a matter of time before her wonderful Franz Kafka/Robbie Begay novels fine the national audience they so richly deserve."
C. Joseph Greaves, author of *Church of the Graveyard Saints*

"Katayoun Medhat is the literary cousin of Tony and Ann Hillerman, her sleuths, Milagro's "K" and Diné (Navajo) Nation tribal police officer Robbie Begay the soul brothers of the Hillerman's Leaphorn and Chee. Steeped in the landscape of the Land of Enchantment with all its harsh beauty, cultural diversity, prejudices, history of exploitation, and present-day challenges, *Lacandon Dreams*, like *The Quality of Mercy*, is a literary page-turner. By the way, 'milagro' in Spanish means 'magic'. There's that, too, in Medhat's prose."
Sara Pritchard, author of *Help Wanted: Female*

"Try Katayoun Medhat. You might just be drawn to her prose like ferromagnetic metal to magnet."
Mark Stevens, author of The *Allison Coil Mystery* series

Flyover COUNTRY

A MILAGRO MYSTERY

KATAYOUN MEDHAT

Leapfrog Press
New York and London

Published in 2022 in the United States by
Leapfrog Press LLC
www.leapfrogpress.com

Printed in the United States of America

Distributed in the United States by
Consortium Book Sales and Distribution
St. Paul, Minnesota 55114
www.cbsd.com

First Edition

ISBN: 9781948585316 paperback
ISBN: 9781948585323 ebook

Library of Congress Cataloging-in-Publication Data

Names: Medhat, Katayoun, author.
Title: Flyover Country / by Katayoun Medhat.
Description: First edition. | Fredonia, NY : Leapfrog Press, 2022. | Series:
A Milagro mystery
Identifiers: LCCN 2019021077 | ISBN 9781948585316 (softcover : acid-free
paper)
Subjects: | GSAFD: Mystery fiction.
Classification: LCC PR9110.9.M43 L33 2019 | DDC 823/.92--dc23
LC record available at https://lccn.loc.gov/2019021077

THE AUTHOR

Katayoun Medhat was born in Iran and raised in Germany. A couple of years in a Catholic boarding school in rural Germany helped her to appreciate the meaning of culture shock. Her decision to study Anthropology in (then) West Berlin may or may not have been related to these earlier experiences. Working her way down the list of courses least likely to yield a job, Katayoun moved to London where she attempted to learn Berber at the School of Oriental and African Studies and, moving on, gained an MSc in Social Anthropology at University College London. Viewed retrospectively Katayoun's portfolio of motley jobs may not have been an entire waste of time, as they taught many valuable life lessons. Training as a psychoanalytic psychotherapist helped to make sense of Anthropology- and vice versa. Clinical therapeutic practice in various settings induced enduring awe and admiration for the human capacity for resilience. A PhD in medical anthropology on cultural negotiation in mental health care led to the Navajo Nation in the Southwestern United States.

Katayoun's debut novel *The Quality of Mercy* featuring renegade cop Franz Kafka was conceived during a grey English November to assuage a yearning for the Southwest's vast landscapes and turquoise skies; and is an homage to the Diné (Navajo) and the unique Diné sense of humour.

The Quality of Mercy was winner of the 2016 Leapfrog Press Global Fiction prize.

Franz Kafka and Robbie Begay soon established that they mean to continue cooperating on solving other cases in their somewhat irreverent, not to say chaotic way, and so are being most willingly obliged by Katayoun with *Lacandon Dreams* Milagro Mystery number 2, *Flyover Country*, is Milagro Mystery number 3, and number 4 is taking shape right now.

PROLOGUE

A colossal moon rose over the crest of the mesa. It rose fast and steadily, casting peaks and valleys, rifts and ravines, rock faces and canyon walls in a cold, silvery light.

At the eastern boundary of the mesa, the coyotes began to *yip-yip* shrilly, urgently; then to howl, one by one, in a tonal wave that gained volume and swelled as it traveled across the high plain.

Near the cave, a light breeze rippled the surface of a puddle that had remained from the last rains. A rabbit came out of the undergrowth and followed the trail of scattered greenery toward the cave, languidly exploring and plucking at the abundance of weeds and grasses and high-plains blooms tickled out of the earth by the spring sun. The rabbit sampled tender blossoms, stripped berries off shrubs, and tore at fibrous leaves. Its cheeks bulged with this rare bounty as it nibbled its way along the trail toward the shadows of the cave.

In the moon's rays the rabbit's shadow was large and grotesque: a humped shape with waggling antennae lurching along the ledge above the sheer drop.

The rabbit's neck snapped as easily as dry twigs breaking underfoot, its final breath rising moonward as a high-pitched scream and mingling, briefly, with the coyotes' shrill choir.

At the foot of the mesa, a thousand Milagro lights twinkled. In the pale moonlight, the cliff face glistened like bones.

CHAPTER ONE

It was one of those days that made it difficult for even the most committed pessimist not to have a murmur of song in their heart. The sky was a deep azure; above the mesa, cotton-puff clouds drifted like flocks of downy sheep, and a soft breeze bore with it the rich scents of springtime.

The little boy, accompanied by his dad, tripped up the steps of Milagro Police Station, bounced through the foyer, stopped at Becky Tsosie's reception desk, and piped: "Hi."

Even Becky couldn't resist the little boy: "Hi," she said, showing a dimple that K hadn't seen for many a moon. "Can I help you?"

The kid's dad, a rancher type in plaid flannel shirt, John Deere cap, and work boots, prodded the kid: "Vernon! Show 'em what you got!"

"I found something," chirped the boy, swinging a Walmart grocery bag.

His father shrugged his shoulders: "Better make sure we're legit, huh? It's private land and all, but you never know what they let you keep these days, right?"

Becky's eyes had gone cold. "Officer Kafka will help you," she said.

"A pleasure," said K, "Becky, the printer jammed again."

"When are you going to learn to feed the paper in right?" hissed Becky. Adieu dimple.

"So, you found something?" said K. "How exciting!"

"Yes!" trilled the boy. He was a happy little dumpling.

The father grimaced, his eyes narrowing.

"Would you like to show me what you found?"

"Yes! But I wanna keep it!" said the boy.

"Well … if you found it on private land, there's a chance you can keep it. Unless it's a really big find, like an ancestral village or something that the archaeologists might want to study …"

"I want to be an arcologist," said the boy.

"Great profession," said K. "There's plenty around here that will keep you busy."

The boy, having decided that he'd had enough chitchat, opened the grocery bag, pulled out and held aloft, a dirt-covered clump.

"Hmm," said K, "what have we here? Let me have a look."

The child handed over the clump. It was heavier than K had anticipated. He turned it around and found himself looking at the hollow eye-sockets and grinning teeth of a skull.

His involuntary exclamation made Becky look up: "What is it?"

"It's …" He addressed the boy brightly: "How about you give me your address and I make out a receipt for you? We may have got ourselves something that the archaeologists might find interesting. Where exactly was this found?"

"On our land in Hawksmoor Creek," said the man. "You can find all kinds of crap there after snowmelt."

"It's not crap!" said the boy.

They watched the little boy skip down the steps to the parking lot ahead of his father, his fists full of lollipops, which Becky kept to comfort the distraught offspring of the arraigned.

"What did he find?" asked Becky.

"A skull," said K.

"What … ?!"

"A—"

"Get that thing away from me! Get it out of here! What is wrong with you?"

"I didn't know what was in there," said K.

"You need to take that thing out! Now!" Becky's voice was pitched high.

K went out of the station and stood in the parking lot, dangling the Walmart bag from his finger. Out here, in the high desert, you literally did walk on the bones of the ancestors—except for the Navajo, who traditionally had done everything to avoid doing just that, burying their dead in hidden, to-be-forgotten-and-never-to-be- spoken-of-again places. The dead passed into the realm of *ch'įįdii'*, malevolent, vengeful spirits–and were friends of the living no more.

"What are you doing?" asked Juanita Córdoba. She was carrying a sealed evidence bag and had her patrol car keys at the ready.

"Thinking of where to put this," said K, and lifted the bag.

"What is it?"

"A skull this kid found in Hawksmoor Creek. Becky doesn't want it in there."

"A skull?" said Córdoba. "Eww."

"I'm pretty sure it's an old one," said K. "What is our protocol with skulls?"

Córdoba frowned. "We had one a few years back," she said. "I think we asked Delgado Forensics to look at it, and then we passed it on to those archaeologists at Creosote Canyon. They like that stuff."

"Oh," said K, "I promised the little boy he could keep it."

"You know you had no business to promise him that," said Córdoba. "Why don't you give me that thing, and I take it up to Delgado. I'm going to meet with Grimes for this evidence." She lifted the bag.

"Erm ... sure," said K. "Well ... thank you. Guess I better go over to Walking Beauty Trading Post to get some sage for Becky."

CHAPTER TWO

"Shit hitting the fan over at McKinnon Canyon," said Smithson.

"Ain't it always," said Young. There was hardly an hour in the day when Young couldn't be found in the station's breakroom. That's what they called 'liaising' at Milagro PD. He had sunk his hand into his mouth up to the knuckle, trying to pry shreds of pulled pork from his molars.

"Must be something in the water," Smithson said.

"Uranium," said K.

Young snorted and retrieved a wad of worm-like matter from his oral cavity. He contemplated it with forensic attention and popped it back into his mouth.

"See you later," said K.

"Hey! I was talking to you!" said Smithson. He had positioned himself in the doorway of the break room so that K couldn't get out.

"Let's go to your office," said Smithson.

"I always forget you got yourself a view!" said Smithson. "You like plants, huh?" He went over to the window, poking his fingers into plant pots. "Guess it reminds you of home, huh? England?"

"Wales," said K.

"That's why you dig plants? Coz it's all green over there?"

"I hadn't thought of it like that."

"How *do* you think of it?" There was an edge to Smithson's voice.

"They are living matter I can do something to help survive," said K.

Smithson shook his head. "You're weird. Anyways: McKinnon. They got this thing going on. It's about a horse …

"There are jokes that start like that." K watched Smithson pace up and down his office, stopping intermittently to pull at a plant-frond. "It would be great if you could leave them a few leaves."

"Huh? Uh. Sure. Anyways ..."

An interminable tale ensued, not made any more riveting by Smithson's lack of commitment to the rules of the narrative arc.

"So the cougar killed a miniature horse?"

"Well, that's what they know now," said Smithson weightily, "but that ain't what they thought then. See ..."

Half an hour of yapping later, and K had what was a sorry tale of neighborly strife. Good Ole Boy X's daughter's miniature horse had been found expiring on the pasture from lethal injuries. Good Ole Boy X hadn't hesitated, and had taken his shotgun over to Good Ole Boy Y and had shot Good Ole Boy Y's dog. Nope. Good Ole Boy X wasn't a good ole boy, but some loaded guy from some-place else ... and he'd sent his groundskeeper, some beaner proba-bly, to do what he had to do.

"*Beaner?*" said K.

Smithson ploughed on like a harvesting machine through an interminable Kansas wheatfield.

Thereupon Good Ole Boy Y had ... *whatever.*

Thanks to his oratory skills, Smithson succeeded in turning boondocks drama into soporific lullaby. Not even his rhetorical crimes against cultural sensitivity helped K much to keep his eyes open.

"What about the cougar?" K asked again.

"I was getting to that," Smithson said. K wasn't holding his breath.

The short of it was, as K eventually gathered, that GOB Y's poor mutt had died in vain, because—as even Loaded Guy From Some-place Else had to accept—the miniature horse had been killed by a cougar. Now the settlers of McKinnon Canyon had turned away from turning against each other, jointly turning against the cou-gar. Right now, a vigilante group was taking turns on armed cougar-watch. The folks of McKinnon Canyon always found a common enemy when they needed one.

"Cougar vigilantes?" said K. "Aren't Fish & Wildlife supposed to do that?"

"I was getting to that," said Smithson.

Somebody—and that somebody had better watch out—had snitched on the McKinnon posse of vigilantes and informed the Department of Fish & Wildlife, which sent round their wildlife officer, who had been run off in not-exactly-neighborly fashion by the irate vigilantes. Now the whole sorry mess was Milagro PD's to clear up.

"Curtis Malone?" asked K. "They ran off *Curtis Malone*?" He had a hard time imagining anyone running off Curtis Malone. Even McKinnon folk.

"They sent some kid," said Smithson, "Just down from, uh, wherever, some fancy Cali school where they study climate change and stuff. Didn't last five minutes in McKinnon." Smithson laughed phlegmily.

Local yokels, working their stubbly jaws on chewing wads of bacca, advancing with shovels and pitchforks on a sun-kissed fucking Cali lib. McKinnon Canyon was that kind of place.

"Why are you telling me all this?" asked K. He was beginning to yearn for City Market shoplifter-spotting duty.

"We can't let them get away with this. If they get it into their minds that they can just run anybody off that they don't take a shine to, we'll have another of those militia outfits there in no time. It's a … uh … preventative measure."

It was another one of those deals where the more K listened, the less he understood. He tried to wrap his noodle around whatever Smithson was trying to say: "So, they are fixing to hire us out as that kid's bodyguards?" K asked experimentally.

"The kid's on his way back to Cali." Another phlegmy laugh. "Nope, they're gonna get the real deal now. They asked for it, they gonna get it. *This time* it's gonna be Curtis Malone."

Curtis Malone was the real deal alright. Curtis Malone looked as if he could survive anywhere with nothing but the clothes he stood up in. Probably had to, if K remembered the musty smell of said clothes correctly. Curtis Malone had wintry gray eyes, a weather-beaten face furrowed by a thousand lines—few of them laughing—and an austere frame with not an ounce of spare fat on it. He was a man of few words, who most definitely did not suffer fools gladly—which made it all the more puzzling that Malone was still working for Fish & Wildlife; after everything that had gone down there, everything that had driven practically everyone from the old guard out, so that all who remained were the shiny, new lickspittles of the oil and gas industry to which the Administration for the End Times had gifted all public lands.

Smithson made a stand-off between Malone and the McKinnon vigilantes sound like a potential High Noon kind of deal: nobody willing to back off, blood and guts drenching into sawdust floors.

Milagro PD was needed to broker peace between the vigilantes and the wildlife officer, make sure that nothing bad happened, like, *really* bad. Dig?

It brought to mind an emergency UN peacekeeping mission.

"You want to be careful," said Smithson. "McKinnon folk can be real touchy."

"Yeah, make sure you're careful," K said.

"No," said Smithson. "*You* be careful."

"Me? Dream on."

"You. I already cleared you with the Sheriff."

"You cleared me with the Sheriff?" Too late, K understood that what he'd taken for Papi Smithson's bedtime story had been a briefing. "I feel you are the better man," K said sincerely.

Smithson did not protest. He shrugged. "Well, yeah ... but I got all these DUIs to process."

"You know me," K tried again, "if it's a big diplomatic job, I don't think I'm your man."

"I know how you like to chew on your foot," agreed Smithson. "But you don't need to do anything. You just need to stand there. You're pretty tall, ain'tcha? Just try to look mean. Keep your mouth shut."

"Like a scarecrow."

"Curtis Malone is gonna do the heavy lifting. You're just there so they get the message. McKinnon Hall, 7 o' clock sharp. Tonight."

"Got it," said K.

He had learned to tell when a battle was lost.

CHAPTER THREE

The light in McKinnon Canyon reminded K of the light on the Welsh coast. It had a peculiarly opaque quality, a pale luminescence, that gave the landscape an aura of otherworldliness.

McKinnon Canyon Road wound along the side of Resting Warrior Mountain. To the north the hillside fell away, and sloped down to the creek. The river's path was marked by a band of cottonwoods that would, in time, fall prey to thickets of pesky tamarisk, the inexorable progression of which was forcing the local ecology to yield to its particular needs.

It was curious, K thought, the degree to which tamarisk was maligned by the same settlers and ranchers whose advent and effect on the land, after all, mirrored the tamarisk's advance more closely than that of any other, shyer, less determined species: neither belonged, neither were particularly sympathetic to their new environment, both were hardy and relentless, and cleaved to the Darwinian imperative to propagate their species at any cost.

Beyond the creek and the verdant battlefield of competing flora, the land gradually rose to the cliff face of McKinnon Canyon. On these slopes, the latest influx of settlers was setting down root. Out of the stony soil that had been ploughed, fertilized, and crisscrossed with water supply lines grew gnarled and knotted vines. Increasingly shorter, milder winters and longer, hotter summers had made their propagation possible.

Above the vineyards towered baronial stone-clad manors, housing San Matteo County's new elite. McKinnon Canyon now boasted a slew of bijou bed-and-breakfast concerns as well as an upmarket rustic lodge, with a five-star resort in the planning. The resort, or rather, the *spa* would offer traditional Southwestern pursuits paired with lavish comfort. There would be trail riding, rodeo instruction, pottery restoration courses, bat-viewing tours, owl-feeding excursions, chuck wagon feasts, hot stone massage, fish pedicures, and goat yoga. At least K *hoped* there would be fish pedicures and goat yoga. Nowt wrong with piranha pedicures and billy goat yoga.

The community hall was at the far western boundary of the Canyon, where McKinnon Canyon Road merged with the Indian service road and the fertile valley opened up into an arid swathe of Navajo reservation land. Scattered compounds there housed trailers, hogans, and sheep corals, and the landscape was dotted with oil donkeys that rose and dipped and dipped and rose in hypnotically repetitive motion.

The community hall was a proud testament to old stonemasonry traditions: hand-hewn rocks held together with discreet layers of mortar, decked with a slate-tiled roof. The hall had been built long ago, before particleboard and corrugated metal had made craft and skill redundant.

A quarter of an hour remained until seven, but already every parking space in front of the building was occupied and the roadside was lined with pickup trucks. K watched leathery cowboys file stiff-legged through the community hall's doorway. The majority of them were packing. These were proper men who had never in their lives been further than a lurch-and-tackle distance away from their guns. They slept with their guns by their beds. They went to the laundromat packing. They had protested in front of the *Happy Moo* Ice Cream Parlor, fully armed, when it considered banning open-carry from its premises.

Given that this whole thing had started with a feud over a shot dog, K hoped that Curtis Malone would know how to handle these folks. He'd better.

Time advanced. More grizzled, plaid-shirted, arms-bearing McKinnonites arrived. Some huddled at the entrance to the hall, sucking on roll-ups and intermittently expelling impressive amounts of bronchial congestion, while mustering the patrol car with rheumy eyes and clenched jaws.

The dropping temperature began to drive people inside the hall. There was still no sign of Malone's Fish & Wildlife Range Rover. It was getting close to seven. Chances for an advance briefing with Malone weren't looking too hot.

In the community hall, groups of weather-beaten ranchers stood about in clumps, wearing John Deere caps and Stetsons, faded jeans and workman's boots, broad belts adorned with fist-sized buckles, substantial torsos encased in plaid shirts and heavy-duty multi-utility vests. The smell was of leather, manure, tobacco, and testosterone.

He'd planned to wait at the back until Malone arrived, but as he entered, the throng of voices stopped abruptly; the men turned, and, facing K, parted, creating a narrow passage that forced him to saunter the gauntlet all the way to the front of the hall.

Walking through, taking his sweet time, he met the eyes of his foes, regarding them blankly and unsmilingly. He walked as slowly, as languidly, as one of those cowboys stepping out of the saloon into the blazing midday sun, walking along that dusty stretch of road, grit crunching underfoot …

At the front of the hall, two rickety chairs had been placed in a depression in the dirt floor, setting out pretty clearly the tone of things to come. K watched the procession of hardened country folk shuffle to their seats.

The clock above the door had by now passed 7 PM by five minutes. K let his gaze roam deliberately over the sea of leathery faces, compressed mouths, and narrowed eyes that regarded him without friendliness. He took care to distribute his attention evenly, and was glad now that he'd left his coat open over his holster—just in case standing around like Lot's wife didn't do the trick.

The clock advanced to 7:08. A certain unrest was beginning to take hold of the crowd.

7:11. Oh, Brother Curtis, where art thou? Feet shuffled, caps were pushed back, necks were scratched, and holsters adjusted.

7:13. Pushing it now, Curtis Malone.

A rangy old boy got up and traipsed to the thermos. The glug-glugging of coffee splashing into polystyrene cup filled the hall. One by one the men got up and formed a row at the coffee urn. Judging from the rustling of sugar packets, most of these old boys had a sweet tooth.

7:15. Still no Curtis Malone.

The McKinnon wake returned to their seats, from whence they regarded K in the manner of carrion birds eyeing a carcass, noisily slurping coffee through tobacco-stained teeth.

7:20 PM. *Screw you, Curtis Malone.*

K lifted the chair out of its depression, turned it round and straddled it, placing his elbows on the backrest. "I guess we better start," he said.

A mutinous murmur arose from the crowd. There was a part of K that empathized with them. It was pretty clear that they regarded their presence here at all—abandoning their cougar vigil and attending this here gosh-darn useless meeting—as much of a concession as they were willing to offer. And Curtis Malone, that damn two-bit bureaucrat, was now throwing their goodwill back in their faces by leaving them high and dry. And if Malone thought anybody was going to give him any fraction of their precious time ever again, he had something else coming. They were going to get themselves that cougar and—

"You are not," K said firmly.

The murmuring stopped. They looked at him incredulously.

"That's what I'm here to tell you," said K. "You are not going to do anything to that cougar. Deter it by any means you have. Scare it off. Feed your dogs inside. Keep your cats in the house. Let your miniature horses sleep in your den. Install electric fencing. Install motion-activated lights. Install motion-activated sounds. Or sprinklers. There's a lot that you can do. What you *can't* do is harm or kill the cougar."

The grumbling became an outraged roar. That cougar had been judged, found guilty, and sentenced to death—and they'd be damned if they let anything or anyone get in the way of his righteous execution.

"If anything happens to that cougar it's going to be treated as a federal offense," K said.

A hiss traveled through the crowd, like water drops sizzling on a red-hot stove. Wild animals that strayed into human habitats forfeited their right to life, was the gist of that hissing. Surely what had made this here country great was that every man had the right and freedom to defend what was hiss*sssssssss*.

"It isn't the cougar that strays into your habitat," said K, "It's y'all that stray into his. This is the price we pay for expanding and settling where we aren't supposed to. An occasional visit by one of those bears and cougars and elk that are being displaced by our houses, roads, and those ATVs that tear up all our wilderness is surely a small price to pay?"

Nope. Boy, had he got it wrong. Any price at all, however small, was too high. Maybe it wasn't the Land of the Free, so much as the Land of the Freeloaders?

Silence, K perceived, could indeed be leaden. He'd always thought it a fanciful turn of phrase, but, blimey, it wasn't. This was a lead zeppelin settling on the assembly and squashing the bejeezus out of it.

Maybe one of these days he should take up that psych assessment. Maybe this affliction of his, saying out loud what he thought was just in his head—and which, indeed, was supposed to stay in his head—merited some kind of a pathological status. *Tourette-Related Involuntary Vociferation,* say. TRIV for short.

The McKinnonites sat immobile, watery, red-rimmed eyes trained on him, jowls bulging with grinding molars.

"The occasional visit by a wild animal, and the occasional out-of-control wildfire; this is the price we pay for settling and living where we aren't supposed to," he said in the jolly manner of everybody's favorite uncle.

That, and the drought that in the near future would once again turn this land into a dustbowl and drive mass migration northward, only to—fingers crossed—eventually come up against a wall that the blessed inhabitants of lusher climes would erect against the invasion of desiccated dryland scrabblers.

The hiss was, by now, a roar filling the hall like the torrents of a flash flood rushing through a canyon.

Curtis Malone had not turned up. Maybe he had known what was coming. Just a couple of miles from here was a homestead that had an effigy of a man hanging by a noose from a tree. Below it, a sign nailed to the gate announced: WE DO IT THE OLD WAY. Somewhere at the margins of K's auditory cortex, an aural mirage of "Dueling Banjos" began to twang.

It was time to make like a guillotine and head off.

K delivered a set of instructions concerning legal wildlife-deterrent strategies, dead-eyed and through barely moving lips; then he rose, hooked his thumb under the backrest of his chair, dangling it—how nonchalantly alpha could you get—and offered to reschedule the meeting with Malone. He'd count it as a bonus if he managed to exit without having to break the chair on some ornery codger's head.

He set the chair back in its depression, smiled emptily, and, tipping his hat, walked toward the compact mass of denim, flannel, BO, and gunholstery at a pace adapted to the introductory chords of "Dueling Banjos," which had continued looping in his head.

Fifty pairs of eyes bore holes into his back. But hey, in the olden days it wouldn't just have been eyes boring holes.

K got into his patrol car, took out his phone, and dialed Malone's cell. The phone rang and rang and rang some more, until it clicked and disconnected.

K turned on the ignition, reversed, and took a left on McKinnon Canyon Road. At least they hadn't slashed his tires.

CHAPTER FOUR

The next day brought with it compensation by way of K's preferred duty: traffic patrol. There were plenty who couldn't stand it when all about them everybody was in motion while they were stationary; but K was not one of these. Watching the world drift by while daydreaming was K's favorite part of his job—or would have been his favorite, had he not been condemned to spend the first part of his shift on the dust-riven soft shoulder on the perpetual disaster zone that was Highway 288.

Half an hour in, and K had bagged three vehicle safety-violation citations. He had kept his head when all about him, the cited were losing theirs. He had spent some time jotting down particularly colorful suggestions in his little black notebook, mostly involving anatomically ambitious acts of self-gratification of which he had been the recipient, in case *The Milagro Gazette* ever decided to go for an X-rated "Police Blotter" edition. Then he set about finishing the pencil sketch of Sleeping Warrior Mountain that he had started during his last time on traffic duty.

Just then, with immaculate timing, a compact car hove into view. At first K thought the heat rising from the asphalt was playing tricks on his eyes, for this vehicle slalomed in a most alarming manner, sailing into the opposite lane, over-correcting, heading for the ditch, overcorrecting again and then heading for the opposite lane. Headlights flashed and horns honked as the driver, keeping to his expansive trajectory, passed K's patrol car.

K careened onto the road, switched on the light show, and gave chase. The compact sailed on, without straightening out or slowing down. There was nothing for it but to wait until the driver was set to head for the ditch again, then overtake him and block his way. Just then, the driver slowed down and pulled over.

The driver wore his gray hair in a crew cut. Blue eyes, round as marbles, looked out of a ruddy, apple-cheeked face.

"Step out of your car, sir, please." K saw no need to even bother asking for license and registration.

"Officer!" said the man.

"How about counting back from a hundred in sevens?" said K.

"Officer!"

"Just do it for me," said K.

"Ninety-three, eighty-six, seventy-nine, seventy-two ..."

K tried to locate the breathalyzer while trying to keep track of the guy's arithmetic—which, in any case, seemed to be more solid than his driving.

"... Sixteen, nine, two, minus-five, minus-twelve, minus-nineteen ..."

"That's fine, sir. Now would you please step over here and walk twenty steps in a straight line?"

The man did as asked, perfectly. "Officer," he said, "I oughta—"

"We'll do what we have to do here first," said K.

For some people, an encounter with the law powered right through their digestive system like a laxative. K hoped the guy wouldn't get caught short, right there at the dusty roadside of Highway 288, with truck and pickup drivers thundering past, leaning on their horns and yelping with schadenfreude, and teenagers in souped-up low-riders craning their necks and hollering obscenities.

"This won't take too long," promised K. The restroom facilities in the county jail were adequate, depending on urgency of need.

Next came the test with the outstretched arm and index finger, which the guy aced too. K had seen people damn near poke their own eyes out instead of getting their finger to alight on the tip of their nose, as instructed. They'd have to invent a whole new sobriety test for guys like this.

"Now, sir, will you blow into this? As hard as you can?"

"I been sober since 1976," said the man.

Kind of odd that the man, who had been so docile about complying with the roadside sobriety maneuvers, now seemed set to resist. Usually it was the other way around.

"Just blow, sir," said K.

"I ought to look after—"

"Later," said K. "As soon as we get this over with."

Whatever the guy was on, it wasn't showing up on the breathalyzer. "Blow me," muttered K, looking at it. "Have you consumed any controlled substances, sir? Cannabis, perhaps?"

"I told you: I been sober since 1976. Got myself clean with the help of the Lord."

"Well done, you," said K.

"And the Lord," said the man.

"Sure," said K, "Him too." He felt that now wasn't the time to start a theological deliberation on the gendering of the Almighty. "Are you on any medication, sir? Antihistamines? Painkillers? Barbiturates?"

"No," said the man. "I been sober since—"

"Nineteen eighty-six," said K. "That is a long time."

"Nineteen *seventy*-six."

"I beg your pardon," said K. "So ... how come you drove in a manner both careless and endangering the safety of fellow road users?"

Today official jargonese tripped off his tongue like candy pearls.

"It's ...," said the man. "It's ... my guys. I gotta look after my guys ..." He looked quite frantic now.

"Your 'guys?'"

The man pointed toward the car. K followed him.

"No!" the guy yelped, as K made to open the passenger door. His cry was so urgent that K obeyed.

"Lord, oh Lord, where have I got my stick? Please Lord, make it so I put my stick in the trunk. Lord, did I put my stick in the trunk? Lord! Oh Lord, have mercy, Lord!" The man crossed himself.

"I take it there's something you need out of your trunk?" said K. This was the kind of thing they taught you in Police Academy 101: Never let a suspect near their trunk, because that's where they tend to keep their shotguns. If suspect-trunk contact is unavoidable, make sure you have your handgun trained on them, safety catch off. That's why so many citizens, armed or not, died face-down in the trunks of their cars.

But K, having made the man perform all those roadside maneuvers while being jeered at and catcalled by passers-by, found he had no appetite to train his gun on this wretched guy.

"Go ahead," he said.

The man opened the trunk and stuck his head into it. K heard mumbled invocations and incantations, pitched higher and higher the more panicky the man got.

"It's on the backseat," the man said, withdrawing his head from the cavern of the trunk. His forehead was beaded with sweat.

"Your car isn't booby-trapped, is it?" K asked genially.

Eyes flickered in a haunted face: "They don't like it when I leave them alone," the man said. He crossed himself, opened the back door of the car, and jumped backward. "Stay back! For the mercy of God, stay back!"

K watched as an indistinct gray mass tumbled out of the car, separating and slithering toward the roadside ditch, accompanied by the distinct sound of rattling.

"You got *rattlers* in your car?" The man nodded. "How many?" From what he'd just seen, there looked to be at least five.

"Twelve."

"Twelve?" asked K.

"Like the Apostles," whispered the man.

K dialed Fish & Wildlife and got the usual endless ringing, forty-seven-point menu, another message, and a rerouting to the forty-seven-point menu. Who the fuck was responsible for emergencies involving hazardous wildlife?

"You haven't fed them adrenaline, have you?"

The man looked at him in disbelief: "No, Officer, I have not."

"Well, you seem to be driving around with twelve rattlesnakes in your vehicle," said K.

"They got their basket," said the man.

"Where is their basket?"

"On the passenger seat."

"Was the basket closed?"

The man shook his head: "It was open just a little bit." He indicated a gap with index finger and thumb.

"That's quite enough for a snake to squeeze through," said K. "So you are driving along the highway with an open basket full of rattlesnakes on your passenger seat …?"

"They like it when I sing to them," whispered the man.

"Was that what you were doing when I stopped you? You were singing to your snakes?"

The man nodded. "We were having ourselves a good time. We're supposed to hold a mass down there on the Indian reservation. Redwater."

Such were the taboo-busting feats of religious conversion. Traditionally, the Navajo didn't rate snakes at all. Now some were apparently okay with attending masses led by them. There was some kind of metaphor in there somewhere.

"I don't think that snake mass is likely to go ahead," K said gently.

At last, he got hold of Pet Rescue. Always good in a crisis, they were sending over Francis. True to his name, Francis knew how to handle this kind of thing. As they waited around, the man positioned himself by the ditch and called out the names of his snakes mournfully, while K did the paperwork. All the man's papers were in order. He was clean. There was no warrant on him. He was a preacher at the Pentecostal Evermore Gracious Church in Terencetown, Texas.

Francis arrived with his snake catcher and donned a pair of heavy-duty gloves, with the help of which he trapped the Apostles that were loose in the car and deposited them in a wire-mesh contraption.

K asked: "How many did you trap?"

"Seven," said Francis. "Are those all?"

"Five of them went that way," K said, pointing at the ditch.

Francis leaned over the ditch and listened. "They're probably way over there," he said, pointing at the wasteland beyond. "Good that you lost them here. Would have been really bad if they'd escaped further up near the motel or the store."

"Are you not going to help me find them?" asked the preacher.

"What kind of rattlers are they?" asked Francis.

"Speckled and diamondback."

"They get along?"

"We are all God's children," said the preacher.

"Did you inject them with adrenaline to make them mean?"

"No! No! No!" The preacher looked very unhappy.

"They'll be okay," said Francis. "There's plenty of mice and stuff for them to feed on around here."

The preacher shook his head. "I'm not leaving them here. No sir, I'm not."

Francis looked at K and shrugged his shoulders. He grabbed a jute sack out of his car and jumped over the ditch, snake stick in hand. They watched him poking about in the undergrowth. The preacher prayed soundlessly, except for the occasional sobbed *Lord have mercy*, which tore at K's agnostic heartstrings. He was quite tempted to join in the preacher-man's incantations—not least because he was damn sure the guy wouldn't budge before every last one of his snakes had been found.

"This is a bit like looking for needles in a haystack," said K.

"The Lord will guide us," said the preacher. K felt it was rather generous of him to include all of them.

"I hope so," K replied.

"Let's pray, brother," said the preacher, and grasped K's hand. His grip had the vicelike firmness of despair. Short of acting extremely unbrotherly, K could see no way of freeing himself of it. So he stood, his hand in the man's, saying *Lord* and *Amen* at what he deemed appropriate intervals.

In the depths of the wasteland, Francis lowered his stick, brought it up and deposited his live cargo in the jute sack. He gave a thumbs-up sign.

"Hallelujah!" shouted the preacher, raising his arms while still holding onto K's hand. K's desperate tugging had no effect; he could see a good chance of featuring in this week's police blotter column by way of a roadside revivalist meeting.

Francis moved through the field with purpose. He stopped abruptly, stooped and swooped, and stuffed another wriggling snake into the sack.

"Hallelujah! Praise the Lord!" sang the man. K had given up trying to liberate his hand.

They watched Francis stalk the stony ground, the preacher's prayers now vigorous and joyous. Under a straggly juniper bush Francis stopped again, swooping and scooping. They watched him advance, writhing sack in hand. The preacher now sang, shouted and sobbed with relief while squeezing K's hand like a harmonica.

"You found them all, brother?" asked the preacher when Francis returned.

Francis nodded. "Got five right here."

K looked on with distaste. The preacher let go of his hand and stretched it out toward the sack. K shook his head.

"I got to take them," said Francis. "It's the law." The preacher looked crestfallen. "It's a miracle anyways we got them all," Francis added gently—and generously, given that nothing could have compelled K to wander the wasteland looking for rattlesnakes, never mind catching them and carrying them about in a sack.

K took the opportunity to hand over citations for driving in a hazardous manner and being in possession of dangerous, uncontrolled wildlife. The preacher crumpled the sheet of paper into his pocket and buried his face in his hands, while Francis stowed away the mesh basket with the rattlers in the back of his pickup.

"What's going to happen now?" asked the preacher.

The truth was that K didn't know. He looked to Francis.

"Don't worry," said Francis, "they're in good hands."

"But—"

"I'm sure some of your Redwater congregation will be relieved if you hold tonight's mass without snakes," said K.

CHAPTER FIVE

After the Apostles drama, Milagro's southside was balm for K's
soul. He parked the patrol car under an overgrowth of brush on
the roadside across Hawksmoor Creek. The creek, dividing Milagro southside from Milagro northside, opened suddenly and
unexpectedly into a yawning crevasse. It was a moderately ambitious Evel Knievel stunt-jump wide and deceptively deep, its
floor covered by sagebrush and tamarisk. Occasional flash floods
had eroded its banks, polished the sandstone cliffs, and carved
grooves into the rock face. Hawksmoor Creek now was an embry-
onic Grand Canyon and would, a few million years hence, be just
as awe-inspiring to amoebae and cockroaches, sole survivors of
the Apocalypse.

Some miles south, the languid outline of Resting Warrior
Mountain shimmered in the heat. All was quiet on this Western
front, except for crickets making a racket in the pursuit of love.
Their stridulations provoked a renewed surge of irritation with Curtis Malone. K grabbed his cellphone and dialed Malone's number
yet again. Squinting at the sun, he listened to the ringing. A butter-
fly came a-fluttering out of nowhere and landed on the windscreen
in a tumble-drunk motion. K watched it fold and open its wings,
as if undecided between moving on and having a siesta, when the
phone jumped to voicemail. Malone's gravelly-voiced message
did little to encourage loquacity. It was likely, anyway, that most
people wouldn't even last the duration of the first deterrent: those
however-many rings it took to finally get to the voicemail. Not
here, in the land of Time-Is-Money.

K kept his message short. Nevertheless, a beep cut him off
mid-sentence.

He had barely disconnected when his cellphone rang. Somewhere up in a tree, a bird echoed the sound. Soon all birdsong would sound like ring-tones.

"What am I supposed to do with this guy?" hissed Becky.

"Which ...?"

"You know who; the guy with the snakes."

"Is he giving you trouble?" The preacher had not looked like the trouble-causing kind. K was surprised he'd found his way to the station.

"He's been here crying, like, for *hours*. Listen!" In the background, K could hear the preacher's sobs, punctuated by his gulping for air.

"He sounds very upset," K said.

"You can say *that* again! What am I supposed to do with him?"

"I don't—"

"Don't you dare say you don't know! It's *me* that's gotta sit with your mess!"

"How is this my mess? Was I supposed to let him drive on with all those snakes partying in his car?"

"Why do you always bring me trouble?" asked Becky, as if he hadn't said anything at all.

"I'll see what I can do," K said, and hung up.

He stared at a trio of vultures drifting high above, riding the currents over the creek in ever-widening circles. A red-tailed hawk tumbled out of the blue and dived into the chasm.

K scrolled for Pet Rescue's number and dialed it. A squirrel shot out of the brush and dashed across the road. The phone was picked up on the fourth ring by Martha, the organization's coordinator. She listened without interrupting, then said:

"Let me have a look at his schedule." K listened to sounds of drawers being opened, papers being shuffled, and intermittent muttering. "He's off for the week ... No, I can't phone him when he's off. The thing with the snakes today was an exception, because it was an emergency."

"Are you sure you couldn't ..." K tried feebly.

"I am sure," said Martha. "There's nothing here my volunteers can rely on. Not on funding. Not on cooperation. Not on happy ends. The only thing I can give them is to protect them from this mess when they are away from here."

"That sounds quite grim," said K.

"It is," said Martha and hung up.

On the whole, this wasn't a conversation that necessarily needed to be passed on to Becky. Better travel in hope, and all that. Though she probably thought anyway that K had just promised to think of something to get her off his back. There was no justice in this world. And no mercy. With that in mind, he might as well enjoy Hawksmoor Creek's peace and quiet before returning to the shitshow that was routine at the station these days.

Traffic was sparse at this time of day. The air buzzed with busy bugs. The hawk returned and landed on the tree growing on the edge of the ridge. It perched, utterly still on the branch, and then suddenly rose high into the air, where it performed three loops before tumbling out of the sky and diving into the depths. Another life done gone.

At the far end of a wide field, halfway to the rise of the mesa foothills, rows of majestic cottonwoods marked the course of the river that had once run there, and which now had mostly dried up. As groundwater depleted, the trees would have to stretch their roots, hundreds of years old, ever deeper and further. Like the proverbial iceberg, they made up three times the volume of the giant ancient trees themselves. Beneath this soil were cities of roots, metropolises of gnarled, twisting rhizomes that ran from here to the mesa and beyond. The trees had been here when the first Anglo ranchers arrived in the valley, and had seen many ice-cold winters and scorching summers; thirty-year droughts and occasional years of bountiful precipitation; ravaging wildfires, raging flash floods, and rampant plagues. Standing mighty and serene, they had survived all this now to be cursed daily by people living nearby, for obstructing their data signals.

This was also the very spot where the militia boys had shot Deputy Sheriff Greer. What had grown to a major incident covered by the national press had started innocuously enough. Greer had come upon three guys stealing a water truck and hadn't called for backup. They found Greer's patrol car a couple of hours later, embedded in a fence. Greer's glazed unseeing eyes were trained on the horse pasture. Blood pooled on the patrol car's floor and soaked into the dirt. Beyond the fence, three horses grazed, unperturbed.

During the ensuing chase the perps engaged the cops in a Wild-West-style shootout, abandoned the bullet-riddled truck and vanished into the badlands.

The whole of San Matteo County hunkered down in the knowledge that out there a bunch of cop-killers were on the loose. Occasionally vigilante troops set out into the wilderness to bring Deputy Greer's murderers to justice.

One day a couple of hardy birders, keen to confirm a sighting of a ferruginous pygmy owl, found a withering cadaver under a bush. The cause of death, later determined by forensics, had been starvation, precipitated by a broken femur. Another corpse was found sometime later by a so-called geological expedition reconnoitering exploitable natural resources. That one had died from a gunshot wound.

The last guy was found by a Navajo tracker, engaged by a McKinnon Canyon rancher to locate a lost cow. The carcass was a desiccated mess with half a ribcage missing, a foot torn off and fingers gnawed to the bone. The coyotes had finished off what a cougar or bear had begun. Nobody was bothered. The men had shot the deputy and deserved no mercy.

K appreciated that story as a reminder that the vast and unforgiving wilderness that surrounded them was really a cartography of death; whatever humans did to subdue Nature, it would keep the upper hand in the long run. That's what he thought on his good days.

A dragonfly with sapphire-blue wings hovered at the patrol car's open window, as if conducting an inspection. What did it see through its huge compound eyes? Tiny Ks, standing on their heads, a thousand times repeated? Did the dragonfly take him for a friend-

ly flower on which to rest? More importantly: what was a dragonfly doing here?

Perhaps it had been lured by the farmers' wheel-line irrigation.
In the sunlight, cascading water projected as iridescent rainbows.
The dragonfly whirred off toward the multicolored mist. A light
wind skimmed the alfalfa fields and turned their surfaces into em-
erald-green waves.

K watched the water spraying skyward. It was near noon, the
air was hot, and the sun stood high. These folks could barely wait
for their dustbowl moment. Was there reason to this madness? What
percentage of water evaporated in this heat? How much precious
groundwater was being lost in this reckless way? What about the
groundwater level? What about those ancient cottonwoods? How
far did their roots have to dig down now?

The glistening water on the asphalt evaporated and rose as
clouds of steam.

The distant grumbling of an engine signaled the approach of
the first vehicle to interrupt K's reverie. A pickup truck roared
around the corner, came perilously close to the edge, overcorrect-
ed, and, before K's astonished eyes, crashed into the picket fence a
bare couple of yards from the patrol car.

The vehicle sat motionless, splintered fence posts covering the
hood. The impact had dislocated the entire length of the fence, so
that it hung over the borrow ditch's perimeter like a drunk about
to be sick.

The pickup was an older model Ford. Its paint was faded
and peeling, its body pitted and dented. On the passenger side, it
had been keyed all the way from door to taillight. Inside, nothing
moved. K walked around to the driver's side and tapped on the
window. The pickup's windows were too dusty to see through. He
tapped again. Nothing.

He tapped once more and called: "Are you alright?" There
was no answer. "I'm going to open the door," K announced. He
didn't think the collision with the fence had been strong enough to
cause injury, but if the passengers were elderly or frail, the impact

might have induced shock. In terms of personal safety, a couple of maimed elderlies would be preferable to some dude loading his gun because there was a lone cop without backup knocking on his truck. Just about anything could be behind that dirty window, that dented door.

CHAPTER SIX

Mostly K was irritated by his job; on rare occasions he almost liked it, and at certain times he positively hated it.

Now was such a time.

Not only was the snake man still sitting in a corner of reception sobbing while Becky, from behind her desk, shot him poison-dagger looks that would have felled him, had he not acquired immunity over the years; but now K had to deal with this woman, who looked so defeated, so broken, so crushed, that it seemed no less than an act of sadism to do his job. His wretched job.

What did Magnusson, Milagro dive bar owner and philosopher manqué, always say about his "applied yin yang theory?" That there wasn't anything on this Earth that was ever just good or just bad—though K could definitely think of few things that were pretty much all bad. Perhaps being caught today would offer the woman a way out of whatever she was trapped in? For she *was* trapped. It was an aura that clung to her, something that emanated from her. He imagined this was all the release she ever got, swigging Southern Comfort while driving her pickup truck, commuting between whatever it was that crushed her soul and sapped her life force.

"I get a feeling you wanted to be caught," K said. "Did you?"

She raised her head and looked at him through dark, dark eyes. Her dilated pupils made her eyes look black. He handed her a mug of coffee, and she wrapped both hands around it. She did not drink. She used the mug to hide her face.

He watched the crown of her head dipping behind the mug, her knuckles showing through her brown skin. He listened to her quick, shallow breathing, and waited. Something in the way she hunched, in the way she pulled her head down between her shoulders, made

K understand that this wasn't obstruction; it was abject shame. She was so ashamed that she couldn't bring herself to look at him.

"We were lucky today," K said. She flinched, as if he'd whipped her. "We were lucky. The only damage today was a picket fence. A picket fence is pretty easy to replace. A life isn't. Why don't we look at this as something that happened just in time? Like a warning sign just before the cliff edge that you've spotted just in time to turn round?"

Behind her coffee-mug shield, she began rocking to and fro, whispering. Her voice was so low, K couldn't make anything out, couldn't even tell if she was whispering in Navajo or in English.

K knew that a certain kind of drunk driver drove drunk because they had no sense that anything they did could be or would be of any consequence: it wasn't irresponsibility, it was a lifetime of learning that nothing they ever wanted or did had any impact.

That these people were themselves society's whipping boys didn't, however, mean that they should be let off: on the matter of impaired driving, K was, in principle, on the side of the law.

The woman shrunk further into herself, the mug's rim pressed to her forehead, her knuckles white. K knew the domino effect that DUI arraignments could have. Livelihoods could be lost, and with them, home, children, security, future employability. Without the support of relatives, people—once caught—could rapidly descend to the level of street drinkers.

What he was seeing here wasn't just shock and shame, though. This woman was mute, or had been muted, by the sum of whatever it was that life had heaped upon her. She bore many of the telltale signs of a battered person. If this was the case, then some good might come out of catching her and removing her from the line of fire. Sometimes a time-out in jail wasn't such a bad thing.

Usually K wasn't bad at getting people in his custody to talk. But he knew—somehow he just knew—that this woman would *not* talk. Before she was arraigned, he decided, he would use his discretion to allow her some time to make whatever arrangements she needed to make. She could make this so much easier for him if she would only talk. But even without her cooperation, there remained various ways to buy her time. K, committed anti-establishmentari-an that he was, knew them all.

K escorted the woman to one of the eager interns who had recently begun flooding the station in the quest for bankable work experience. Learning to handle the bureaucratic burden surely counted as valuable learning these days. The interns were all blue-eyed, corn-fed Anglo boys who would vote red, as their daddies did. This one was, as far as K remembered, called "Hunter" or "Cody" or "Turner" or something—as the boy's gormless mien never changed, it was hard to gauge whether or not he was calling him by the wrong name. Well, let the thrusting young buck and fu-ture pride of Milagro town deal with the woman's ID, license, and all the stuff K had omitted to ask for because he'd been too busy role-playing addiction counselor.

"You just take the details off this lady and enter them into Form TR/105.3.4, okay?"

The woman hunched opposite Taylor/Randy/Colson. When K said goodbye, she did not look up. He walked off with the mixture of shame, sorrow, and opportunistic relief that so often marked his days here.

The snake man had gone. "Did he leave?" asked K.

"He was running late for his mass," said Becky.

"Good."

"Good that he was running late?!"

"Good that he left," said K. "I thought maybe he'd just stay. Forever."

"*You* did? How do you think I feel? He was here for hours, cry-ing. You said you would do something about his snakes. Did you?"

"The guy I need to speak to is going to call me back." Little white lies and all that.

"Better make sure he does, because that guy is going to come back here straight after his mass. Whoever's doing the night shift is going to have a ball."

"Dilger," said K, and fought hard to suppress a smirk.

In his office, K busied himself with stuffing unfinished re-ports into files and stacking the files to a gravity-defying height.

He opened the window to the rumbling of pickups over asphalt and the sweetness of diesel fumes. It was no good. The collective misery of humanity was seeping into his pores.

The phone rang.

"Some guy called that there's a truck smashed into his fence," said Becky.

"I'm on it," K said and hung up on Becky's snort.

"I'm sorry, man." Darren's voice cut through the rumbling of his tow truck.

"You *are* driving the tow truck right now?" asked K.

"Don't worry. I got hands-free."

"I was wondering if you could do me a favor and pick up a wreck on southside?"

"Gonna be a while. Been going nonstop. Hardly get no breaks at all."

"That busy, huh?" said K.

"The city will get loaded on pound fees," Darren said cheerfully.

K had forgotten that there were fees to be paid to get impounded vehicles released from the municipal tow yard.

"How much is it?"

"You talking hour or day? It's $10 an hour, up to ten hours. Then it's $130 a day."

"One hundred and thirty dollars a day?"

"That's twenty-four hours," said Darren.

"How are people going to afford that?"

"It's $420 a week," said Darren, "so it gets cheaper the longer you leave it there."

For some people that was the monthly rent for a condo or a trailer.

"Some people just leave their car right there at the pound," Darren said. "They just never come back for it, you know?"

"I'm not surprised," said K.

"Then we auction 'em off," said Darren.

K rang the picket fence owner, armed with a battery of apologies and cutlery at the ready for a super-sized portion of crow. Folks could get pretty irate when they had a truck embedded in their picket fence.

Not this picket fence owner, though. "It still drives good," he said. "The keys were in the ignition. It's on my property. Anytime you want it, you just come on and get it. I left the keys in."

He didn't seem too fazed about the fence itself. It happened often enough, he said. A few weeks back, a pickup had misjudged the corner and trashed all three letter boxes. The occasions on which somebody had crashed into the utility pole and cut off the electric supply were countless. "It's bothersome when you're watching a game," he added complacently. His son was on his way over now to help him repair the fence.

K thanked the man for his sanguine outlook and promised to be in touch as soon as he'd gotten the requisite insurance details. He hung up before it could occur to the tolerant picket fence owner to ask how come he hadn't already got the insurance details.

The man had helped K to buy his lost lady some time, at least. He was pretty sure she didn't have the money to get her vehicle out of the pound. In letting her go, he had relied on using her truck as leverage. It, if nothing else, would bring her back.

He spent some time standing behind dusty blinds, staring at the road and attempting to calculate the percentage of misery, existential dread and enraptured rattlesnakes this tarmac carried past the station at any given hour of the day. He drew squiggles in the dust with his fingertips. They did not improve the appearance of the blinds much. The squiggly line he had drawn in the dust brought forth unpleasant memories of the rattlesnakes.

He took out his phone.

"Pet Rescue, how may I help you?"

"What is going to happen to those snakes?" asked K.

"It's you again," said Martha without enthusiasm. "... I guess they'll be euthanized."

"Euthanized? I thought you're a humane society?"

"Where do you think we got space to keep a bunch of rattlers? They'll have to go somewhere else. I'm not holding my breath that we'll find anybody that's keen on keeping rattlers—unless it's those kinds of people we definitely wouldn't want to be *keen* on keeping rattlers."

"How can I get hold of Francis?"

"I told you …" There was a pause. K crossed his fingers. "I got an old dog here that needs a home," said Martha.

"A dog … It wouldn't be fair on a dog. I'm barely at home as it is."

"What about a cat, then?" said Martha so quickly that K realized he'd walked into a trap.

"Wittgenstein won't like it," K implored.

"This is a house cat. A real old tom. His owner just died. All he does all day is sleep. How about you adopt him as your store cat? Just needs to be fed and watered, and you got plenty of room for a kitty-litter tray in your bookstore, haven't you?"

"You put some thought into this."

"I have to. Are you in your store tonight?"

"I guess so."

"Get the litter tray on your way there. And food. He prefers wet food. If you get the dry stuff, make sure you get the one for seniors. Francis will bring you the cat."

Martha had hung up before K had time to even clear his throat.

CHAPTER SEVEN

It was the day of parallel universes. From drunk drivers and Pentecostals with musical snakes to this quiet sanctuary harboring the whole world with its wonders and terrors, its enlightenment and despair alike on these dusty shelves, each volume a doorway to another realm, another wardrobe leading to another Narnia. Whenever he approached the stone steps that led to the wood-paneled door with its milky-glass windows that opened into the bookstore—his bookstore—his heart beat faster. He supposed, therefore, that the bookstore meant something to him, and felt a little pilot light of warmth igniting somewhere in his frozen soul. Time to do some re-shelving.

It was getting on toward conventional closing time when the doorbell tinkled. "You wanted to talk to me," said Francis.

"Sure do," said K. Francis seemed to have come empty-handed, unless he had stuffed the old tom under his t-shirt or into one of the utility pockets of his cargo pants.

"Shoot," said Francis.

He listened quietly to K's account of the inconsolable preacher, who probably was at the station right now, sobbing into stone-cold Dilger's ear.

"You know we can't give him back his snakes, right?"

"We can't? Is there not a way ...?"

"No way," said Francis.

K's heart felt heavy in his chest: "Martha said they'll probably be euthanized."

"Do you think the guy cares what happens to those snakes when he isn't going to get them back anyways?"

"I don't know," said K. "But I do."

"You do, huh?"

"It's bad enough to be ruining people's lives as the main part of your job. I don't need a bunch of dead animals as well to sit on my conscience."

Francis laughed. "Your take on your job sure is confidence-inspiring." He peered at K: "You are serious, aren't you? Look, there's nobody that will rehouse those snakes. And we cannot let that guy have them back. But … how about I release them somewhere they got a good chance of survival, and where they'll be out of people's way? I'm thinking of giving them a ride over to Quorum Valley."

"Quorum? Why not drop them off at XOX Big Energy HQ with compliments to Lucky Easton, CEO?"

"You sure change fast," said Francis. "Did you just go from hardcore animal rights activist straight into assassin mode?"

"They're both worthy causes."

"Speaking of worthy causes, I got somebody for you sitting in my truck." K didn't know whether he was disappointed or relieved. "I didn't want him to get scared, and I wanted to check you out," Francis grinned. "Be right back."

The cat was huge. And it was beautiful, with long, dark, silky fur that surrounded its head like a lion's mane, and remote, green eyes framed by aureoles of long, silvery hair.

Francis held up the cat.

"Hello," K said.

The cat looked at him—or rather through him, as if there was something of infinitely greater significance somewhere beyond K.

K gently scratched it behind the ear. The cat lifted a paw and softly laid it on K's hand, guiding it higher up on its head.

"I think we got ourselves a done deal here," said Francis, and put the cat into K's arms. It pushed its head up at K's chin, its whiskers tickling K's neck.

"You got yourself a nice store here," said Francis.

"Listen," said K, "are there any books you like? Natural history? Local ecology? I'd like to give you a book."

"Sci-fi," said Francis.

K set the cat on the floor. He watched the tom, tail held high, stalking through the store, meticulously inspecting every corner and nook. Soon enough, it found the litter tray that K had put in a corner of the storage room. The cat climbed into the tray, pawed the litter experimentally, and climbed out again, much like a guest inspecting a hotel room's facilities.

"Suit you, sir?" K asked.

The cat sat there, tail neatly wrapped around rump, looking at K pensively. They regarded each other in silence. The cat got up, padded over and rubbed against K's legs, purring.

Francis appeared with a book wedged under his arm. "Are you sure about this?"

"Sure I'm sure."

"I figured I should read one of the old guys," said Francis.

K craned his neck. "Asimov. He's supposed to be good, if you are into that kind of thing."

"I guess you aren't?"

"They say that sci-fi isn't about the future, it's about the present. I don't feel I need any more present."

"I see what you mean," said Francis.

"So … are we okay with the snakes?"

"Sure. They'll be fine in their mesh cage for a couple of days. Just need to make some time to drive over to Quorum."

"Do you need to feed them?"

"They like chicken. They don't need much. Just a bit, you know, so they don't start feeling mean. A hungry rattler is a mean rattler."

K accompanied Francis to the door. Something occurred to him. "Hey, does the cat have a name?"

Francis turned around and shrugged. "None that we know of. He must have had a name, I guess, but that old guy died all alone. No relatives. So nobody could tell us."

The cat had come to the door, and now sat next to K like a good host seeing guests off.

"Any idea what you're going to call him?" asked Francis.

"I think so," said K. "Benjamin."

"That's a good name for a cat," said Francis, and climbed into his pickup. "That's 'Benjamin' after Walter," said K to the cat, who pressed his head against K's shin and purred.

"That'll be a 'yes,' then," said K.

CHAPTER EIGHT

"The sheriff wants to see you *now*," said Becky, making no effort at all to suppress the glee in her voice.

K schlepped along a corridor saturated with the burning-tire-*cum*-decomposing skunk aroma of Sheriff Weismaker's coffee. He stopped at the sheriff's door, lungs burning, breathing shallowly through pinched nostrils. Right now he'd go through another session with the McKinnon folk rather than being made to drink a cup of the sheriff's brew.

"Sheriff," he said.

Weismaker was working on a crossword, and didn't look up. "'Misguided?'" he said.

"Sir?"

"Six letters."

"Crosswords aren't my thing, Sheriff," said K.

The sheriff frowned and chewed on his pencil: "'Misguided ... six letters ... third letter's a w ... come on ... ah! 'Unwise.' That's another word for 'misguided,' ain't it?"

"I suppose so," said K.

"'Reckless?' Thirteen letters?"

"I think I know what you're doing, sir," K said.

"Do you? Help me with this," said the sheriff, peering myopically at a message slip: "'This ain't the Land of the Free, it's the Land of the Freeloaders.'"

"I don't say 'ain't,'" said K.

"You go on like this, son, and they'll revoke your naturalized status," said the sheriff.

"Maybe it's time for me to pack up and go back to Wales and grow leeks or something," said K.

"You got some commitments here. Remember your book-store?" said the sheriff. "If you're starting to think about leaving now, it's about running away. I'll be darned if I put all that work into changing y'all's rota for nothing. Anyways ... what got into you with the 'freeloaders?'"

"Good sense got into me," said K. "All I said was that if hu-mans insist on settling where they aren't supposed to settle and take away all that habitat from wildlife, they should be prepared to occasionally pay a price for that."

"Uh-huh," said the sheriff. "I was hoping that Curtis Malone would tell them that. He's got some practice saying those things to folks and making them listen."

"I don't?" asked K mutinously. Weismaker regarded him over the rim of his spectacles and sighed.

"Malone didn't turn up," K said.

"He didn't turn up?"

"No."

"Why didn't he?"

K shrugged. "I don't know."

"He didn't say?"

"I rang him a couple of times. I left messages for him. So far, he hasn't gotten back to me."

The sheriff frowned. "I spoke to him a couple of days ago. We set up that meeting together. He was all for it. He'd got some great stuff together about humane methods to deter wildlife. He had me convinced, alright. You're saying he didn't get in touch with you?"

"He didn't."

"Left no message?"

"No, sir."

"Did you call Fish & Wildlife?"

"Just his cell, sir."

"We better call the office," said the sheriff, and began rum-maging through the papers on his desk. "I recall some restructur-ing. Fish & Wildlife got moved to ... where did they get moved to ..."

"I couldn't say, sir." All that he *could* say, had he been asked, was that the monstrous bureaucratic apparatus serving infinitely fragmented federal services cleaved to ye olde divide-and-rule ruse.

"Get yourself a coffee while I hunt for the number."

K got up reluctantly and walked as slowly as reasonably feasible to the sulfurous fount. He took his time choosing a mug among the chipped crockery on offer and was just lifting the coffeepot in the manner of someone removing a blowfish from a plughole when the phone rang.

"Please, God," prayed K the agnostic, "let this chalice pass by me ..."

The sheriff replaced the receiver: "Gotta postpone your coffee. Call-out. Take Young."

K didn't bother miming regret. He made like an exorcist and got the hell out.

"Did the sheriff tell you not to pass on work you're supposed to do to the interns?" asked Becky.

"No. Gotta go."

"*No?* Why did he want to see you, then?"

"Because of all the complaints that you practice your handwriting on," said K. "Look, I'm in a hurry." Becky was getting that pinched look around her nose. "Can't we be friends again?" asked K. "We used to get on fine, didn't we?"

Becky snorted. "Did you pass on stuff you were supposed to do to Chase?"

"Chase?"

"That intern."

"Isn't he called 'Cody?' Or 'Hunter?'"

"He's called Chase. And he's got big problems, I'm telling you, *real* big problems with ARGUS. Even bigger problems than you have," said Becky.

"So what's the problem with Cody's problem?"

"*Chase.* His problem is where you are supposed to save each entry as you go, and then save the whole file; Chase didn't get that. 'Cause if you don't save every entry as you're inputting it and you only save the file, it's gonna save just an empty file and delete all your entries. He's been doing that all the time he's been here, like two weeks. Did you give him important stuff to do?"

When Becky was in a mood, she liked to rub K's nose in his IT inadequacies. K found he was warming to Taylor/Colson/Randy. "Why don't we have this out later?" he asked. "I really have to go."

And he wasn't even lying. This time the benign spirits that had protected K from the sheriff's coffee were diligent in the distraction they had staged: a fire had broken out on Milagro's south-eastern fringe, setting a trailer ablaze.

K found Young standing in the foyer, wedging his thumb under his holster and trying to scratch his pit. Catching a noseful of Young's peculiar mélange of stale sweat, BBQ sauce, and spearmint, K accelerated past him with a cheery wave.

K had thought that after a near-decade living and working in Milagro, he knew most of it. But now and then he came upon places he'd never noticed, and had never suspected were there. This was such a place. It looked like a place way back in time . . . Milagro before Milagro. It looked like those places deep on the Rez that you passed—so remote, so untouched, so forbidding, that you wondered how anyone had ever found their way here. Steep mesa walls rose out of hillocks of rocks and rubble, the debris of millennia of landslides. No ranches, no alfalfa or hemp fields here. No irrigation ditches. Toward the west, the land sloped off into the plain that stretched to the far mountain range. Vermilion Crest still bore a tiara of snow. To the south, the metal sheet roof of the Walmart Supercenter winked in the sunlight. The acrid chemical smell of something burning made K's nose tingle. A plume of black smoke spiraled skyward, lending the air a leaden hue. K parked the patrol car behind the fire engine.

The HazMat team, in their suits already, were examining smoking debris. Whatever there had been, was now gone. One of the HazMats came over, tipped his plastic hood and handed K a mask and a pair of high-top boot covers.

"This looks bad," K said.

"It is," the HazMat guy, whom K now recognized as melancholic Dave Oberg, said.

The mask was paper, and didn't do much to shield him from the awful toxic fumes. But maybe the mask was just about preventing him from coughing his DNA all over the place.

"Finding anything?" asked K.

"Trying to assemble the remains," said Oberg.

"Remains?"

"Two, at least," said Oberg, "could be three. We aren't sure yet."

"People died in this fire?"

Oberg nodded.

"Anybody saved?"

Oberg shook his head.

"How come?" Somehow, K had gotten the idea that this was a routine fire that had been caught in time.

Oberg raised his hand, snapped his fingers and opened his palm: "These old trailers," he said, "they're combustible."

The smoke tickled K's nose and burned his throat. He tried not to think of the micro-particles of burnt human flesh that were entering his body.

Oberg was looking at him as if he knew what was going on. K cleared his throat and asked, "Any idea what made this thing burn?"

"If something goes up that quickly, it's usually arson," said Oberg. "But we still have to check it out."

K picked his way around HazMat tape and smoldering rubble heading toward the trailer of the person who had called in the fire. The high polish of the vehicle parked outside contrasted with the lopsided trailer's flaky paint. One window was nailed shut with a sheet of plywood. An overflowing trash can in front of the trailer hummed with the delirious buzz of flies. K climbed the steps to the trailer and knocked. Inside, a dog began to yap hysterically. K waited for a minute and knocked again. He heard the dog rush to the door and throw itself against it.

"Hello," K called, and knocked again. He heard a door inside open, the sound of the floor creaking underfoot. "Police," K called. The footsteps stopped. "It's about the fire." The floor creaked again.

A chain was pulled off the door. A woman's face peered at him through a three-inch gap. The little dog struggled to squeeze through, baring impressive fangs.

"Harvey!" said the woman. "Shush!" She scooped up the dog and held it under her arm. The dog, emboldened by the height it had gained, yapped shrilly and snarled.

"May I come in?" K asked.

The woman made an attempt to smooth back her hair, thereby dropping the dog. It made a dash for K and fastened its teeth onto K's boot. "Harvey!" said the woman and grabbed the dog by the scruff of the neck, carrying it aloft to the back of the trailer. She shut a door on Harvey's shrill complaints. "He is very protective," said the woman. There was pride in her voice.

She stood aside and motioned to the interior of the trailer. There wasn't any free surface. Piles of clothes and cardboard boxes occupied every conceivable space, even the cooking stove. Under the sink an open trash bag, brimming with take-out containers, spilled part of its contents on the floor. The woman stood, uncertain, in the middle of the mess.

"I just got here," she said, "I'm not staying here long. Just until I find something, you know? I never lived like this before. Hauling water and making electricity with a generator. It's like a hundred years back or something."

"You called the fire department?" asked K.

She nodded. "I was getting back from work. I worked the early shift. I was driving down Dead Creek Road, and there was smoke, and I thought, 'Gee that's some fire'—but I didn't think it was a real fire. I just thought it was them burning trash, you know? You burn trash and it comes up all thick and black. I was going to ask them to burn my trash, too, you know, while the fire was going. I was driving down when I remembered I forgot Harvey's food. I turned back right there and drove to Walmart. There's only one kind of food he likes, you know? He doesn't like dry food at all. He only likes that fancy stuff that looks like a big old sausage. But he only likes the chicken 'n liver flavored one. He won't try anything else; I tried *everything*. But Walmart didn't have that stuff. I had to speak to the manager, and the manager said they'll have a delivery in two days, but what am I supposed to do? Harvey just won't eat anything else. Then I tried City Market. City Market didn't have any of that stuff either—I don't even think they carry it, 'cause it's real fancy and expensive. It's kind of weird that Walmart has it, don't you think? Then I went to Safeway, and they didn't have it, either. But this nice lady at the checkout said, 'Why don't you try Country Market, they got all kinds of stuff?' So I did, and guess what? They had it, and there was a 3-for-2 deal on it, too! And then I drove home ..." Her voice sank to a whisper. "It was black. All black. The smoke ..." Her eyes filled with tears. "If I hadn't ... if I hadn't run out of food for Harvey ... do you think ...?"

She had chuntered on about Harvey's food preferences and her odyssey around Milagro's supermarkets, as happily and as unaffectedly, as if all that was on her mind was dog food. K marveled at the phenomenon of narrators reacting to a turn of events in their story as if they hadn't foreseen it, hadn't already lived through it. They knew the story; they knew how it ended. And yet it was as if each telling bore with it sudden shock, fresh devastation, like a kind of psychic Groundhog Day.

K tried to remember who had told him that his own tendency to lose himself in reverie was really a type of escapism, a defensive maneuver against the unbearable harshness of reality. Perhaps they had been right, because right now he had begun to lose himself in the miraculous dynamics of narrative displacement precisely when the woman asked him if her dog-chow excursion had occasioned her neighbors' deaths.

No. It hadn't been a question. It had been a confession. She knew her neighbors might have been saved had she gotten home earlier.

"Thank you for calling the fire department," K said. She had had to drive up the road to where there was reception, so she had gone out of her way, in a way.

She nodded, her eyes searching his face as if looking therein for absolution. "Did you know your neighbors?" asked K.

The woman shook her head. She had just moved down from Idaho. She'd gotten a job as a caregiver at the Mesa Vista Care Home. She was renting the trailer from one of the managers until she found something better. Now she really, really wanted to get out of here. Her eyes filmed with tears.

"You never saw your neighbors?" asked K.

She shook her head. "I haven't been here that long." She hadn't ever seen them; she hadn't seen anybody. But she had seen a truck parked in front of the trailer, at night. She didn't know if the truck had been there every night, though. She hadn't really paid attention. And she started to cry again.

"Would you be able to come to the station and make a statement?" asked K. She suddenly looked frightened, so K added: "It's fine. We could do it here and now, if you prefer."

She did prefer. While K shifted his weight from foot to foot and Harvey snarled and yapped shrilly and hurled himself against the door, the woman wrote down her statement, resting the form on top of the edge of the stove and now and then wiping her eyes with the back of her hand. She wrote slowly and stopped frequently, chewing on her lip and casting her eyes toward the ceiling as if to summon inspiration from there.

"Just write as you told me," K advised.

She nodded like a pupil eager to please the teacher and wrote, tears rolling down her face and dripping onto the statement form, smudging her script.

Mike Grimes rose out of the smoking rubble like a plastic-shrouded colossus and shambled over. With his unkempt mane, abundant facial hair covered in a hair-and- beard-net, and thick glasses, Grimes was a remarkable rendition of the mad-scientist stereotype.

"Meet Heidi," Mike said. He gestured to a young woman with rosy cheeks and net-covered, straw-colored hair hanging in thick braids over her shoulders, who was poking around in smoldering debris. Rarely had K beheld someone so suited to their name and, appearance-wise, so unsuited to their profession. Heidi waved cheerfully.

"So ...?" said K.

Grimes drew his foot over a pile of rubble. "We got us one of those situations where a couple of minutes make all the difference," he said. "These old trailers are drenched in formaldehyde. The fire takes a while to get going. Then it takes hold, and ... *whoosh!*"

Damn Harvey and his special food, thought K, and asked: "Cause?"

"Arson. Melted gas canister over there." Grimes cocked his thumb toward the far end of the tar-black mass that had been the trailer. "I'll put it all in the report for you." Grimes was familiar with K's attention span.

"Are you sure? I mean, why? Who'd do this?"

Grimes shrugged: "Could have been a domestic situation; someone carrying a grudge; burglary gone wrong ..." He pulled his glasses down to the tip of his nose and looked at K over the rims. His eyes were the pale green of gooseberries. He took a step toward K. "But that's not what I think, see?"

"What do you think?"

Grimes's eyes shone with a chemical-green light. He looked over his shoulder. "There's been a bunch of these all over the county," he said in a low voice.

"Arson attacks?"

Grimes looked over his shoulder again and stepped closer. "All folks that had gotten offers from property developers and refused to sell."

"Property developers?"

Grimes grimaced, hissing, *"Shh!"*

"Property developers?" repeated K in a whisper.

A trickle of rubble bounced down the wall of the mesa. K looked up along the sheer wall and, above it, at the azure sky. Suddenly he felt as if there was an eye, a giant eye somewhere, trained on them.

"It's been going on for years," Grimes said in a hoarse whisper. "One fire here, one fire there ... plenty of time gaps."

"You think this might be such a case?" K murmured. Paranoia was contagious.

"You heard of Highlight Living?" asked Grimes in an even lower voice. K shook his head. "They developed Mesa Sunshine Gated Community."

"Oh," said K. Mesa Sunshine Gated Community was an assembly of hacienda- and alpine-chalet-style houses, girdled by a spiked, wrought-iron fence, at Milagro's eastern boundary, that sat on the desiccated plain like a piñata on a funeral buffet.

"First they got Delgado," Grimes murmured. "There's nowhere around Delgado now that ordinary folks can afford to buy."

"You think they would torch a trailer with people in it to get to the land?" whispered K.

Grimes raised his eyebrows and shrugged. "I'll get the report ready for you." He stalked over the rubble, his white HazMat suit billowing, wreathed in smoke like the genie from Aladdin's lamp.

CHAPTER NINE

K had barely set foot in the station when Becky pounced again: "You know you're not supposed to go and see people on your own, right?"

"It was just a short statement we needed. No big deal," K said.

"When you're accused of harassment or something, then it will be," said Becky.

"Accused of *what*?"

"Harassment. Sexual assault. Stuff like that."

"There are many things I may not know," said K, "but one thing I do know is my boundaries."

"The folks who are going to accuse you are not going to know that," said Becky.

"I forgot to smoke my bong today," said K. "I'm not getting what you are saying."

Becky's nostrils flared. "I'm saying you are not supposed to go see people on your own."

It was a verbal-riff equivalent of hyenas on the savannah, turning round and round before bedding down.

"What did you say?"

"What did I say?"

"Did you just say I'm like a hyena?"

Oh, crap. Ye olde Tourette's striking again.

"No," said K, "I was thinking about lunch, and probably speaking Welsh, coz I really feel like a bowl of *cawl* and a *hye-ee-nah*. That's a tea cake in Cymraeg." He doubted she was going to Google to verify. The way Becky looked at him, she wasn't buying it, anyway.

"You can't go on call-outs on your own."

"We're alone when we do the traffic patrols," K objected.

"That's in a public place," said Becky, "and you got dashboard cameras. Anyways. You're not supposed—"

"Young hadn't had his lunch," K said.

"You were supposed to take me!" yelled Young. He had crept up on them and was now leaning on the reception counter, breathing heavily. His shirt showed traces of ketchup and mustard. There was a smear of chocolate on his chin.

"I thought it was just a little fire," K said.

"Was it big?"

"Well, worse than I thought. Delgado Forensics were over there."

"Delgado Forensics? Wow. Must be serious, then. What did they say?" asked Becky.

"They were just starting," said K. "They think it was arson."

"Arson, huh? Did anybody get hurt?"

K nodded. "Two died. At least two. Maybe three."

It was always when he said things out loud that reality hit him. "Two, definitely," he added, "the neighbor called in the fire. I got her statement."

"What did she say?"

"Nothing much," said K. He didn't feel up to repeating the Harvey saga. It was one of those stories that made you feel worse every time you repeated it.

"'Nothing much' took you that long?" There were all kinds of speculation in Becky's eyes. K felt a hot knot of anger forming in his gut.

"You really think I'd go and assault or harass a witness to a fatal arson attack? Just because there's no one there to stop me?"

Becky shrugged. "You never know."

"Really? You never know?"

"No," said Becky.

"That must be a pretty hellish place to be in," said K, and stomped off to his office, where he tore frayed leaves off the dragon tree, proceeding from there to tear up old message slips. When he found nothing more to tear up, he stood at the window looking at the cracked tarmac of the parking lot, tracing some more patterns into the dusty slats of the blinds. He felt the madness of the world creeping up on him. It wasn't an empire of surreal imagination or florid psychopathology. It wasn't a grand and noble type of madness. It was madness fashioned of petty preoccupations and small-minded paranoiac projection. It was a kitchen-sink drama of low cunning and banal opportunism.

He looked to the mesa foothills, lying innocently in the sunshine, where today a couple of people had died because of an ill-tempered lapdog's food preferences.

CHAPTER TEN

In Milagro PD's meeting room, Delgado Forensics' wholesome Heidi was drawing a diagram on the whiteboard depicting the trajectory of the fire, and showed photographs of the molten, shriveled lump of plastic that had been the gas canister used to start the fire.

The fire had started inside the trailer. Gas from the canister found at the scene had been sprinkled along the length of the structure and set alight. The destruction was too thorough to determine whether a lighter or matches or another implement had been used. Likewise, it was impossible to determine whether or not entry had been forced. The charred remains of two victims were in the morgue, awaiting the attention of the pathologist.

"Why ain't *you* telling us?" asked Dilger, who had busied himself with stuffing down a half-dozen Little Debbie Swiss rolls set out in pyramid shape on a hostess trolley for the forensic team's delectation. He pointed at Grimes.

"Am I not doing a good enough job for you?" Heidi asked merrily. "Any more questions?"

"Yes," said Smithson. "Why don't you tell us about those arson cases up in Delgado?"

"That's how Highlight Living are supposed to get their land, right?" asked Myers at his usual volume, apparently unaware of the KGB-level infiltration exercised by ruthless property developers.

Grimes's pale gooseberry eyes widened behind his Coke-bottle lenses.

K fancied that Grimes would blame him for the careless talk, though he'd been too disturbed by Grimes's paranoid fantasies to tell anyone. And there wasn't anybody he would have wanted to tell, except Córdoba and maybe Gutierrez, but Gutierrez wasn't on duty anyway.

"Would they not have torched the other trailer too, if it was property developers?" asked K.

"They're counting on the folks in the other trailer to get scared and move out by themselves," said Myers gaily. "They're way too clever to do more than they have to."

"Arson," said Juanita Córdoba wistfully, shuffling her court files. "I wish I could work on that."

CHAPTER ELEVEN

Córdoba's office was sober, meticulously organized, and somewhat impersonal, when disregarding the evocative scent of citrus fruit and lush, tropical foliage after a rainfall that surrounded her, and the incongruous snow globe on her desk, encasing a lasso-throwing cowgirl mounted on a rearing horse.

"It's a waiting game," said Córdoba.

"Sure is," said K.

"It gets to you after a while."

"Doesn't it just," K said vaguely.

"I like things that I can do something about. These cases, there's so little I can do."

K was beginning to find Córdoba's unusual chattiness somewhat unnerving.

"You want something you can do something about?" he asked hopefully. But Córdoba was concentrating on something beyond the vanishing point, and did not hear.

"That lawyer is like a coyote digging up bones," she said.

"That lawyer?"

"He's a real creep, too," said Córdoba. "I guess it takes a creep to defend a creep."

Obviously K was meant to know what case and which lawyer Córdoba was referring to; wrack his brains however he might, K couldn't recall the case she was grinding on about right now. There were so many; Córdoba kept busy. She was a one-woman social-justice band, and nobody dare yell that all pigs were dirty and needed to be defunded because Córdoba embodied all the highest ideals of the job. For her it wasn't a job, it was a calling—and whenever K spent time with Córdoba, he felt almost proud to be a cop. Almost.

"Is he going to get him off?" asked K.

Córdoba shrugged. "I have only the one witness. And she's starting to scare."

"Just the one witness ...?"

Córdoba looked up at K. The color of her eyes always stunned him. They were the purest obsidian. "You don't know what case I'm talking about, do you?"

"I ... erm ..."

"The serial assaulter," said Córdoba. "The guy who preys on Native women."

"*That* guy!" said K.

That guy had made it his specialty to lure into his vehicle and subsequently rape inebriated Native women, mainly street drinkers. He would cruise between the dive bars on Main and City Park, biding time until his prospective prey was on her own. He was not just an opportunist and a rapist but a sadist, too. What he tended to do to his victims was so degrading that they would not go to the cops even if they hadn't been incapacitated and weren't socially marginalized to begin with. But there were never any witnesses to these attacks anyway.

Córdoba had spent the better part of a year working on this case, which nobody else was interested in. Female Native street drinkers occupied the lowest level of society's debris. These women were generally regarded as barely human, their rape and torture given as much thought as this community of ranchers tended to grant to the ethics of animal husbandry. Maybe that's why Córdoba wished she were working the arson case.

"That lawyer creep's going to throw everything at this." Córdoba drummed her fingers on the table. "He's scaring my witness."

"The one witness you have?"

"She's real frightened. I don't blame her. The guy is fixing to drag her through the mud. I'm getting worried about putting her through this." Córdoba laid a palm flat on her forehead and ran it over her hair. "What do you think?"

K couldn't remember Córdoba ever asking him for advice. His mind went blank.

"It depends how you look at it," he said eventually. "If you happen to believe in justice being done, then you at least owe it to try. If you happen to know the guy is going to continue victimizing others, you owe it to try. If you are into probability of conviction, you might want to desist. If you are worried about vulnerable women being given a hard time and maybe feeling even more vulnerable, then you might want to desist."

Córdoba nodded thoughtfully.

"But if you want to give the victims a chance, however small, to overcome and become survivors, then you owe *them* to try."

"I'll think about it," Córdoba said. "Thank you." She laid her hand on his elbow briefly: "And now tell me what I can do for you."

"You really can't find anything?" He'd been sitting next to Córdoba at her desk for over an hour, watching her work her way methodically through whatever database she could get her hands on: census data, utility services, voter registries, San Matteo's refuse collection database, Medicaid and Medicare records, tax records, vehicle licensing … It was the first time, as far as K could remember, that Córdoba had not fulfilled his expectations. He had thought this would be the simplest thing to find—for anyone but him.

"*Nothing*," said Córdoba, "I don't get it. How can that be? Right now, I can't think of anyplace else we can search. I guess we could try City Planning …"

The more blanks they drew, the more fascinated K became. This was like an old-fashioned mystery, in which they were trying to find a place that didn't exist—though mysteries usually had it the other way round, with places that were on maps but remained elusive in reality.

"You didn't grow up here either, did you?"

Córdoba shook her head: "Albuquerque."

The majority of the squad had indeed grown up in San Matteo County, but there were few among them K felt like asking.

"How about Smithson?" said Córdoba. "He really knows his way around here."

Smithson appeared, proudly bearing a plate of scavenged Little Debbie rolls, which he passed around. Córdoba declined but K accepted, because he didn't want to seem churlish. It was his first Little Debbie cake in all his time in this country—and if he'd tried one before becoming a naturalized citizen, there was a good chance he wouldn't have gone through with the naturalization process.

"We can't seem to find any official address for this place," K explained, putting his finger on the blank space to the west side of the mesa on the map.

Smithson squinted at the map: "Why you askin'?"

"We're trying to ID those arson fatalities," said Córdoba.

"Ahh, those arson fatalities ..." said Smithson. "Darn clever way to grab yourself some cheapo land and make some real whoopee with it."

"You don't sound as if you see a problem with this," said K.

"Depends how you look at it," said Smithson vaguely. "Did you try—?"

"We tried everything," said Córdoba sharply, rattling off all the databases she'd worked through.

"Could be this is one of those blind spots," said Smithson.

"Blind spots?" said K. The blind spots he knew were those of a conceptual nature, like the one Smithson had just demonstrated.

"You ain't heard of blind spots?" said Smithson. "There's loads of them on the Rez. But we got ourselves a couple of blind spots in our county, too. There's some particular parts of Milagro that are blind spots—there's no record for them, see? I'm saying there's no official record for them."

"*For* them, or *of* them?" asked K.

"For them," said Smithson, unperturbed. "There's gonna have to be an official record *for* them for there to be an official record *of* them, see?"

K hadn't taken Smithson for an existentialist.

"You ain't gonna find those blind spots on Google, or your GPS. There's no postal delivery there, and no trash pick-up. Because there are no utilities, there is no address. Because there's no address, folks living in those blind spots can't vote, see?"

K knew something about this. It was how large swathes of the Navajo Nation's residents were excluded from participating in their democratic right to vote. The Rez was vast, remote, and mostly lacking in the natural resources that evoked Anglo avarice. "Name and Claim" had been the white colonists' preferred method of land theft. Name—create an official title—and file a claim; in a heartbeat, land that had been in use for centuries by Native tribes was then closed to them. And now, in a perfidious historical turn, the very places that had not been deemed worthy of the European acquisitive drive were a means to further disenfranchise the Native population by excluding them from the electoral process.

"Are you listening?" said Smithson. "You *are* into this crap, aren't you? The whole mesa used to belong to the Ute. You ought to know that, right?"

K nodded. He knew that crap. The Ute had had the use of a huge area of land, covering a sizable part of what was now New Mexico and Colorado, running from sandstone desert to the Rocky Mountains. By historical accounts, the tribe had been more than liberal in signing away their land. It was hard to understand quite why.

Perhaps Chief Ouray—*aka* "White Man's Friend"—had been trusting enough to believe that the invaders' rapacious appetite for land could be appeased by preemptive gifts; perhaps Chief Ouray had known that the colonists would, in any case, take what wasn't yielded to them voluntarily. Perhaps the Ute had simply not sub-scribed to the concept of land ownership, or, as the majority of other tribes did, defined land ownership as a perpetually transitional state: at any given moment, you owned only the land on which you stood.

"How come not everything that used to be Ute land is blind spots?" K asked, thinking this a fair enough question. Judging from Smithson's expression, though, it apparently was not.

"They are blind spots because they were ... overlooked. Or forgotten. See?"

"Pity that didn't happen more often," murmured K.

"There's nothing there," explained Smithson. "There's no wa-ter. The soil's kinda bad. Nothing will grow there. Probably there was nobody that wanted that land. I guess it must have been Indians in that trailer. Or some meth cookers. Or maybe both."

Córdoba was looking at the pattern the swaying branches of the tree outside the window were casting on the wall.

"'Indians or meth cookers,'" repeated K.

"I figure the only folks that will live without utilities got to be Indians. They're used to hauling water and using generators for electricity."

"Oh," said K.

"What?" asked Smithson.

"The neighbor … that lady I went to ask some questions about the fire … she mentioned something about a generator and hauling water."

"You're telling me *now*?" asked Córdoba, exasperated. "If I had known that, we could have saved ourselves an hour of trouble."

"I just remembered," said K sheepishly. "I thought she was exaggerating. She said something about how living there was like being a hundred years back. I thought she was just using a figure of speech. Was there a generator in the burnt trailer?"

"It was you who went there, remember?" said Smithson. "Indians can deal with living there. It's basically the same way that most of them live out there on the Rez anyways."

"If there had been evidence of a meth lab, Grimes would have mentioned it," said K.

"You sure?" said Smithson.

"What is *that* supposed to mean?" asked K.

"I'm saying nothing," Smithson said, meaningfully.

K decided he wasn't going to give him the satisfaction of pursuing whatever beef Smithson had with Grimes.

"If there's no address," he asked innocently, "how do the people who live there register to vote?"

"They can't vote," said Smithson in a long-suffering tone, just about skipping the addition of "dumbass."

"Is that legal?" asked K.

"It's illegal to vote when you ain't got an address," said Smithson.

"So what are you saying? That these people who live in blind spots right here in Milagro city limits have no legal identity?"

"Yessir. That's what I'm saying."

"So it's like they're dead." Too late, K realized what he had said.

"Nope," said Smithson. "It's like they never been alive."

CHAPTER TWELVE

Cuauhtémoc was balancing on a ladder with a duster, taking out books, dusting them off, and slotting them back. Benjamin sat under the ladder watching specks of dust adrift in the light. Cuauhtémoc jumped off the ladder. K remembered that he had no employee accident insurance.

"I see you met."

"That's a great cat." Cuauhtémoc smiled happily. "He's been keeping me company. And he's real good for business, too."

K still praised the day that had put Cuauhtémoc in his way—Cuauhtémoc, and his high school teacher and champion Siwan Davies, thanks to whose powers of reasoning and persuasion K had finally decided to risk taking on Agnes Prohaska's bookstore. Their first meeting had not been especially auspicious, given that Cuauhtémoc had been a suspect in a case. K's interview technique on that occasion hadn't been something to merit a three-star evaluation in the police interrogation manual.

"There's some people I know …" said Cuauhtémoc, and cleared his throat. "There's some people I know that are starting up a Water Alliance…"

"Water Alliance?"

"We are in a drought," said Cuauhtémoc, "but people don't care at all. Maybe they don't see it. They're worried about air pollution. But why is nobody talking about water? If there's no water, we are all going to die."

"I'm with you on that," said K. "A Water Alliance sounds like a great idea. Where are you meeting? I might drop in."

"I … I was thinking … could we meet here? Maybe if everybody gave a bit of money, we could rent the back room for the meetings? The library closes so early."

"You'd like to meet here?" Why hadn't he seen it? The back room was the ideal space for gatherings. After all, it had a long and distinguished history of old hippies meeting up to chew on the Gramsci-versus-Trotsky conundrum. "Great!" K said enthusiastically. "This is exactly what this store is supposed to be for! Who are these people? Students from your school?"

"There are some that split off from the other Water Alliance. They never used to do anything. No educating people. No outreach. Nothing."

"Where did you meet them?" asked K.

Cuauhtémoc blushed. "My boyfriend." He said it very quickly, and K guessed that he hadn't had the opportunity to say it very often yet. There was all the wonder and excitement and audacity of a new and perhaps first relationship in Cuauhtémoc's voice.

"Anytime you want to meet up here, just go ahead," K said, trying to keep his voice casual, so as not to scare this earnest and intensely private young man. He still cringed when he remembered how his clumsy questioning had forced Cuauhtémoc to come out to him. "Matter of fact: if you know of any other groups that need a place to meet up ..." He began to see a way for the bookstore to become a community hub ... maybe a center to foment revolution. He was beginning almost to feel thrilled, until he remembered that he might have to be there and play the gracious host. Maybe there was a way to create a lifelong position for Cuauhtémoc. Maybe he should just go ahead and transfer the store to Cuauhtémoc now.

"Is the cat going to stay here?"

"He seems happy enough, doesn't he?"

Cuauhtémoc nodded. "Real happy. He's already picked where he's gonna sleep."

"Let me guess; the armchair with the crochet blanket?"

"How did you know?"

"Wouldn't you, if you were a cat? Now we better have a proper introduction: Cuauhtémoc, meet Benjamin; Benjamin, meet Cuauhtémoc," K said gravely.

Cuauhtémoc held out his hand. The old tom tilted his head and regarded the hand. Very slowly, he raised his paw and laid it on the boy's hand.

"Now we are all one happy family," said K. He wasn't even sure if he was joking.

"Some guy came in," Cuauhtémoc said, and went to the desk with the vintage cash register, and produced a handful of glossy flyers. "He brought in these. He wanted us to put them out for the customers." K took one. "I didn't know…" Cuauhtémoc began. "I wasn't sure if this is the right thing for the store …"

K studied the flyer: "You were right." Never underestimate the forces of serendipity. He looked at his watch. "How are you for time?"

"I got the afternoon free," said Cuauhtémoc.

"Would you mind staying on? There's something I'd like to check out."

"Sure."

"And don't work too hard. Promise? How about taking some time to organize your Water Alliance group, while I go and check out these high-gloss folks?"

CHAPTER THIRTEEN

K parked his clapped-out old Datsun at the roadside. He walked along the dusty road until he came to an ornate and spiked wrought-iron gate, where the polished vehicles of visitors filled the landscaped driveway. A young man wearing a faded NAVAJO COMMUNITY COLLEGE sweatshirt was raking the gravel walkways—a Sisyphean task if ever there was. He moved with a limp, and his dragging leg grooved the gravel, thereby undoing the work he had presumably been employed to do.

K strolled into the show-house, where an assembled crowd of would-be buyers filled the den pretty much to capacity. Actually, it wasn't a den or even a living room, but—as a sun-kissed dude with flaxen locks that spoke of a bathroom-shelf full of alchemical hair products informed them—a *kiva*.

K raised his hand and inquired as to whether or not there was a trending demand for holding ceremonies in domestic dwellings. Underneath the man's perma-glaze, his smile lost a few degrees of warmth. A young woman passed among the audience with thimbles of iced tea and bowls of Hershey's Kisses. Her name tag, which read ORLANA LOMATEWA, identified her as someone who might conceivably have experience of *kivas* as ceremonial spaces.

On the whitewashed wall of the *"kiva"* a projected slideshow depicted the vision of the Kachina Village Development in a loop.

"Kachina Village?" Did these fools know where they were? At least now the *kiva* made sense. Maybe the developers had originally aspired to buy up some land Santa Fe way, or somewhere around Sedona—one of those places that were magnets to Anglos on a quest for the "authentic" Southwest, consisting of Pueblo pottery, Zuni fetishes and Hopi *kachinas*, who would rate dens-dressed-up-as-*kivas* as a spiritual bonus. In redneck Milagro town, alas, the secular appetite for Native sacred spaces needed some developing.

The projected image of ornamental wrought-iron fences topped with lethal spikes gave way to presentations of the styles of homes available: "Chalet," "Ranchito," and "Hacienda," sterile eyesores that made the soul bleed, all accessorized with three-car garages. Gleaming white gravel paths led to blindingly lacquered front doors. Kitchen "nooks" opened onto backyards decked out with chemical-green AstroTurf and the inevitable basketball hoop in one corner. Immaculately tarred roads led in loops to nowhere. The general impression was a New Jersey Turnpike take on *Natural Born Killers*-meets-*The Truman-Show*, designed by a twelve-year-old on a bad batch of meth.

Small mercy that the development itself afforded not from any one of its vantage points even the tiniest glimpse of the mesa. K drew some comfort from the thought that the Ancient Ones' stronghold wouldn't be sullied by the eyes of these perverse creatures, who would be shielded from all this infinite natural splendor inside a spiked fence.

"Which one do you prefer?"

K's initial impression, that the buxom woman who posed the question was asking him to appraise her chest, probably didn't speak in his favor.

"Have you made your choice?" he asked evasively.

"The 'Hacienda' is the only one that's got a *kiva*," said the woman wistfully, "but it's kind of more than our budget, you know? The 'Ranchito' is cute, though."

"A couple of years ago, you could've bought this whole land for $20,000," K said.

"Are you kidding me? Twenty thousand dollars?"

"Well, it used to be the overflow site for the municipal dump," said K cheerfully. "They managed to make it look real neat though, haven't they? You should have seen the cleanup operation of all those toxic barrels."

He beamed at the woman and accosted Orlana Lomatewa, who was refilling bowls with Hershey's Kisses. "I just noticed your name. You don't happen to be related to Douglas Lomatewa?"

Orlana nodded: "My uncle. You know him?"

"I worked with him on a case years ago," said K, "over at Keams Canyon."

"You are a policeman, too?" asked Orlana.

"I was wondering about these *kivas*," said K.

Orlana emptied a bag of Hershey's into a bowl and set out fresh thimbles, which she filled with iced tea. "Do you like them?" she said eventually.

"No," said K.

Orlana nodded and hefted up the tray: "I don't think my uncle would, either." She set off on her way through the merry throng.

The blond dreamboat was giving a speech that left the assembled moist-eyed and fumbling for their checkbooks. Here they were at the apex of the magic-imbued world of the Ancient Ones, who had chosen to settle here because of the portentous fortune delivered to those residing in these spots by the *Vortex*. This magic land offered everything that the wild at heart could desire, with the added bonus of a Walmart Supercenter in immediate proximity. It would be, the dreamboat promised, a community of like-minded people, a place where winners in this life congregated and mingled and raised the fruits of their loins. The community was safer than Fort Knox, thanks to the artisan-designed eight-foot fence, which would impale and disembowel miscreants seeking to scale it. In fact, were politicians to consider erecting a similar fence along—

At this precise moment, and as proof of the ever-present possibility of divine intervention, the door of the "Hacienda" show-home opened and Óscar Gutierrez, accompanied by his wife Conchita carrying their youngest child in a sling, entered to the dreamboat concluding his sentence with "—the Mexican border."

The prospective buyers turned as one, assessed the Gutierrez family, and then turned expectantly back to the dreamboat. Perhaps they thought that the entrance of a Hispanic family was being staged for the purposes of providing a demonstration of the property developers' strategies concerning intruders.

"Can I help you, folks?" asked Dreamboat. His joviality had an edge.

In the time it took K to contemplate a suitable intervention that would make Dreamboat publicly choke on eating crow, Gutierrez flashed his shield and said: "There's been a report of vandalism on the property. The squad cars are on their way."

Gutierrez nodded gravely at the assembly; laying his hand on his perplexed spouse's shoulder, he steered his family out the door. Quite a few of the prospective feudal lords of the *kiva*-manor took the opportunity to skedaddle in their wake, among them the lady who had fancied the "Hacienda"-style domicile.

Dreamboat was having a hard time being heard over the din. Some folks sank their hands into the Hershey's bowls on their way out, depositing fistfuls of the candy in various pockets. Maybe this outing had just been cosplay, a cheap day out for these visitors. The thought cheered K up some.

Orlana came through with a tray, collecting thimbles. Dreamboat was chasing visitors around the room. His effect was damn-near magical: as soon as he got close, people vanished through the door. Too late, K noticed that he was the last man standing.

Dreamboat approached with one of those grins that K tended to find more unsettling than reassuring. He reckoned he could see the spotlights reflected in the patina of Dreamboat's capped teeth. Close up, the man's skin looked impossibly smooth, with not an enlarged pore in sight. His eyes were a very pale blue, his pupils Benzedrinoid pinpricks.

"So," he said expansively, "what do you think?" He spread his arms to encompass the "*kiva* room" and pivoted on his heels. "Neat, huh?"

"You're a franchise of Highlight Living?" asked K. The pupils contracted to an even smaller diameter.

"Highlight Living?" said the man through compressed lips. "Certainly not."

"No?" asked K mildly.

"No."

"I just recently went to view one of their new gated communities, and it was so similar that I thought you must be connected. I was so happy when I saw that Highlight Living expanded to our little town."

"We are not connected," said the man grimly.

"Maybe you hired the same architect," said K. "So, anyway, what *is* your outfit called? High Life Living? High Desert Living? High Life? High Five? Pie in the Sky?"

"Cities on a Hill."

"Cities on a Hill," savored K. "As in: 'As a city upon a hill, the eyes of all people are upon us'...?"

"Huh?" said Dreamboat.

"The Reverend John Winthrop, 1630."

"Huh?"

"The Reverend ... John ... Winthrop, 1630. My great-great-great-great—oh, never mind." As so often, K's flights of fancy were not only mistimed, but directed at eminently unsuitable recipients.

"Uh."

"You *have* heard of the Mayflower?" asked K. When you riffed on WASP identity to goyim, you better went the whole hog.

"Sure," said Dreamboat.

"My great-great-great-never-mind was first off the ship. He was the first man to set foot on American soil. And he organized the very first Thanksgiving, which they celebrated with the Indians in their *kiva*."

"Really?" said Dreamboat. He had woken up some.

"Sure. You can read up on him in Wikipedia. That's why I really love your *kiva* room here. Anytime I sit here, in front of a roaring fire, it will put me in mind of my great-great-great—"

"Neat!" said Dreamboat. In his pale eyes, K could see dollar signs spinning. To have a descendant of a Mayflower pilgrim purchase a Cities on a Hill *kiva*-endowed "Hacienda"-style domicile would be a great sales pitch for sure. Dreamboat seemed to have forgotten that the development's *kiva* rooms boasted no fireplaces, but sported, as advertised in the glossy brochure, underfloor heating.

He insisted on leading K around the edifice, a disheartening experience if ever there was. The house had as little to do with a hacienda as the underfloor-heated "*kiva* room" had to do with a kiva. Even from the upper-floor windows, there was no view of the mesa. The view was of a suburban hellhole where Arthur Miller's salesmen went to die, bankrupted.

"So, how did you find this place?" asked K.

"Pardon?"

"How did Cities on a Hill find this piece of land?"

"Oh, we have scouts. You know, just like your great-great-great-granddaddy had, when the Indians showed them around."

"You have Indian scouts?"

"No Indians," said Dreamboat. "We have scouts that know the area. People who live here."

"This land belonged to Indians," said K.

"That was a long time ago."

"Who does your land tend to belong to?"

Dreamboat shrugged. "Sometimes it's ranchers. Or families that want to move on. Ranchers that can't pay their taxes." He seemed to spy something in K's eyes, and added: "It's mostly worthless land. We take it off their hands, and they can get themselves a nice little house somewhere that's not so isolated."

Interesting how all Cities on a Hill's advantages were now being reframed as disadvantages.

"We give value to the land," said Dreamboat, somewhat heatedly. "We take something that's worth nothing and we ... transform it into a place where dreams can grow."

"You should be a poet," said K. "There is of course a great burden of responsibility on being 'a city upon a hill'. Luckily, this compound sits in a depression. There's much more freedom in being looked down upon than being looked up at, don't you think?"

"Pardon?" said Dreamboat.

"You got yourself a lovely piece of land here," said K.

Dreamboat brightened. "It sure is."

"Pity that this plot is so prone to wildfires, though."

Dreamboat shook his flaxen head in the manner of a groggy boxer.

"I better let you deal with that incident of vandalism," K said. "Where are the police, I wonder?"

He grabbed a couple of brochures from the display table. Outside, Orlana was stowing away signposts.

"Do you enjoy your job?" he asked.

The way she looked around while considering her answer told him a lot.

Dreamboat came crashing through the door. "You need to check the windows! Now!" he bellowed, cantering off on gravel-strewn and raked pathways, a hire-for-profit knight without valor in pursuit of the vandals of the American dream. Orlana Lomatewa looked after him and gave a little shrug.

"Say hello to your uncle from me," said K.

CHAPTER FOURTEEN

Googling fire incidents, as K was starting to appreciate, wasn't a task taken on to fill a few free minutes with. He hadn't known that there were so many kinds of fires, ranging from uncontainable wildfires spreading with devastating speed, gas leaks demolishing whole apartment blocks, spontaneously combusting vehicles, self-immolation (of which lamentable act there was more about than K would have guessed, mostly committed by women—he'd have to ask Córdoba about those).

Entering "HIGHLIGHT LIVING" + ARSON into the search engine had brought forth a neon-hued warning of cyberthreat and ransomware, which K, who was even more afraid of cyberspace's diabolical machinations than of the sheriff's toxic brew, had duly heeded.

"There's some lady here that wants to talk to somebody," Becky said. The phone amplified the background noises in reception.

"What would the lady like to talk about?"

"That's for you to find out," said Becky.

The lady that wanted to talk to somebody entered the office uncertainly, and stood at the door. She was a slender woman of middle age who wore her black hair in a tight bun fastened by a silver and turquoise barrette. Around her neck hung a beaded lanyard with an ID card. K offered her a chair and she sat down slowly, her back straight. She set her Pendleton purse on her knees. Her hands kneaded its shoulder strap.

K opened his doodle notebook. The woman cleared her throat.

"How can I help you?" K asked, too brightly. Roleplaying affability wasn't K's strong point, even though he'd gotten in plenty of practice recently. The woman's frown deepened. "How can I help you Mrs. ...?" he repeated more somberly.

"Yazzie." The woman zipped her purse open, rummaged through its contents and brought out a Kleenex, which she used to dab her nose. Then she began to methodically fold the tissue into harmonica creases.

"Mrs. Yazzie, would you mind telling me what your visit is about?" K asked eventually.

The woman twisted the tissue into a coil and crushed the coil into a ball in the palm of her hand.

K folded his hands into a pyramid, as he'd seen the Annoying Counselor do. Among all of the Annoying Counselor's tics, habits, and ruses, this gesture had been the most annoying of all. It spoke of coy self-regard, of oblique narcissism, and—as K eventually had understood—of that most unforgivable state of all in a counselor: helplessness. He unfolded his hands and nodded at the woman— another meaningless, time-buying gesture courtesy of the Annoying Counselor.

Maybe character development was just this: a chain of unpleasant habits acquired from those one least respected, and therefore most closely scrutinized.

Mrs. Yazzie was still twisting the tissue. It had to be a strong tissue to withstand that amount of mistreatment.

She cleared her throat again. "I came here because of that trailer fire."

"The trailer fire?"

She was a manager at the Mesa Vista Care Home, she said, holding up the lanyard with her ID for K to see "Arlene Yazzie." In her ID photo she was smiling and looked different enough that K would not have recognized her from the ID alone.

Arlene Yazzie had heard about the fire from a new employee. Her voice was now so low he could barely hear her.

"Excuse me?" K bent forward. "You are renting out your trailer to your new employee?"

Arlene Yazzie nodded, twisted the tissue in her hands, drew a breath as if preparing to dive off a cliff, and said: "The other trailer ...?"

"What about it?"

"It burned down?" she asked.

K nodded.

"What …" said Arlene Yazzie and drew a faltering breath. "What happened to the people?"

"Do you know the people who lived there?" asked K.

"Lived?"

"Do you know the people in the trailer?"

Arlene Yazzie twisted her tissue rope some more and pulled at it until it came apart.

"Who lives in that trailer?" asked K carefully.

"My relatives," said Arlene Yazzie. "How are they?"

"What are the names of your relatives?"

"Samuel," said the woman, "Samuel and Emma."

"Samuel and Emma Yazzie?"

"Nakai."

"Emma and Samuel Nakai are your relatives?"

Arlene Yazzie nodded and narrowed her eyes: "Emma is my maternal aunt, I guess you would say; Samuel is her husband." She was trying to translate, for the benefit of this *bílagáana*, the intricate Navajo kinship system into much less specific Anglo terms. K recalled the Diné term for maternal aunt: *shimá yázhí*. Little mother. "How are they?" asked Arlene Yazzie hoarsely. "Are they okay? Did they … get out?"

"Are both trailers yours?" asked K, hating what his job made him do.

The woman made a movement that looked like something between a head shake and a nod. "They belong to the family. The family used to live there. It was our outfit, but a lot of us moved away. There's no utilities there. No water. No services. No trash collection. No nothing." She looked at K and said, quickly: "Miranda really needed somewhere to stay."

"Miranda?" asked K.

"Miranda who rents the other trailer," the woman said. "My relatives …"

"Can you tell me something about them?"

"They are elderly," said the woman. "Emma, she has one of those sicknesses; I forgot the name." She looked at K and shook her head: "I know that name. We have a resident at Mesa Vista that has the same sickness. He can't hardly move; sometimes he's better, and then the sickness gets bad and he can't move. Why am I forgetting the name?"

"Because you are stressed and worried," said K.

Tears brimmed in Arlene Yazzie's eyes. She ducked her head in an attempt to hide them.

"Parkinson's?" asked K. "Is Emma Nakai's illness Parkinson's?"

Arlene shook her head: "Parkinson's—that's what they are saying Samuel has got. He shakes a lot. What Emma has got ... it's one of those sicknesses that no one knows how long they will take, or how fast they will make people sick. There's nothing the doctors can do ... " Her hands scrunched the tissue. "I don't think that the sickness Samuel got is Parkinson's," she said fiercely. "Sam used to work in the uranium mines, over there on Black Mesa. When they closed the mines, he got some work in Redwater Valley, where they put all the uranium waste. I think that's how he got sick. It's not Parkinson's that made him sick. This other person we have at Mesa Vista, he did the same kind of work."

"So your aunt and uncle were both—are both—unwell?"

Arlene Yazzie nodded. "Emma, some days are better; she can get around some. Some days she's real sick, she's paralyzed. Samuel, he is getting worse all the time. He can barely move at all," she said.

"They are both incapacitated?" asked K. Arlene Yazzie rummaged in her bag and produced another tissue, which she proceeded to mistreat. "How do they manage?"

She looked at him blankly. K rephrased: "Is there anyone who helps them? Someone who looks after Emma and Samuel?"

"Their daughter," said Arlene Yazzie. "She moved back here to help them."

"There are three people living in the trailer?"

Arlene Yazzie nodded.

"What is the daughter's name?"

"Alice. Alice Nakai."

"Have you heard from Alice since the fire?"

"No." She twisted the tissue again.

"When did you last hear from them?"

"A couple of months? Three months? Maybe six months? We meet up when there are family gatherings." She dabbed at her eyes. "We are all busy," she added, as if she felt she had to defend herself.

"Since the fire you haven't heard from any of them?" K asked.

"Emma and Samuel, there's no way of getting in touch with them. You have to go there to speak to them. They don't have cellphones or anything. There's no utilities. They pretty much still live how our people used to live."

"They hauled water?"

"Alice does. She hauls water and gets wood for the stove. And they run a generator a couple of hours a day."

"So Alice didn't get in touch with you? Did you try to contact her?"

"I tried to call her. That's why I'm here." She twisted the strap of her purse and did not look at K: "Do you know if ... do you know if they ...?"

K's mind went blank. He tried to recall Heidi's presentation on Delgado's preliminary forensic findings. He attempted to remember Grimes's preliminary report, which he had read with his mind chasing after ruthless property developers; he attempted to drag up the squad's discussion of the case, but all he could remember was constructing a Venn diagram pertaining to the convergence of the mindsets of property developers, Big Energy and the good ol' boys of McKinnon Canyon. He was pretty sure there had been talk of two bodies, not three. But being pretty sure wasn't sure enough to impart information to a grieving relative. Anyway, they hadn't got the final report yet.

"The fire is being investigated," said K, opting for half honesty. "Because there are no utilities and services, it has been complicated to find out who lives there. There are no official records for these trailers at all."

Arlene Yazzie frowned: "We told them to move. We told them to come live with us. They wanted to stay ..."

"Of course. Sometimes people just like to stay in a place they know," K said.

"That's what they said. They said, 'We always lived here. We will die here ...'"

She stifled a sob.

K tried to be casual about getting Arlene Yazzie to write down her relatives' details for him. She did not know their dates of birth, though she reminisced about a party they had held for Emma on the occasion of her sixty-fifth birthday, which Emma had greatly enjoyed. It had been a short while before she got sick, about four years ago. Or maybe three. Or five. Samuel was a couple of years older than Emma. But he was a shy man, and did not like to be the focus of people's attention, so the family had held no celebrations for him. So Arlene didn't know how old Samuel was. She guessed he was older than Emma, but he had had a lifetime of working hard over there in the uranium mines, and maybe he seemed older than he was because his health hadn't been real strong for a long time. The whole family had had a great time at Emma's birthday party at Gopher Lake, though, butchering a sheep and having a cookout. Nearly everybody had been there. Alana had come up ...

"Alana?" asked K.

"Alana is Emma and Samuel's daughter. Alice's sister. She lives in Albuquerque. She moved there with this guy ..."

"Are there any more children? Do Alice and Alana have other siblings?"

"Arnold. He moved away someplace ... I don't know. We hardly see him anymore. He didn't come to Emma's party."

"Would you give me their phone numbers? Alice's and Alana's and Arnold's?"

"Their phone numbers?" said Arlene Yazzie.

"This is a police inquiry," said K.

Her lip began to tremble, and her eyes brimmed with tears.

Who was he kidding. Of course, she knew. How were two elderly, infirm people with significant mobility issues supposed to have escaped a fast-spreading fire in their trailer? In K's experience, though, hope did spring eternal. As long as there was a thread, however worn and thin, people would hang onto it. And sure—anything was possible. As yet, they weren't 100 percent certain that the burnt corpses in the trailer were those of Emma and Samuel Nakai. It was conceivable that those burnt remains belonged to somebody else. But in the grand scheme of things, that possibility would merely transfer the burden of grief onto someone else.

The speed with which Arlene Yazzie located Alice Nakai's phone number made K feel pretty certain that she really had tried to ring her cousin Alice not that long ago. For Alana, she only had a redundant work number. For Arnold she had no number.

"Does Alice work?"

"She works over at The Magic Dollar." Arlene Nakai tapped her forehead. "I should have called The Magic Dollar! Why didn't I think to call The Magic Dollar!" Hope shone in her eyes. She didn't wait for a response, and got busy on her phone. Already she looked like a different woman. Amazing what a bit of hope could do. She held the phone to her ear for what seemed a long time.

"It got cut off," she said eventually. "That's what happens when you let it ring too long. They're real busy over there."

"They are," K agreed. The Magic Dollar was indeed always busy. A lot of folks lived on the breadline in San Matteo County. Also, The Magic Dollar was chronically short-staffed.

"Maybe I'll drive by later. Maybe I'll drive by now—" She looked at her watch, then picked her collection of twisted Kleenex off her lap and shoved it into her purse. She had the air of a horse ready to bolt. Hope and impatience enlivened her face.

"We'll call you as soon as we have more information. And do keep in touch," K said, as if they were old acquaintances. Anything not to kill off the hope in her eyes. She'd find out soon enough.

She nodded, her eyes already on the door.

K fed the Nakai family's contact details into the computer, compiled a short report on Arlene Yazzie's visit, and, gazing out the window at the distant foothills, entertained himself with buoy-ing daydreams of a Nakai-Yazzie extended family reunion.

Led by his yearning for a happy ending, or at least a happier ending, he started to believe his own evasions and so managed to forget, for a short while, what they already knew with reasonable certainty.

CHAPTER FIFTEEN

"Emma Nakai. Samuel Nakai. Alice Nakai." Weismaker seemed to have some trouble deciphering K's handwriting. "Who are they?"

"Two of them, probably, are the people who died in the fire," said K. "Emma and Samuel lived in the trailer with their daughter Alice. According to Arlene Yazzie, their relative, who came to see me just now, they were both infirm and needed care."

"She's a relative?"

"Arlene Yazzie is a ... niece, I guess you'd say. She's the manager at Mesa Vista Care Home. She heard of the fire and came in to ask about her relatives."

"How did she hear about the fire?"

"She rents out the other trailer to a new employee at the care home. The employee is the neighbor who rang the Fire Department. That's how Arlene Yazzie heard about the fire."

"The same neighbor who needed to get that dog food?" Apparently Weismaker did read their reports and statements.

It was all Harvey's fault.

"What did you tell Arlene Yazzie?" asked the sheriff. K stared at his shoes.

"You didn't tell her anything."

"No, sir," mumbled K. "Just that the investigation is ongoing ..."

"Good," said the sheriff.

"Sir?"

"I'm glad you didn't tell her anything, when we don't even have the results from Delgado back yet."

When you did something right by accident, because you were too chicken to do what was right by your standards, did that still count as doing right?

"Who cared for them?" asked the sheriff.

"Sir?"

"This couple. You said they were old and infirm?"

"Their daughter Alice was their caregiver," said K.

The sheriff held up the piece of paper. "Where is this lady?"

"She ... she, uh, couldn't be reached," said K.

"Did you try to get a hold of her?" asked Weismaker.

"No," said K. "Her relative did."

"What do you know about her?"

"She looks after her parents ..." stammered K.

"Occupation?"

"She works at The Magic Dollar. That's what her aunt said."

"You want to go there and see if you can catch her. Does she have a vehicle? Was there a vehicle?"

K tried to remember what the neighbor had said. Most of what he remembered was that stuff about Harvey, and Harvey's teeth digging into his boots. And that Melinda, or was it Melissa, worked shifts at the care home, got home at odd hours, and didn't tend to look outside when she was at home. She had never seen her neighbors. At least that's what she had said.

"Do you make her for a suspect?"

"No," said K.

"So there was no vehicle at the burnt trailer?"

Melinda had mentioned a truck parked by the trailer. Had K asked her what type of truck? Nope. Had K asked her when she had seen the truck? Nope.

"There must have been a vehicle," said the sheriff. "You just said they don't have any utilities over there. So they must have a truck to haul water and get firewood, right?"

Weismaker's computer pinged. "How's this for timing?" he said, peering at the screen. "Here's Delgado Forensics' report now." He pushed his glasses up on his nose and scrolled down the screen. "So. We got two people. Older folks, probably between sixty and eighty years old. Bone density isn't an accurate science. It says here it depends on the life people have. The kind of exercise they have. The nutrition. Genetics. Environmental pollution ..."

"Of which there is a lot," said K.

"One male, one female," said the sheriff. He read on. His eyebrows knitted and his frown deepened. He shook his head.

"Sir?" said K.

Weismaker looked up. "The bodies of the deceased were found at opposite sides of the room with a space of 2.5 yards between them."

"They had separate beds?" said K.

"Maybe. Or maybe they were separated."

"Separated? Who by?"

"Probably by the same person who drugged them with barbiturates before they set the trailer on fire."

"What?"

"Let's get a hold of the daughter and eliminate her from the inquiries." The sheriff's face was grim.

"Sir ..."

"Did you ask the relative about a vehicle? Did you try to get a registration number?"

"No, sir. She came in to inquire about her relatives. It didn't seem appropriate to interrogate her." "Let me tell you again, son: we are not counselors. We are cops. We need to get a warrant out on this Alice. She's our Number One suspect."

"Sir ..."

"There's a person out there running free, who most probably drugged and killed her elderly, disabled parents. Drugged them, and burned them alive. Get her vehicle registration and ID. We need to get that warrant out ASAP. We don't want murderers running around our county. Get on it. Now!"

CHAPTER SIXTEEN

K's ears rang from listening to the Department of Motor Vehicles' holding music, a laudably bold choice of Janis Joplin's "Mercedes Benz," which somehow lost poignancy and allure after the thirty-ninth loop. He decided to drive by the DMV, where a line of people bearing documents snaked out the door and around the corner. As an officer of the law on urgent business he would, of course, be entitled to sail past the hapless hoi polloi. K duly recalled the principle of not exploiting privileges afforded by one's position, and drove on.

On the grassy verge at the corner of Mesa Vista Road and the Juniper Street Mall a rotund prairie dog was feasting on a carton of Tater Tots that somebody had dropped.

"Don't mind me," K said, but the prairie dog retreated into its burrow anyway. The Tater Tot-scoffing prairie dog went some way to reconciling K to the concrete purgatory that yawned at him under the midday sun. In the parking lot, gaping cracks in the asphalt brought to mind the precarity of the Earth's crust. An infant whirlwind crossed the lot, practicing gathering up discarded candy wrappers, flyers and tissues in a Nature-meets-Civilization display that would get to be an awesome spectacle, once it had grown up. The parking lot was empty but for a half-dozen vehicles, vintage pickups, all parked in front of The Magic Dollar.

The Magic Dollar had been the first store to open in the Juniper Street Mall, which sat on a reclaimed strip of rock-strewn land five blocks south of Main Street, previously settled peacefully by generations of gophers. Milagro Municipality had planned Juniper Street as a shopping district to rival New York's Fifth Avenue or Los Angeles's Rodeo Drive, with bijoux boutiques, elite chain stores, and metropolitan coffee shops.

And this was the Juniper Street Mall now: The Magic Dollar, one phone shop, the Wedding Apparel Boutique—whatever that was— and the Busy Beaver Alteration shop were what the displacement of all those guileless gophers had gotten them. And while The Magic Dollar would most likely survive, the other stores gave the Juniper Mall the feel of a ghost town in the making. Except for the Busy Beaver, which looked as it had looked on the day of its opening: closed, and like a half-assed front for classified substances trafficking.

The till at The Magic Dollar was unattended. K had nearly completed a round of the premises before he encountered an employee on her knees beside a heaped shopping cart, untangling a mess of what looked like Mardi Gras beads. On beholding his uniform, the employee rose to her feet very slowly, in a manner that made K think she would have held up her hands had she been able to get up without supporting herself by clinging to the edge of a shelf.

He wondered about the hinterland of this woman's life: meth labs, partners, children, relatives on outstanding warrants, falling foul of a territorial gang war … She stood and looked at him in the manner of a deer caught in the headlights. There weren't that many jobs where one's mere appearance would have such an effect. Had K nurtured sadistic impulses, he might have been tempted to say, "I see you have been expecting me."

She wasn't in charge anyway, and scuttled off to find the manager. K wouldn't have been surprised to hear the sound of squealing tires, followed by the sight of a vehicle vanishing in a cloud of dust.

The store manager was a middle-aged woman with a pronounced limp that warranted the use of a walking stick. "Yes?" she said, not particularly encouragingly. She too looked edgy. K flashed his badge and asked if she could spare a few minutes in her office. The woman turned, her limp more pronounced now. K, following her, thought of an old work-horse that deserved to be put out to pasture. Perhaps her days consisted of putting her feet up in her office and being beastly to her staff.

She opened the door to the cubbyhole office with a key hanging from a bunch that reminded K of keyrings in old prison movies.

The cubbyhole's dimensions encouraged intimacy. It also smelled as if somebody had spent approximately a year in there, eating Cheetos and hard-boiled eggs and never changing their socks. "Maybe we should leave the door open," suggested K, "so you can hear if a customer needs you?"

"Ginger is out there," said the woman, and drew the door shut.

"I'm here to ask about Alice," said K. "Alice Nakai. She works here?"

"What's the matter with her?" asked the manager. "Where is she?"

"Is she supposed to be here?"

The woman shrugged. "She hasn't shown up. No excuse or anything. She didn't pick up her phone when I tried to call her. When you see her, you can tell her she was fired. I just got somebody else."

"I don't think I shall," said K. "Do you have an idea where Alice may have gone?"

The woman shook her head. "She looks after her parents. They're elderly and pretty sick. She's always real anxious to get home on time. I allowed her to work split shifts, so that she can go home and give them their medication and, you know, take them to the bathroom and give them their meals, and then she comes back here and works the other half of her shift."

"How many days a week does Alice work?"

"She's supposed to be here every day," said the manager.

"Every day?" K asked.

"Well, she got those long breaks," said the woman. "She has to make up for them somehow."

So Alice Nakai was made to work unpaid overtime in exchange for accommodating her shift pattern. It was the same principle that ruled historical indentured servitude. K said: "I thought she works split shifts?"

"There's not many places that let their employees do that," the woman said.

"She is not at home," said K, taking care to keep his voice even. "Where else do you suppose she might be?"

"She's always with her parents," said the woman. "They need a lot of looking after."

"I'm sure she is very grateful to you for letting her work split shifts."

The woman's eyes searched his face. Her chin was set. K couldn't discern a massive amount of goodwill toward him. People had a tendency to get pissed when you implied they were moral pond scum. Perhaps she really thought she had been generous and tolerant and supportive. Who knew how she herself was being treated? Getting the oppressed to use their pent-up frustration generated by oppression to oppress others was another one of capitalism's box of magic tricks.

"I shall need to see any information you hold on Alice Nakai. Social Security, bank details." The manager looked uneasy. "This is a police inquiry, ma'am."

"We don't have anything for her."

"You haven't got anything for Alice Nakai? Surely you must have something to process the payroll?"

The woman turned her eyes toward a patch of peeling paint on the wall. "She was paid in cash. Many of them don't have bank accounts."

By "them" K assumed she meant Native Americans. "Social Security?"

"We deduct it at source," the woman squeezed through compressed lips.

K was willing to bet that here was one who'd yell "Build the Wall!" while being the minion of an enterprise that profited from the undocumented-but-taxed labor that kept this blessed country afloat. "I see," he said. The silence seemed to accentuate the rankness of the Cheeto-and-boiled-egg-saturated air. Maybe he suffered from synesthesia. "We would like to find Alice. Anything that comes into your mind might help."

Had it not been for the infernal stink he'd have waited some more for her to crack. "She's real quiet," said the manager. "She was a good worker, but real quiet. Kind of shy. But a lot of them are like that. Not real friendly."

"*What you hear in the echo is the sound of your own voice.*"

"Huh?"

"Confucius," K said.

The woman took her eyes away from the peeling paint and regarded him with something resembling concern.

"Did Alice Nakai share anything about her private life?" asked K.

"No," said the woman. Her voice had softened somewhat. Maybe it was the effect of K'ung Fu-Tzu. "I don't think she got a boyfriend. No kids. Just her parents."

"When exactly was she supposed to come in?"

The woman pointed at a shift plan on the wall: "That's when she was supposed to come in."

"Has she been in at all since?"

"No. I was thinking of promoting her, too. Go figure." She clicked her tongue.

"So she hasn't been in contact?"

"No. She knows you get one chance here. That's it."

"Is there anybody else here who may have heard from her?"

"No." She rubbed her knee. "There was a woman in today, though, that asked the same questions. A relative."

"Mrs. Yazzie?" asked K.

"I didn't get her name."

"What vehicle did Alice Nakai drive? Do you know?"

"Some old truck," said the store manager. "Maybe white. Or brown. Or blue. I can't remember. You want the registration number?"

"That would be great," said K. Sometimes an unpromising encounter would turn out to be very successful after all.

"I haven't got it," said the manager.

"Did you not just ask me if I wanted the registration number?" said K tightly.

"I just asked because that's what they always say in those cop movies." There was a glint of malice in her eyes.

"Don't leave town right now. We may need to speak to you again," K said. *That* too was something they always said in those cop movies.

CHAPTER SEVENTEEN

There was some truth to the trope that everything was relative. Relative to time spent in The Magic Dollar's reeking cubbyhole, time spent in K's own office perusing the computer was almost bearable.

The amount of information Big Brother stored on his citizens was truly astounding. Take Alice Nakai, who practically lived off the grid and who was one of the least connected people that K could remember coming across in recent times: no access to even the most basic utilities, no mail delivery, no trash collection. Yet she was easily located on one of those websites that spilled all your vital statistics without even demanding a fee; so easily that even K found her. Right away.

So, too, were Alice's parents, Emma and Samuel Nakai—though without any address or DOB. But this frail elderly couple, who had never registered with the real world, who had been excluded from utilities, services, and participation in the democratic process, existed in cyberspace, alright. They would not have known this and never would now, but here they did exist.

The address listed for Alice was in Gallup. K assumed it had been a while since she had lived there. And here were Alana and Arnold Nakai. Alana resided in Albuquerque; her phone number had to be harvested from another spy-site. It wasn't hard to come by, as K was in possession of Alana's full address. In the olden days, getting those results would have taken Sam Spade and Philip Marlowe the better part of a month. They would ricochet across the land, hole up in seedy motels, and hang out in dive bars, accumulating expenses. They would run into some tough dudes, bed some shady dames, and keep their morale up with gallons of bourbon and rye (but never beer. For some reason, never beer). Nowadays everything that had made Phil Marlowe's life interesting could be done and ticked off in the space of five skull-numbingly boring minutes.

Alana Nakai was a couple of years younger than her sister Alice, and she had, as far as K understood, three children and possibly no partner. At least the Big Brother site had not listed a partner, but then again it only listed people with the surname Nakai; so maybe there was a modicum of privacy left in this world.

"Here we go," thought K. His mouth was dry and his temples throbbed. He could not remember why he had offered to be harbinger of gruesome news to the Nakai orphans. He dialed Alana's number and listened to the phone ringing. How long did a phone have to ring before it was okay to hang up and state honestly that the desired party could not be reached?

"Hello," said a voice.

"Am I speaking to Alana Nakai?" K asked.

"I'm okay with the contract I have," said Alana Nakai.

"Contract?" asked K, to the sound of static.

He dialed again. This time Alana Nakai picked up after the second ring. "I told you—"

"Ms. Nakai," said K. There must have been something in his voice, because now the silence hit him. On the other end of the line, Alana had gone very quiet. He couldn't even hear her breathing.

"Ms. Nakai," he said again. "I have sad news for you." He had debated with himself whether to use *bad* or *sad*. Now he didn't know whether or not he had made the right decision. As soon as he said "sad," he heard Alana gasp.

"My dad?" she said.

"I'm afraid—"

"My dad. Something has happened to my dad?" Alana wailed.

"I'm afraid there has been an accident. I'm calling from Milagro Police Department," said K. *What the fuck was he saying? An accident? There had been a fire, and it had been arson.* "There has been a fire," K continued. "A very bad fire. I'm sorry to say that both your parents—"

The woman on the other end of the line began to weep.

"I'm so sorry," K said. "So, so sorry." And he hadn't even told her the worst yet.

"Are they both …?" Alana Nakai sobbed.

"Yes," said K.

"What… where is Alice?"

"When did you last talk to your sister Alice?"

"… A couple of months …? Three months?"

"Are you not in regular contact?" asked K.

"Alice is always busy," Alana said. "She works every day."

"And she cared for your parents," said K. He hadn't meant to say it that way.

Alana was silent. "I have three kids," she said eventually. "And I'm carrying a baby right now. I'm due in two months."

"So Alice has not been in contact?"

From another room came the sound of children playing. At K's end, a convoy of pickups rumbled along the street. A couple of geese held a honking competition in the park. A motorcycle with a faulty exhaust puttered past the station.

"Ma'am, has your sister been in contact?"

"Um …" said Alana Nakai. "… There was a missed call from her on my cellphone …" Her voice sounded small and far away.

"Ms. Nakai? When was that?"

"That was … last week sometime? A couple of days ago?"

"Would you mind checking for me?"

K listened to Alana look for her phone. He heard her read out the date of her sister's missed call in her call log. It had been an evening call, which made K wonder if Alana had missed her sister's call deliberately.

"I meant to call her back …" said Alana feebly. "Do you think … did she want to tell me …"

"Your sister made that call approximately eighteen hours before your parents died," said K flatly.

Alana Nakai gasped. "Oh God. Oh God," she whispered. "When did … when did my parents …?"

There was a part of her that knew, and a part of her that did not want to know.

"Why are you telling me now?" the woman sobbed, when K told her the date of the fire. "They've been ... they have been gone for a week?" Her sobbing grew wilder, as if the fact that she hadn't known of her parents' death for a week was worse than her parents dying. Was it the time she had spent not knowing, the time she had gone about her daily business believing that her parents were still around? Was it that the imagined bonds had not, after all, been strong enough for her to sense their deaths? Or was it the time she had lost not grieving? But then there were many cultures that believed that there was a limited time—and how long this time was varied between cultures and belief systems—during which the departed inhabited a twilight zone between the living and the dead. The average time for this, cross-culturally, seemed to be four days during which the soul threw off its earthly shackles and bonds, left the body and traveled towards ethereal eternity.

"I'm so very sorry," K said again.

"What about the funeral?" asked Alana. "Where are they now?"

What there was of them would have been scraped into some forensic Tupperware, or whatever Delgado Forensics had used to transport the charred and pulverized remains of Samuel and Emma to their lab.

"Is there any chance you can travel up to Milagro?" asked K.

"I'm due in two months," Alana repeated. "Where is Alice?"

"We don't know," said K, and said more firmly: "It would be helpful if you could come up to Milagro." They damn well needed what remained of the family here. He wondered when Alana had last seen her parents. "Would you like to inform your brother before we speak to him?" asked K.

"No," said Alana Nakai.

Arnold Nakai lived outside Seattle.

"Arnold's Awesome Autoshop," announced a voice.

"Can I speak to Arnold Nakai?" said K.

"He's busy," said the voice.

"It's important," K replied. There was the sound of buttons pressed. Whoever had taken the call hadn't bothered to mute it, or didn't know how to.

"Boss!" said the voice. "Somebody wants to speak to you."

"I'm busy!" said the boss.

"Said it's important."

"Who is it?" Arnold asked.

"Sounds like a cop," the voice said.

K damn near swallowed the receiver. *What the fuck? A cop?* Despite his Welsh lilt, his lily-livered liberalism, and his bleeding-heart, social-worker attitude, he sounded like a cop?

"I'm just putting him through," said the voice.

"What makes me sound like a cop then?" asked K.

"Er, um, I was just guessing, sir," said the voice evasively.

"I guess it's just experience, huh?" said K amicably.

"Arnold Nakai. How can I help you, sir?" People using their manners when speaking to a cop usually had a dirty conscience, or something to hide.

"I have bad news for you, Mr. Nakai," said K. To the sister he had brought *sad* news; to Arnold, it was *"bad."* Was this unconscious gender bias at work, or was it that people who recognized cops across a phone line would be more familiar with *bad* than *sad* news? "I am very sorry to have to tell you that your parents passed away."

The line was silent. K waited. He looked at the second hand of his watch as it made a full circle, then inroads into the next one. "Mr. Nakai ...?" Silence. K waited some more. He couldn't hear anything. Had the man fainted? "Mr. Nakai? Arnold? Did you hear me?" There was a sound at the other side of the line: low, guttural.

"Your parents died in a fire in their trailer. It was a devastating fire." Silence. "They died last week. I'm sorry for the delay in contacting you." Silence. "Mr. Nakai?"

"Yes," the man's voice sounded thick. "Are you done? I gotta get back to work."

"Can we call you later?" asked K.

Through the silence, K could feel the man contemplate saying "no." "We need to speak to you," K said. "When is a good time?" He extracted a cellphone number from the reluctant man, and hung up.

Nobody could accuse him of not learning on the job.

CHAPTER EIGHTEEN

The plot of scorched earth at the foot of the mesa was visible from across the plain. A length of police tape wrapped around a fence post flapped in the wind. The smell of burning still hung in the air. The sun stood high in the sky, and in its harsh light the rocks of the mesa walls stood out like bleached bones.

In the far distance, the sound of trucks could be heard, rumbling along the highway. A dust devil pirouetted over the plain, reminding K of a Sufi whirling dervish. Mist obscured the San Matteo Mountains and made them look like a distant mirage. To the south, red sandstone ran into desert ocher. To the west, a verdant band of trees marked the twisting course of the Merced River.

Why had the Ancient Ones bothered to scale the mesa, there to build their impossible citadels that hung in space like eyries? Of all this available and accessible land, why had they opted for their fantastic colonies, suspended over gaping chasms?

There was something ostentatious, something defiant about these castles of the sky that didn't seem to fit the archaeological theories of cliff palaces as storage spaces, as fortresses against marauding enemies, as safe retreats from fire and drought. Who was to say that the Ancients had not indulged in cliff palaces, just because they could? Maybe they had happened on one of those ceremonial gatherings at Chaco, the purported Rome of North American antiquity, and—filled with audacious vision—had set forth to build their own proverbial cities on a mesa, their high and airy and hard-to-reach castles, a New World equivalent to the splendor of marble and gold rested on wooden posts sunk into the mud of a shallow lagoon, that reckless privileging of appearance over reality, that glorious folly that was Venice.

There was something special, something extraordinary about living, literally, in the shadows of this ancient paradox. K looked up. The rock face was so steep and sheer he had to tilt back his head to see all the way up. The mesa crest stood dark and sharp against the deep blue sky.

"Alice?" he called. "Alice?"

A gust of wind swept over the trailer's charred remains and raised the acrid, metallic smell of cold ashes. In the wind, trailer debris rattled and groaned. A sheet of metal thwacked against a boulder. Within these noises was a trickling sound, as if the mangled, ruined structure itself was moaning. K shivered.

The sound amplified; now there was a pattering sound. A trickle of grit rolled down the rock face. It became a cascade of bouncing stones that gathered speed and force, displacing ever more rocks in the course of their fall.

K backed away from the mesa wall, and sprinted toward the patrol car. Behind him, the swooshing of gravel grew louder. A thick cloud of dust made it difficult to see where he was going. He threw himself into the patrol car, stepped on the gas and reversed. The sound of rockfall rose to a thundering crescendo. A boulder rolled down the slope, bounced off protrusions on the rock face, gradually gathered speed and crashed down. Around it, dust rose in plumes.

The boulder had landed where the trailer's front door would have been.

The mesa stood black against the blinding sun, and the air was still and heavy.

CHAPTER NINETEEN

"Did you get the warrant out?" The Sheriff wore that steely expression that had taught K not to attempt obfuscation, distraction, or self-justification.

"No, sir."

"Care to give me a reason?"

I do not care to live in a world in which the first suspect in the death of two elderly, helpless people is their daughter and caregiver would have been one reason. It was the kind of reason that, according to the Annoying Counselor, tended to guide K's professional conduct, therefore making it unprofessional.

It was this kind of guided fantasy into a labyrinth of cul-de-sacs that had especially endeared the Annoying Counselor to K.

"We are waiting on the DMV," was an acceptable answer, and it was true to the extent that, if one were so inclined—as K certainly was in this case—one could wait on the DMV 'til Doomsday and beyond.

"Have you ..." The Sheriff regarded K over the top of his glasses. He shook his head. "Go chase them up. Now."

"Sir."

In his office, K entertained himself for half an hour listening to the DMV's holding muzak; this time it was, go figure, Mozart's *Eine Kleine Nachtmusik* played on a loop on a hand-cranked hurdy-gurdy. He hung up when he no longer could distinguish hurdy-gurdy from tinnitus.

It was lunchtime, anyway. He composed an email to the DMV and sent it in the full knowledge that obtaining an email response from the DMV was approximately 0.75 percent as likely as having your phone call answered within the eight hours of your working day.

On his way to the bookstore, K made a detour to the library, where he dropped off a supply of various Milagro PD info manuals that signified conscientious maintenance of public relations, then joined a man with a broad back in perusing the pinboard.

The man at the pinboard was Felix John, chairman of the local Human Relations Commission and inceptor of Native Networks, promoted as a pan-tribal grassroots association. "Pan-tribal" in this context meant Diné and Ute, a nothing-short-of-daring initiative considering the long-standing animosity between the tribes, judiciously fueled by the colonial overlords.

"Hi," said K.

Felix John nodded without smiling. K studied various cards offering litters of kittens. Some specified "to good homes." Most did not. A blonde woman in her middle years, swathed in a caftan sporting a petroglyph pattern, came sailing into the library.

"Hey, Felix! How are ya?" Felix John nodded. "Too bad about the Mesa Center, huh? Have you found an alternative place for your meetings?" Felix John shook his head. "Aww, tough, huh? It's hard times for everybody."

"It's just once a month that we are meeting," said Felix John.

"Maybe that's the problem," said the woman. "Maybe they want you to rent their space weekly. Gotta fly! Good luck."

Felix John nodded. He didn't look as if he was holding his breath. K looked at an imaginatively designed flyer:

WATER ALLIANCE
Wednesdays 7 PM
THE BOOKSTORE, 679 N Main

"You're looking for a place to meet?" asked K.

Felix John turned to face him: "Native Networks. We used to meet at the Mesa Center. They kicked us out."

"How big is your group?"

"We had almost twenty …" John reconsidered. "But that was just a couple of times at the beginning. People like something when it's new. Most haven't got the commitment."

K recognized a disappointed man when he saw one. He pointed to the Water Alliance flyer: "You could meet at The Bookstore."

"The Bookstore?" asked Felix John. "That old Russian lady's bookstore?"

"Czech," said K.

"Huh?"

"She is Czech, not Russian," said K. "And I'm running the store now." Felix John narrowed his eyes: "You're a policeman."

"Are being a policeman and running a bookstore mutually exclusive?"

For the first time, the shadow of a grin showed on Felix John's stern face: "I guess."

"I'm going to the store now," said K. "Drop in and have a look if you want."

The Bookstore was locked, but bore signs of recent productive activity. In the ledger, written in Cuauhtémoc's calligraphic hand, were entries pertaining to eleven sales, two of collectible tomes, bringing in a tidy sum. And they weren't even books that K was particularly sorry to see go.

Benjamin was curled up in the armchair, one paw stretched out. The crochet blanket sported a number of fresh loose threads.

The store-bell tinkled. Felix John was standing in the entrance, looking around. "It's been a while that I was here. They used to have a great Native book collection." It sounded as if John expected K to have sold off the collection, profiteering *bílagáana* cop scum that he was.

"We still have," K said coldly.

John's expression thawed some. K wondered if his cold tone had done that. Some folks did better when they got a sign of how they made you feel. K, however, had a grudging admiration for people like Felix John, who had the integrity to stick to their borderline hostile manner, even with those they stood to potentially gain from.

"Shall we have a look at the meeting room?"

The meeting room, at the back of the store, had borne witness to decades of meetings of the hard Marxist core of Milagro town—a hard core of which, as far as K was aware, only Agnes Prohaska remained. Where did old Marxists go when they died? *Why* they were all dead was not much of a riddle. You just had to sniff the rich patina of nicotine on the walls, to know that capitalism's gain had been Marxism's loss. Odd, that such politically aware folks thought nothing of maintaining in profit one of the most pernicious industries capitalism had to offer. But this was America. (Fleetingly, K considered whether or not he was running the risk of being sued for letting people congregate in an environment marked by historical nicotine. Maybe he needed to draw up disclaimers?)

Felix John examined the room and counted the chairs set around the large round table. "A round table!" he said with the slightest trace of enthusiasm in his voice.

"The King Arthur principle," said K, adding, when John frowned: "Where there's no head, people may sit with each other without hierarchy."

"Ten chairs is good," said Felix John.

"You could always ask people to bring folding chairs, just in case."

"We need the room five hours once a month, last Tuesday of the month. The meeting is about three hours; I come in an hour early to set things up, and I stay on to write up minutes and our resolutions."

"There is a bathroom and a tea kitchen with a kettle and coffee maker."

"How much ...?" asked Felix John.

"It's free," said K. "I'd like this space to be useful to the community. But I'd be grateful, if there's a group of people, that you replenish what you use in the kitchen."

"Sure," said John. "We'll bring our own stuff."

It occurred to K that perhaps he had better ask cursorily what Native Networks was about.

"You worried?" Felix John's voice had an edge.

"Would you be okay sharing premises with, let's say, white supremacists?" asked K.

John looked him squarely in the eye: "You are a policeman."

So this was how people saw him. There was practically no difference between a cop and a Nazi. There was a part of K that wanted to say *fuck you* and escort Felix John to the door. That part was quite strong—so strong, in fact, that it blocked out any other impulses. He stared at John and started counting backward from 666 to try keep this temper of his in check.

He'd gotten to 647 when John shrugged and said: "There's still people in this town that believe 'BLM' means 'Bureau of Land Management.'"

These people were quite right: BLM did stand for the Bureau of Land Management, as much as it had come to stand for Black Lives Matter and Brown Lives Matter. He knew that what Felix John was saying was that there were people in this town who believed that the *only* BLM that counted was the Bureau of Land Management, and saw even that BLM as a mark of liberal snowflakery, trying to interfere with the freedom of citizens to destroy as much of Mother Earth as they damn well pleased.

K stopped counting, but kept quiet. Let Felix John do his own damn work.

They eyed each other like two tomcats in Trashcan Alley. Fuck it. Sometimes it was almost good to feel the veneer of civilization strip away.

"You know what this administration is doing to our sacred lands?" asked John.

K nodded. This administration, the most shameless of a whole lineage of shameless administrations, had opened practically all public lands, sacred and protected, to fracking, drilling, strip-mining. As the Earth lay gasping and withering, as the ice caps melted and the deserts expanded, as one endangered species after another croaked, and each new year brought a novel and uncontrollable zoonotic plague, the administration had stayed consistent to its one mantra: profit. What wasn't commercial did not exist. This administration's swivel-eyed greed even had tinpot dictators, who had hitherto gamely followed in the US of A's venal footsteps, recoil in consternation.

"Our people are waking up," said Felix John. "It took them a long time, but they are finally waking up. Underneath all this, we are still warriors." It sounded like a warning. "There are some angry people in our meetings." John's eyes were narrow, and his nostrils dilated: "You don't want some angry Indians in your book-store, Mr. Policeman; you still got time to change your mind."

"You want an angry policeman? Go right ahead making as-sumptions," said K. He felt an ice-cold rage—the kind, people had told him, that terrified them, because of the look in his eyes. He could see that something registered in John, who now began to look somewhat uneasy.

647 ... 646 ... 645 ... 644 ...

Benjamin stalked into the room just then, and, oblivious to the charged atmosphere, stroked first round K's, then around Felix John's legs. Maybe Benjamin had been reared in the O. K. Corral. Felix John looked at the cat pressing against his legs. He looked at K. The cat hunched his back, stretched, rubbed his head on Felix John's sneaker, climbed up, and sat on his shoe. Felix John looked at the cat and shook his head. K stopped counting. John bent down and scooped the cat up in his arms. He scratched Benjamin's head with a deft hand, and sneezed when the cat's whiskers tickled his nose. His face softened, and he smiled. He looked a transformed man.

K watched the tableau with conflicted feelings. "You made a friend there," he said eventually.

John set the cat down and assumed a stern expression like a man recalled from a personal paradise island. "Is this your store cat?" he asked.

"He's a new guest," said K. "He's just been here a couple of days from the Pet Rescue. His owner died."

"If you need somebody to look after the cat ..."

"You mean in the store, or for good?"

"He's a great cat," said Felix John.

"We'll see."

CHAPTER TWENTY

The standoff with Felix John had eaten into K's lunch break. He wasn't even sure if they had agreed to Felix John using the room for Native Networks meetings, or just to Felix John maybe adopting Benjamin.

Most improbably, K found in his inbox a response to his inquiry to the DMV. The email was headed with a variety of disclaimers pertaining to confidentiality, and warnings regarding the possible consequences of breaching it. K liked it when the modern world collided with quaint, old sensibilities. These entreaties harked back to the days when a man's word was his honor.

Milagro DMV held quite a few records for Alice Nakais. The Alices were of different age ranges, so K had to discount his theory that they had all been named shortly after the release of a Disney movie. Besides, he didn't even know if Disney had gotten around to ruining *Alice in Wonderland*.

According to K's calculation, it was most likely that the Alice he sought would be in her mid-thirties to late forties. He was rolling in full Marlowe mode, doing it the old way. Why waste two minutes on a phone call to Alice's relatives asking her birthdate, when a good part of a workday afternoon could be spent nosing through files, following false leads and flying high on some good, old-fashioned conjecture?

There were three Alices in the estimated age range. One lived on Oak Street. The other had an address in the Cottonwood Trailer Park. The third just had a mailbox address, which made this one the most likely subject.

Of course, there had to be a mailbox. Even if people lived without water and utilities, even if they lived where there were no trash collections and no mail delivery, even if they had no bank accounts and were paid in cash ... even then, they would have a mailbox. No matter that most of the mail they received would be coupons, and those letters you got when your cellphone provider sold off your details to some commercial ads list. For some people, those soliciting letters were the *only* mail they ever received.

Now they had a possible mailbox, and they had her cellphone number; but all that did not make it any easier to locate Alice Nakai if she wouldn't answer her phone. K felt for the note in his pocket. It wasn't there.

So the sheriff still had the scrap of paper on which K had written Alice's cellphone number. Well, it wasn't he, anyway, who was in a hurry to get out a warrant on Alice Nakai. Let Weismaker call her.

As a modicum of penitence, K resolved to write up his reports like a good boy. He regarded the lopsided Tower of Pisa on his desk with trepidation. He felt like someone about to sink his arms into a muddy drain and expecting to be bitten by a mamba. He pulled at a dog-eared file sticking out of the pile and opened it.

It was that incident with the guy who had tried to steal an electric blanket—on a day when the temperature measured 95° F—and there had been sixteen witnesses who all insisted on being interviewed, and who all talked as if they'd just come out of a decade of solitary confinement. He'd had to recruit Myers and Smithson to help take down some of the witness statements. Maybe there had been a bank heist going on, and this loquacious lot were the decoys. He picked another file. This was the one with the run-over dog that had belonged to the old lady, and K didn't feel he could stomach that one either right now.

He contemplated the pile. There were seven left, so if one was possessed of a slight tendency to OCD, as the Annoying Counselor had surmised K did, then you obviously would take the middle one, leaving three at the bottom and three at the top.

But K hadn't wasted his time in therapy. No sirree. He plucked the second file from the top out of the pile, thereby disproving the Annoying Counselor's pet theory that compulsive characters were attracted to the aesthetics of symmetry. Suck on that, Annoying Counselor!

He opened the file. Arrest Report Card. A handwritten witness statement, signed. Easy-peasy. He had left the card mostly blank, except for the date and a brief description of the incident. He took the statement out of the file. It was written in a fairly neat though slightly unsteady hand. Ah, this one he remembered.

K leaned back and began to read. "Oh, sweet Lord, no," he said.

CHAPTER TWENTY-ONE

K flung open the door, missing Myers's nose by a quarter-inch.

"Where are you going?" Becky called.

"Hey! Hey! Look what you done! You made me drop my donuts!" protested Myers.

K accelerated out of the parking lot, narrowly missing a pickup. He didn't bother pulling an apologetic face, and propelled past the shaken civilian. He barreled along Main Street, ignoring speed limits, and took a left.

He considered switching on the flashers and decided against it. It would have advertised his failure to every citizen of Milagro town. At the crossroads he took a tight left turn, and missed the ditch by a hair's breadth. The replaced section of picket fence gleamed white. To the side of the driveway, broken fence posts and splintered wood lay gathered into a pile, perhaps awaiting a bonfire.

K turned into the drive. The farmhouse itself was a squat, wooden-clad building with a terraced porch, at least a hundred years old. An aged Ford was parked in front of the house. Along the fence stood a trailer hitched to an ATV, and a tractor. The yard was surrounded by scattered outbuildings: sheds and barns and metal sheeted awnings hosting a moderate junkyard's worth full of decommissioned vehicles.

K got out of the car and walked up to the farmhouse. There was nobody in the yard but for an old, battered tomcat of strikingly mean appearance sitting at the door, who opened his toothless mouth in a mute *meow* when K approached.

K knocked on the door. Inside the house, he heard stirring.

"Come in!" a voice called.

K entered the farmhouse kitchen that spoke, indeed, of a hundred years of continuous use, most probably by a large family. The farmer and his wife were sitting at the table. The kitchen was fragrant with the aromas of coffee and cinnamon.

"Come right in!" called the farmer's wife. She had gotten up and was now placing a mug and plate on the table. "We got apple pie!" she said. "It's still warm!"

K had heard of this kind of hospitality, the old kind, where any stranger stepping through the door must be first accommodated and fed before any questions are asked, even before introductions are made. It was the kind of hospitality one found around the world, mostly in communities that had little, offered by people who knew what it was to go without, revered the little they had, and understood the joys of sharing.

K knew that such hospitality granted so freely must not be refused, so he sat down with the kindly, taciturn farmer couple and dug into a large piece of apple pie with a crisp, buttery crust and a filling fragrant with spices and the rich aroma of orchard-grown apples, and sipped strong, black coffee out of an earthenware mug.

"How about another slice?" asked the farmer's wife.

K shook his head: "If I do, I'll have to hold a siesta. This is the best apple pie I've had in ages."

"I put some cardamom in with the cinnamon," the farmer's wife said. "A Swedish lady I met in church taught me."

So churches were good for something. K cleared his throat: "I have come for the truck."

The farmer was eating his apple pie in a measured, deliberate manner harking back to an era when children were taught to chew every bite thirty times, no wolfing down, no snacking between meals. The farmer completed his chewing, swallowed, and looked up from his plate. "You need me to fill out something?"

"No," said K, "I don't think that's necessary. I would just like the truck."

"You got the truck," said the farmer.

For a second, K thought that Darren might have come and towed the truck out of sheer enthusiasm for his job. Oh, how that boy liked towing. But then he remembered that he had not told

Darren where the truck was at. Who was he kidding? He'd known anyway. Deep down, he'd known.

He saw the realization dawn in the farmer's face: "You haven't got the truck?"

"Don't worry," K said. What he could see on this man's open face was the worry that he would be punished for what had been his act of well-meaning helpfulness. The folks around here didn't trust officials much, and often they were right not to. "Do you know when the truck was picked up?"

The farmer nodded. "That day we spoke? Must've been the same day. When I got out the next morning, it had gone. I reckoned you took it," he said.

"At what time in the morning did you notice it had gone?"

"'Bout 4.30 AM."

"You didn't hear anything?"

"When we got the television on, we can't hear hardly anything at all," said the farmer's wife. "We're both going deaf."

"When did you last notice it was there?" asked K.

"Would have been around 6 PM," said the farmer. "Is there going to be a problem?"

"Not for you," said K. "That, I can promise."

"So somebody got the truck that shouldn't have it?" asked the farmer. Something in his eyes made K think that he wasn't as good an actor as he ought to be.

He forced a grin. "Happens all the time. Part of the job." He got up. "Thank you so much. One day, I'm going to get the recipe for that pie from you."

"Anytime you come by, drop right in." The farmer's wife sounded as if she meant it.

The farmer got up and walked him to the door. At the door he turned and trained his clear, frank eyes on K. There was compassion in his face. "Oftentimes, what we worry about doesn't come true," the farmer said.

"Thank you," said K. "For everything."

No need to mention that what he worried about had damn well already happened.

K's vehicle bounced over ridges left by tractor tires. He took a left on County Road H. To his left was Hawksmoor Creek; to his right, the slope of the mesa. He drove along farmland, alfalfa fields, small herds of grazing cattle. At the crossroads he took another left and drove along the field where the two horses stood, day-in day-out, under the merciless sun. Every time K saw those horses, he contemplated reporting their owner for cruel neglect. But here animals counted as possessions, and the first law of the Land of the Free was that nobody had the right to interfere with what people did with their possessions.

K drove on autopilot, insensible to where he was going; driving, staring sightlessly through a windscreen smeared with the corpses of bugs committing kamikaze. Today was a good day for bugs to die. K could hardly see the road for all the splotched insects.

At a fork in the road, he took a left without signaling and drove on, past farms and trailers and four garage houses, past a plant nursery, past some crooked-toothed alpacas watching him curiously over a fence, past a howling dog chained in a yard, past an old man walking along the road with a watering can, past a flock of sheep in an orchard, until he came to a second fork in the road and a sign reading PRIVATE NO TRESPASS, beyond which the gravel road dropped deep into the canyon.

K woke from his troubled reverie when a spit of gravel from a passing vehicle hit the side of the patrol car. He took out his cell and dialed.

CHAPTER TWENTY-TWO

The coffee at the Resting Warrior Diner was a shade darker than dishwater, though somewhat less aromatic. K was on his third refill when Robbie Begay came through the door. Setting his eye on his old buddy, K temporarily forgot about his own concerns and started to worry about Begay.

"So, you got yourself into some other mess, huh?" said Begay.

"Lunch is on me," said K, and pushed the egg-stained, laminated menu toward Begay. "They have some nice omelets, with bell peppers and mushrooms. And how about an orange-carrot juice? It's their new item."

"Bell peppers and carrot juice?" Begay shook his head like a pony trying to rid itself of a horsefly. "You still trying to turn me vegetarian?"

"Vegetarian? No. No, I'm not!"

Begay regarded K with raised eyebrows. "What's going on?"

"I just think you should eat healthier," said K. "We all should ..."

"No shit?" said Begay. "That's why you wanted to meet me? To give me some lecture about nutrition?"

"Of course not," K mumbled. But the fact was that Begay looked dreadful, his usually cherubic cheeks gaunt, his eyes bloodshot and puffy and circled with dark rings, his skin color a hepatic puce. Fuck it. What were friends for, if not to look out for each other. "You look dreadful," he said.

"Gee, thanks," said Begay. "If that's all you got to say, I'll hit the road. Got to prepare the sweat lodge."

"You're doing a sweat lodge?"

"Got a regular gig with this lady that Gloria works for," said Begay.

"This lady? The lady Gloria worked for in Sedona?"

"Taos," said Begay.

"The Anglo woman with the souvenir shop?"

"'Native Spiritual Gifts and Merchandise,'" said Begay.

"The one with the 'Spirit Safaris?'"

Begay muttered something.

"The one with the 'Spirit Safaris?'" repeated K.

"So what?" growled Begay. His irises were dull and crowded with burst blood vessels fanning out from the corners of his eyes. "It's a great gig. She pays good. All I gotta do is sit around and sweat some with these *bílagáana* tourists that really dig Indians."

"You certainly have a great take on commodifying your spiritual traditions," said K.

"Double cheeseburger and fries," said Begay to the server who had appeared at the table, "and a Dr. Pepper, forty-four ounces."

"Diet?" asked the waiter.

"No," said Begay.

"How often do you run these … sweat lodges?" asked K.

"Depends on the season. Right now is peak season, so I'm real busy."

"How busy is that?"

"Every day," said Begay proudly. "On Saturdays and Sundays, I got two sessions."

"Two sweat lodges a day? You hold *two* sweat lodges a day? Four over a weekend? Nine sweat lodges a week?"

"Well … yeah," said Begay. He drummed his fingers, and frowned at a ketchup stain on the table. He dipped the corner of a paper napkin into his water glass, and rubbed it over the stain. "When's this damn burger gonna be ready?"

"Drink your water," said K.

"What?"

"You should drink your water," said K.

"What is this?"

K looked at his old friend, his old, old-looking friend, at his sallow skin, graying hair, and those terrible bags under his eyes that were apparent even when he was looking down. "What blood type are you?"

"What are you, a damn vampire?" Begay said.

"If you need a kidney, I would give you one of mine," said K urgently.

"What's wrong with you?"

"Nothing … nothing. I'm just saying if you ever needed a kidney …"

What K could see in Robbie's eyes was not anger, but bewilderment and worry. And, he realized, Robbie wasn't worried about himself, but about K. Here was a guy who did nine sweat lodges a week and still had time to worry about someone else.

"I am worried about what you are doing to your body," said K. "That many sweat lodges can't be good. It's not just 'not good,' it's dangerous. I can't believe that Gloria isn't worried."

"She's in Taos."

"Why …"

"She's running the store," said Begay.

But hadn't the whole point of Robbie giving up his job at Redwater PD been to join his beloved, long-suffering Gloria for the good life in leafy Milagro?

"Want to order?" asked the server, setting down a plate with a burger and sloshing coffee into K's mug.

"Err, a side salad, please," said K.

"We don't have that."

"Never mind," said K, "I'll stick to coffee."

Begay slathered his burger with ketchup "Where's the salt?" He looked around the table, reached behind the paper-napkin holder and began shaking salt over a mountain of fries. "Yum, this hits the spot."

"You'd rather fuck up your kidneys than look like you're listening to me, is that it?" K said furiously.

Begay sank his teeth into the burger. Ketchup flowed over the edges of the bun and dripped down his fingers—some of it onto the plate, most of it onto the table. K fought an impulse to start mopping up.

"You try treating me like a kid, that's what you're gonna get. You think I didn't see how you tried to hide the salt?"

K could think of a good many replies, all of which were sure to *not* get a good reply from Begay. He bit his lip and shrugged.

"Why am I here?" asked Begay.

K ignored Begay's smirk and upended the sugar dispenser into his coffee mug, stirred until by rights there should have been a hole in the cup, sipped the coffee, and looked out the window. He fished a napkin out of the holder, spread it out on the table, pleated it and began to fold a paper boat. K was surprised he still remembered how to make one. He pushed the boat around the table.

Begay plucked the boat up and sat it in his water glass: "Either you shoot, or I beat it."

"What is it you think you got wrong?"

The paper boat had disintegrated into sodden shreds that drifted in the cloudy water like krill.

"I didn't take away the car keys. I didn't have the truck towed away. I postponed the referral to court. And ... I didn't click. I just did not think ... It's like being too dumb to add two and two together."

"So what's new?" Begay said.

K was momentarily stunned by Begay's harshness. He hadn't known his old buddy thought him dumb. It was one of those times that made him remember why he didn't really like people. He shouldn't have reached out to Robbie. All that was happening was that he now felt worse. It was almost like being in a session with the Annoying Counselor.

Begay shook his head: "What's eating you now? We know you don't think like a cop. We know you don't *want* to be a cop. We know that every time you try to act like a cop, you make a big ol' mess. Did you forget?"

"Not every time! There are times I do okay."

"Uh. So you agree that mostly when you try to act like a cop you make a big ol' mess. That okay with you?"

"Not really."

"Ain't that your whatchamacallit ... vocation? Some do-good social worker? And now you're whining about it?" Begay pushed away his plate. "Anytime you think you got something wrong, ask yourself what you should have done instead to get it right."

"Huh?" said K. He had difficulties wrapping his head around that sentence.

"Here we go," Begay said, and leaned forward. "WHAT SHOULD YOU HAVE DONE TO GET IT RIGHT?" he boomed.

"Hey! You're scaring my grandson!" the matriarch sitting at the next table said.

K smiled apologetically at the woman, turned to Begay, and hissed through clenched jaws: "What was I supposed to do? Arraign her immediately? Fast-track her to court and try to get her into a program straight away?"

"Speak up! I can't hear you!" said Begay. "With that kind of DUI, they ain't gonna put you in no program. They just tightened the laws. Leastways for our people, they did. Not only was she driving drunk, she was drinking *while* driving. That's even worse. She's Native. She did some damage to a *bílagáana's* property. That would have gotten her straight in jail anyways."

"Who says that isn't what she wanted?" whispered K. He sank his head into his hands. "What a mess. Oh God, what a mess."

"Hey," said Begay. "C'mon, Franz. Let's get us another refill, huh?"

"You want to find her?" Begay asked.

"I *need* to find her," K said. "She's murdered her parents. How come I didn't realize? She as good as told me."

"She told you she was going to kill her parents?"

"Of course not," K snorted. "But she was so distraught. I should've realized that it wasn't just about herself. I should have realized that she couldn't cope. I mean, I *did* realize she couldn't cope, I *did* realize the drunk-driving was like a cry for help, that she'd given up. That she couldn't go on any longer. I should have asked some questions."

He forced himself to say, out loud, that terrible thought: "I think she wanted to be caught and put in jail. Then they would have had to find someone to look after her parents. That's what she wanted—and I gave her exactly the opposite."

"Did she say that?" asked Begay.

"She ... not in so many words ..."

"What words did she say?" Robbie could be quite literal-minded at times.

"That's what comes out of wanting to play God," said K.

"What did she say?"

"She ... she didn't say much."

"What did she say?" insisted Begay.

"She didn't say anything. Nothing. But —"

"I'm not hearing this," said Begay. "Are we having a replay of what happened with that boy?"

"Probably," said K. "I catch someone, and people die."

"That Counselor they sent you to didn't help you any, huh?"

"Nope."

"You never learn, do you?" Begay said. "You just never learn."

"You tell me, then. What should I think? What should I have done?"

"That's what I'm saying," said Begay. "You are asking the wrong question. Matter of fact, you shouldn't be asking any questions at all. When will you get that people got to take some responsibility for themselves? You tell me that lady has a bunch of siblings. Why didn't she phone her bro and her sis and tell them they need to come up and help out?"

"She tried," said K. "At least I think she did."

"She did?"

"She called her sister the night before ... before everything happened."

"And?"

"The sister missed the phone call."

"How come you're not looking there, if you want somebody to blame? Huh? Did the sister call her back?"

"No."

"She could have called her back. She knew that your woman is looking after their parents, right? She ought to have called her back."

"She's got a bunch of kids …"

"See what you're doing?" cried Begay triumphantly.

"No," said K.

"You're talking for them. Let them come here and talk for themselves. How come you like to put yourself in charge of everyone else's lives so much?"

"Me? I like to be in charge?"

"Didn't you just hide the salt and try to get me to drink carrot juice?"

"You need to grow up."

"Look who's talking," said Begay.

"So tell me what to do about her? What am I supposed to do now?"

Begay shrugged. "You get out a warrant on her. You look for her truck. You find her. You bring her in. You do your stuff."

"And what do I tell Weismaker?"

Begay brightened visibly. "The sheriff! You go tell the sheriff everything, and he'll deal with it."

"I tell Weismaker how I screwed up? Seriously?"

"It wasn't just you, though, was it? You got some help from that intern?"

"Cody? Err … Taylor?"

"The kid that deleted all those files? Bet he ain't feeling too great either."

K didn't quite know if Cody/Taylor's shortcomings made the situation better or worse.

"You don't want to worry about the sheriff," Begay added. "That dude knows you anyways. You know what they say, freedom's when you got nothing to lose, or something? There's nothing you can say to him that will make him change his mind about you."

"*That* bad," murmured K.

"There you go again! Dammit! Who says it's bad—or good? It just is what it is. Your man knows how you are. He knows you, that's all I'm saying. You got that father-son thing going."

"Father-son thing?" choked K.

"You're blushing and I'm going," said Begay. "I'll visit with you in your store sometime soon."

"You didn't eat your fries," said K.

"They're too salty."

K watched his friend's broad frame retreating, and sighed. He swallowed the last of his coffee and got up to go.

The sky was an angry gray now, and the air crackled with static.

CHAPTER TWENTY-THREE

What the sheriff did was much worse than anything K had imagined could happen.

"Take a couple of days off, son," he said. "Go and work some on your store. Those books of yours need attention, too." So Weismaker would deal with finding the truck and presumably getting a warrant out on Alice Nakai.

"Should I not call Alice Nakai's brother and sister to tell them there's a warrant out on her?"

"There isn't, yet. We're going to wait until we get out the warrant. Then we'll tell her relatives."

"They may know where she is. Or at least they may be able to guess where she is."

"Let me worry about all that, son. You go home. Just go home."

Leaving an investigation with none of the potential leads explored, with a killer left roaming, a family left grieving, a crime left unpunished—not to speak of the sheriff deeming him expendable enough to send him off in the middle of an open case: none of this did much for K's mood issues.

He unlocked the door of the bookstore. Above his head the BOOKSTORE sign creaked on its chains. Not everything about running a bookstore had to do with books, unfortunately. If, for example, the old, creaky sign came loose from its rusty fastenings and just happened to land on the head of a prospective customer, and if that hypothetical customer happened to be of a litigious disposition ... (This scenario overstretched the limits of probability somewhat, given the number of prospective customers in the bookstore at any given time.) Whatever. K would have to deal with the sign.

It was not the only thing he had to deal with. There were the dripping taps in the bathroom and kitchen, too. Somewhere he had read that domestic dripping taps made for 68 percent of water wastage.

K spent a couple of satisfactory hours on his back, his head stuck under sinks with wrench, spanner, stopcock, and an assortment of washers. At the end of it all, he had the rare feeling of having accomplished something. Then he wandered about his realm, stopping here and there, pulling a book out to read the back cover or index, making a mental note to return to this one or that at an opportune moment.

He followed a tributary of shelves to his right and found himself in a nook, a kind of secret garden within the bookstore. In the corner stood another old, high-backed leather armchair with crochet cushions in psychedelic colors. Maybe it was those colors that kept Benjamin away from this chair.

What was it with all this crochet? Somehow K could not imagine Agnes Prohaska being into crocheting.

He grew startled when he saw his own name on a spine. Weird, how he always did this when he came upon a book by Franz Kafka. For some reason, he had never felt particularly curious about reading Kafka. He had, of course read him, at school, when they all had to read "The Metamorphosis," and out of loyalty to Grandpapa, who had after all been the one who had named him.

Agnes Prohaska had devoted a whole section to Kafka. Here were his works in German, English, French, and Russian. There was a whole shelf of secondary literature. There were bound volumes of collected words, tattered paperbacks and hardbacks in glossy covers. What would Kafka have made of his work being known around the world, his name being fashioned into an adjective that stood for his peculiar vision? Even people who had never read Kafka knew what *kafkaesque* meant.

Kafka had died a horrible death, barely a couple of years older than K was now. Still, when one considered what had come later, it maybe was just as well that Kafka had been out of it. At least he had died in a sanatorium, and not, as so many others, in that satanic, coldly administered hell that the Master Race had devised for Jews.

If the Horsemen of the Apocalypse hadn't ridden, if history had not taken that particular course, K would not be the bearer of that famous name; it would have been his father Josef, "Joe" Kafka, who would have borne the name "Franz." As it was, Josef "Joe" Kafka, Grandpapa's first and only born, had been named after Grandpapa's friend Josef Guggenspiel. They had both been sent to the same place and only one of them had made it back out.

Grandpapa had never talked about his experiences, never mentioned them. He had never really spoken about Josef Guggenspiel, either. It had been Josef "Joe," K's father, who'd spilled. Joe had been the absolute antithesis of everything Grandpapa was, and had represented. Young Joseph Kafka had insisted on being called "Joe" as soon as he was old enough to ponder the significance of names, and, as far as K understood, had considered being named after his father's gassed friend an act of macabre and mawkish paternal disregard.

Joe was more in line with his giddy, feckless mother, who had possessed the careless arrogance of the survivor—for her family had had the foresight to get out in time, and had made it to the Promised Land. No use crying over spilled milk, right? She had met Grandpapa in a kibbutz near Haifa. He was older, and marked by his experiences, but she liked his calm, quiet ways, his kindness. Perhaps she thought that she would change him, make him into the extrovert she desired. That hadn't happened. She had given him a son, stuck around some, made her child into the resentful narcissist that he was, and had left her family for a young, brawny extrovert. As far as K knew, his grandmother could be still alive, the sole survivor among all his forebears, kicking around somewhere near Haifa with her hairy-chested beau.

K got to know about the camps and the gas chambers at a very young age, when his father, buzzing on a bongful of black Afghan and a few glasses of Mateus rosé, opined how much better the name *Franz* would have suited himself, and how much of a "chick-magnet"—or had he said "bird-magnet"—that name potentially was. Joe considered the old man a blight on his life, a crow casting a shadow on joy, a human cenotaph marking the atrocity of man, when Joe really just wanted *fun, fun, fun, hey*. Not even aggrieved Joe Kafka could have accused his father of ever burdening him with his experiences or outlook, though. No, to Joe it was affront enough that his father had lived, had survived what nobody should be made to experience. It was long after his parents' deaths that K began to understand that his father's resentment had been pure guilt. Survivor's guilt.

Thanks to the powers of displacement, K forgot most of what Joe had told him, until one summer day on Gower beach, Grandpapa's shirtsleeve had ridden up, and K had seen the number tattooed on his arm. Somehow he knew he must not ask Grandpapa about this, and so he didn't.

And now he stood in front of a shelf groaning with editions embossed with the name that his father had envied him for, not because it was associated with exceptional talent, but because it would have helped him *pull* more *birds*. K read the spines of the books and then pulled out one that he had never read, not even heard of, really. *Amerika*. He opened it. Its pages were yellow and brittle, and it was in German with a preface by Max Brod.

K had mixed feelings about Brod, Franz Kafka's buddy, perhaps his closest friend and the executor of his will. Kafka had not wanted his legacy published; he had wanted his writings burnt. Instead, Brod voraciously collected and collated everything Kafka had ever written, from letters to his father and paramours, his private diaries, and unfinished manuscripts. Yes, the world was probably a richer, or at least a more profoundly perplexed place with Franz Kafka's writings in it, but ...

Maybe loyalty was an overrated virtue. Maybe Kafka, freed at last from his tortured mortal shell, was twirling all about them, atomized and happy-as-Larry about his posthumous fame.

It had been a long time since K had read German. Grandpapa had read to him and his twin Lili in German when they were children. K didn't think that Lili had retained any German. She hadn't been particularly keen on those German storytelling sessions.

K made himself a cup of coffee, fluffed up the psychedelic crochet cushions and settled into the armchair. As if summoned by a
bell, Benjamin appeared, jumped on his lap, draped himself across
the open book, and began kneading the cushion with widespread
paws.

"Behold Kafka reading Kafka," said K, lifting the cat off the
book and placing him on the armrest. Benjamin regarded him
through one green eye. He stretched his front leg and laid a paw on
K's arm.

"Would you like to hear what I'm reading?" K asked the cat.

*Als der sechzehnjährige Karl Roßmann, der von seinen armen
Eltern nach Amerika geschickt worden war, weil ihn ein Dien-
stmädchen verführt und ein Kind von ihm bekommen hatte, in
dem schon langsam gewordenen Schiff in den Hafen von New
York einfuhr, erblickte er die schon längst beobachtete Statue
der Freiheitsgöttin wie in einem plötzlich stärker gewordenen
Sonnenlicht. Ihr Arm mit dem Schwert ragte wie neuerdings
empor, und um ihre Gestalt wehten die freien Lüfte.*

As K read aloud in a language he had only ever spoken to one person, he felt in the molding of those vowels the presence of Grandpapa—his voice, so gentle, deep, and contemplative, so melodi-
cally Viennese. Who cared that Franz Kafka the Greater's German
had been Czech-accented? He'd brought Grandpapa back to him. K
felt all ambivalence toward his namesake dissolve. In any case, far
from the doom-laden kvetching that was so often associated with
Kafka, this story began as an albeit slightly sinister ode to the enraptured *flâneur* Karl Roßmann, who was being sent by his parents
into American exile after impregnating a servant girl.

To Roßmann, everything is new and curious, strange and won-
dersome. Worries pass through his mind as fleetingly as clouds; he
is so prone to distraction that even in the presence of danger, he
forgets to focus on his own safety. Each new encounter and situation provoke in Roßmann fresh mirth, curiosity, and delight.

In Roßmann's propensity to be distracted, K recognized an absence of priorities, the truly even-handed openness to new experiences characteristic of that innocent stage in life when experience has not yet tainted the fresh gaze.

On K's lap, Benjamin rolled onto his back, stretched and laid one paw flat against K's neck.

Ich habe meinen Regenschirm unten vergessen und bin gelaufen, um ihn zu holen, wollte aber den Koffer nicht mitschleppen. Dann habe ich mich auch hier noch verirrt.

As he read aloud, Benjamin began to purr, so that pretty soon K felt like a ventriloquist of limited repertoire. This was turning out to be a good day after all.

The only thing that marred this idyll were K's worries about Wittgenstein. Wittgenstein had begun to display, on K's porch, neatly filleted parts of birds, bullfrogs, and rodents. The other night, when K came home, he had nearly stepped on a mouse's heart. K knew that these were gifts, rare expressions by Wittgenstein of affection, or insecurity, or insecurity-inspired affection. K knew what Wittgenstein would do if he caught him here with Benjamin on his lap.

"You are reading to the kitty?"

"I didn't hear the doorbells," K said, and shoved the book on a shelf.

"I wish you hadn't stopped reading," said Siwan Davies. "I was enjoying it."

"Do you speak German?"

"No, but it sounds lovely. It sounded lovely, how you were reading it. What is it?"

K shrugged and bit his lip. "Kafka," he mumbled.

"Kafka?" Siwan Davies smiled. "Did you change your mind about him? Now I really wish I hadn't interrupted you. Won't you go on reading?"

"To a cat and a German-language fetishist? I'd feel like a circus act."

He saw the blood rise, crimson, to Siwan Davies's cheeks. He saw her swallow hard.

"Okay, then," she said. "Bye-bye." Her voice was rough, and she didn't look back.

K set Benjamin on the floor.

"Hey!" Magnusson was carrying a cardboard box. Ever since K had taken on the bookstore, the big Swede had taken to sauntering over from Barbie's, the local dive bar that he had acquired as his retirement project and which, despite his organizational ineptitude, he had not yet succeeded running into the ground.

"Just missed your lovely friend. Pity. We could have had a nice *Kaffeeklatsch* together."

"I doubt it," said K.

"You're looking glum," said Magnusson. "Lover's tiff?"

"We aren't lovers," said K sharply.

"She likes you—you know that, right?" said Magnusson.

"That's because she doesn't know me," said K. "Anyway, not anymore."

"Ah ... I almost feel like I'm back in kindergarten," said Magnusson dreamily. "What are you looking at me like that for? Never mind. I don't want to know. I just came by to give you these." He set the carton on the table. "Cinnamon buns."

"Uh," said K. "Well, that is kind of you."

"Not really," said Magnusson. "I can't stand them. This Swedish friend came to visit, and brought a whole box of them. Homemade. The real deal. She's been trying to make me eat them ..."

"Just think of me as your compost heap," said K ungraciously.

"I thought you love cinnamon buns."

"Depends on the spirit they are given in."

"One of those days, is it?" said Magnusson. "Well, well, well ... what have we here? You got yourself another cat?"

"I got him in exchange for some rattlesnakes," said K. "Long story."

"I won't ask, then." Magnusson tickled Benjamin's chin and began to sneeze.

"Oh, crap," said K, "are you allergic to cats?"

"Could be," Magnusson shrugged.

"Benjamin has only been here for a couple of days. I hadn't thought about allergies."

"Benjamin?" said Magnusson, "Let me guess—Walter?"

"Am I that predictable?"

"You are. Don't worry about allergies." Magnusson sneezed again. "There's not much harm in sneezing."

"Americans are very serious about their allergies."

"Tiny flecks of humanity in a vast, ill-gotten land," said Magnusson. "That's why they are so afraid of everything." He sneezed again. "It's their bad conscience projected into the environment as malign adversary."

"… That reminds me of something," said K. "I'd like to ask you a favor."

"Hmm, I don't know about that," said Magnusson, after K had outlined his request.

Hearing himself saying it out loud, K had wished he could summon back the words and the idea. But now it was too late. "It might help save a life," he said. "Or at least someone's health."

"Why me?" asked Magnusson. "Why the subterfuge?"

"I don't want to lose a friendship."

"Are you really sure this is a good idea?"

"No," said K, "but it may be worth a try. It may not go anywhere, anyway."

"I'll think about it," said Magnusson.

"Yeah, do that," said K. "I don't even need to know what you've decided to do."

"Trying to keep your hands clean? They are already dirty, you know?"

Benjamin, who appeared to be mistaking Magnusson's sneezing for a pre-mating ritual, rubbed his head against the big Swede's legs, purring.

"Would you like to take him along?" asked K.

"You don't mean that," said Magnusson complacently. He cocked his head to read the title of K's book, picked it up and leafed through it. Magnusson had had a couple of years studying economics at the University of Heidelberg, of which—apart from improving his German—he had retained only extremely fond memories of easy access to beer and schnapps, and of romancing wholesome, buxom maidens.

"I haven't read this one. What an interesting beginning. 'The Goddess of Liberty.' She doesn't carry a sword, though, does she?"

"I don't think so," said K. "Isn't it a torch?"

"And she isn't a goddess, either. Do you suppose that Kafka really believed she's carrying a sword? Or is this his willful distortion? Carrying a sword and being a deity would make her into a goddess of vengeance rather than liberty, don't you think?"

"A sword would be more adequate preparation for what awaits migrants on American soil, that's for sure."

"Isn't he brilliant?" said Magnusson. "A bare two sentences in, and we're already neck-deep into an existential discussion."

An odd and entirely uncharacteristic thought came to K of a foreign-language-based book club, where polyglots could meet, discuss international literature, and get away from narrow Anglophone sensibilities and the tedious obsession of white American males in the prime of their years with penning the Great American Novel. The last such tome K had attempted had been several hundred pages too long, and had been a distinctly 'so-what-ish' experience.

"Great idea!" said Magnusson, nodding and intermittently sneezing. "Count me in."

"It was just a thought," protested K.

"And now it's a project," said Magnusson.

CHAPTER TWENTY-FOUR

Domestic tasks brought with them a state of reverie that helped displace K's unease. He decided that he had reached out to Magnusson because the big Swede's disposition made it pretty unlikely that he would do anything about K's request.

K began separating Benjamin from his crochet blanket, carefully liberating loops of fabric from claws: a good twenty minutes' labor of love. Taking advantage of the sun, K carried the blankets and rugs outside and spread them out on the little patch of anthills and weeds behind the store. Then he tended to the battalion of pot plants that had been store-warming gifts from Milagro's bookish crowd, and which, so far, mostly seemed to be thriving.

K was scrubbing the kitchen basin with an environmentally friendly paste of bi-carb when the doorbells tinkled and Felix John appeared, bearing a large cardboard box.

John, unsmiling, nodded curtly and set his box on the counter. It was crowded with coffee cans, sugar, sweetener packets, and cartons of creamer.

K's tenuous moral elation at playing gracious host evaporated; he suspected that this might have been the effect Felix John had been aiming for.

"Great," said K. "How about you take that cupboard to store the stuff for your group?" Check.

"Sure," said John, and began storing his provisions away. Then he drew a small bag out of the box and set it on the counter. "Where is the cat?"

"The cat?" It occurred to K that he hadn't seen Benjamin since he had evicted him from his blanket.

Benjamin wasn't in the reading nook on his favorite chair. He wasn't in the Marxist secondary literature room, nor in the Nineteenth-Century Novel section, or the Americas Collection section, or in the First Editions room; he was not under the desk, nor in the bathroom or storeroom. K opened the front door and stepped out. Traffic roared up and down Main Street. At least there wasn't a bundle of flattened fur, blood, and guts smeared on the asphalt, as far as he could see. The knit-shop's door stood open, and he walked in.

"Well, hello," said a woman arranging wool on shelves according to color. "I'll be with you in just a minute."

"I just wanted to ask if you've seen my ... a cat," said K. "A big, dark—"

"Can't say I have," said the woman. "Are you the veteran that bought up the bookstore from that Russian woman?" That was an average of one inaccuracy per five words. Not bad. She could have been a career politician. "We're real happy a vet bought that shop. That store's been a disgrace. You know she's a communist? Has she died or something? You want a flag for your storefront, you just let me know." She pointed to the counter over which star-spangled and Confederate banners of various sizes ranging from state-funeral to anthill-marker lay draped.

"Better go and find my cat," K said. With some luck, she would take his lack of courtesy for PTSD.

K worked his way through the neighboring stores. They were a mixed lot: a bohemian art gallery, a health-food shop, a hardware store, and a diner. None of them, flag-bearing or otherwise, contained anyone who had seen Benjamin.

K walked to the intersection, each squealing of brakes, tooting of horns, and grating of tires on asphalt shaking his nerves. It would, perhaps, be easier to confront a *fait accompli* than to witness the tragedy unfolding. A woman of slight build passed him, dragged along the boardwalk by a ferocious dog. There were so many dangers out here.

But perhaps Benjamin had just taken a little stroll around the corner, and was sitting on the pleasantly warm paving stones at the back of the municipal offices. As K walked past the building, the automatic doors opened. Would they open for a cat? K entered. The cold air momentarily stunned him. He couldn't imagine that Benjamin, who was an elderly cat after all, could possibly enjoy hanging out in such a freezing ambiance. A woman carrying a bulging tote bag hurried past him.

"Excuse me ..." said K, but she was gone without backward glance.

"For some folks, it's 'hurry, hurry, hurry all the way into the Devil's arms,'" said an old man leaning on his cane and wheezing.

"You don't happen to have seen a cat? A big, gray cat ...?"

"I don't see real good," the old man said. "Hey, how 'bout you read me them notices on the board? You can see alright, right?"

"Sure," said K. "Are you interested in anything specific?"

"Why don't you read all of it?" encouraged the old man.

Some hurried, hurried, hurried all the way into the Devil's arms. Others didn't. Though it was conceivable that they'd all land in that same place, sooner or later.

Council meetings. Council meeting resolutions. Meeting minutes. Whoever typed up these notices sure loved their grocers' apostrophes: ALERT'S TO PUBLIC HEARING'S. TOWN HALL MEETING'S. PLAN'S FOR THE PROPOSED CHANGE'S TO MAIN STREET. The city fathers were keen on luring business to downtown Milagro, and to that end had engaged a city planner whose bold designs seemed to owe rather more to The Green Light's extra-potent recreational cannabis products than to practical considerations. It was difficult to explain those to the sight-impeded gentleman.

"Sir," said K, "I really do need to find my—"

"Any warrants?" asked the old man. "I always like knowing about those. One day I might catch me a criminal, and get me paid some reward." He wheezed merrily.

There was just one warrant. It bore a black-and-white image of blurred gray-tone pixels, like those photos of ghosts that haunted-house detectives liked to show off. Under WANTED and MURDER in bold capitals was her name.

ALICE NAKAI. It was like a punch to the gut. Maybe that's why the sheriff had wanted him gone. It had nothing to do with compassion, or wanting to give him a break. Weismaker had just wanted him out of the way, to get out the warrant on Alice Nakai, without K yapping at his heels.

"What does it say?"

It was the word MURDER he couldn't stand, the word MURDER over her tortured face.

"What does it say?"

But she *had* murdered her parents, hadn't she? In the cruelest way imaginable. She had drugged two helpless elderly people, taken a gas canister, and sprinkled the gas all around the trailer while her parents lay comatose. She had set fire to the trailer. She had let two old people burn alive. Two old people who couldn't move from the separate beds they lay in. Two old people who had gone into death without even the solace of each other's touch.

"Hey! I want to know what the warrant says!"

No. She hadn't committed murder. Alice Nakai had committed euthanasia. She had had to commit euthanasia because she could not see a way out. Not for herself. Not for her parents. What she had done had been to protect her parents from the consequences of her DUI.

"Hey! You! I'm waiting!"

"You'll have to wait some more, sir."

In the store, Felix John was sitting in the rocking chair, with Benjamin on his lap.

"Where did you find him?" asked K brusquely.

John tilted his chin toward the back door. "He was sleeping outside on that blanket."

"He likes his blanket," said K.

"You okay?" asked John.

"Sure," said K.

Felix John regarded him through steel-rimmed glasses: "You got a real fright about that cat, huh?" His expression was almost amicable.

"Do you happen to have a couple of hours to look after the store?" K asked. "Something's come up."

"Sure," said John. "I got nothing on until the group." On his lap, Benjamin stretched and yawned.

CHAPTER TWENTY-FIVE

"You aren't supposed to be here," said Becky.

He had been right about the conspiracy to keep him out. He nodded and walked past Becky Tsosie into his office, which smelled dusty and abandoned even after just a day's absence. K opened the top desk drawer and took out the good old-fashioned notebook that was to him what USB sticks and clouds were to the other cops. He dialed a number and listened to the phone ringing, knowing that he would prefer it if his call wasn't answered. But he needed to have tried.

Just as he was about to hang up the call was answered.

"Milagro Police," K said. He heard the sharp in-drawing of breath. They knew. Somehow, they always knew.

"Alana?" K said. The sound he heard resembled the type of squeak a terrified baby animal makes when it has been cornered. "I wanted to let you know that there is a warrant out on your sister. There is a warrant out on Alice. It is a murder warrant."

Now there was no sound at all on the other end of the line. Though silence was a sound, as that old song said. It was thick and foggy and clogged up the ears and made K confused and forget why he had thought it was so important to phone Alice Nakai's siblings in the first place.

"Alana?" She was breathing now, quickly, raggedly. She was hyperventilating. "Try to slow down your breathing," said K. "You had a shock ... I ... I am sorry ..."

He listened helplessly as the woman gulped and her breath whistled, and she finally began to cry, or rather to howl, *no,no,no, that is not my sister, my sister has never hurt anybody, my sister is a good person, my sister is a good person, she never hurt anybody,* like a prayer, an incantation, the same two sentences, again and again.

"We don't really know what happened. The warrant just means that we are looking for your sister in connection with the mu— with the death of your parents. She hasn't been convicted of anything yet." Oh, cowardly peddler of false hope that he was. "But it would help if you tell us if she has been in contact with you. Has she been in contact with you?"

The woman gulped. "No."

"If she does contact you, would you ask her to turn herself in?" The line crackled with her ragged breath. K fancied he could hear her tears falling—splat!—on the hard surface of a table or counter. "Would you like me to contact your brother?" asked K. The gulping stopped. "Was that a no?" asked K. He could hear her, faintly. She was saying that her brother did not like cops because of some bad experiences, and it was better that she told him. K made an effort to put some vibrant professionalism in his voice and said he understood this, and to call him anytime. He gave her both his office and his cellphone number, which was something he tended to avoid doing.

He was stowing away his notebook with that slightly smug feeling that sprang from fancying having done the right thing against one's selfish inclinations, when he remembered Arlene Yazzie. By rights he should have phoned her first. After all, she had had enough interest in her niece's welfare to have voluntarily visited the police station.

He dug out his notebook again, rang her number, listened to her voicemail come on, and disconnected. He hadn't prepared himself for the voicemail. And anyway, how did one pack a murder warrant into a few seconds speaking to a machine? He drummed his fingers on the desk, redialed, and left a brisk message to call him back.

In the corridor, K ran into Córdoba.

"Are you not supposed to have time off?" asked Córdoba.

"How come everybody knows that?" growled K.

Córdoba regarded him with a slight frown and shrugged. She didn't seem to see the problem. "I was going to visit your store today," Córdoba said.

"My store?" What a pleasant turn of events.

"With my fiancé," K heard Córdoba say.

"All book-lovers welcome!" he said a little too brightly, "I'll have the coffee ready."

CHAPTER TWENTY-SIX

"I'm returning your call," said a low voice. The line fell silent, and by that silence that stretched and stretched and wasn't broken, K guessed that his caller was Arlene Yazzie.

"Mrs. Yazzie?" He took the sound she made, a faraway *uh-huh*, as an affirmative. "I called you because I wanted you to know that there is a warrant on your niece. There's a warrant on Alice. For murder," K said quickly.

"I know," came Arlene Yazzie's soft, low, distant voice.

"You know?" said K, and added, "I just found out a couple of hours ago myself." Was that the impulse to apologize, or was it the need to position himself apart from the heartless powers that presumed guilty until proven innocent, that did nothing to save a soul but so much to punish it, that so rarely offered solutions or healing, but generated that much more hurt and misery?

"They tried to make us put up one of those warrant posters. I said no," Arlene Yazzie said flatly.

"It doesn't mean that Alice has been convicted, Mrs. Yazzie," said K, "it just means that they are looking for her in connection with the ... deaths of her parents."

"Murder," whispered Arlene Yazzie. "It was that word that's so hard to see. My niece isn't a murderer." Her voice cracked with injury.

"Has Alice been in contact with you, Mrs. Yazzie?"

"No. No ... She hasn't. I have this feeling ..." her voice broke.

"What feeling?"

There was a click. Arlene Yazzie had disconnected.

K scooped up Benjamin, who had been sitting by his feet. "Oh God," he said into the cat's fur. "Oh, God."

Benjamin, perhaps not that well versed in human language, purred contentedly and snuggled into K's chest.

It was afternoon, and a steady drift of browsers and even occasional customers helped to dispel the leaden feeling of doom that was weighing on K.

He was toting up sales, when his mind-expanding excursion into the realm of account-keeping was interrupted by his cellphone ringing. When he finally located the phone, he didn't recognize the voice at the other end of the line: "Is this a bad time?"

"It's fine. How can I help you?"

"It's Francis. From Pet Rescue. Are you sure this is a good time?"

"Benjamin was sitting on the phone, and I thought he had swallowed it," K said.

"Benjamin?"

"The cat you brought me: Benjamin."

"Good name for a cat," said Francis.

"That's what you said last time."

Francis laughed. "At least I'm consistent. You want to come along for a rattlesnake liberation trip?"

"Um … As an alibi, or partner in crime?"

"Both. I figured I'd better take along a cop, in case I get caught with those snakes. Of course, it is still illegal, whether you are there or not," Francis said cheerfully. "But most folks aren't going to know that."

"You had me at 'illegal,'" said K. "When?"

"I was thinking if we leave around 4 AM, we're gonna make it back by 9 AM."

"Pending no unforeseen circumstances," said K.

CHAPTER TWENTY-SEVEN

Newcomers kept trooping past K, who was sitting behind the counter trying to make headway with *Amerika*. Felix John's gathering was well attended. From the meeting room came the scraping of chairs, laughter, voices that rose and fell, the gurgling of the coffee machine. Then somebody closed the door, and the subsequent silence made it easier for K to concentrate on his book. His German wasn't what it once had been.

K surfaced from *Amerika* to raised voices. There was no laughter now.

The door to the meeting room opened. People hurried past K. Outside they congregated in clusters, heads together.

Benjamin stalked out of the recesses of the store and nudged his head against K's leg.

"Have you been whoring yourself out again?" K asked, and lifted Benjamin onto his lap.

"That's no way to speak to a cat," said John. The lamplight reflected in his glasses, and there was no way of knowing if he was joking.

"Normally I don't talk like that when there are witnesses," said K. Felix John's sardonically raised eyebrows told him that this was exactly what he expected of the fuzz. They were on the way to another one of those eyeballing standoffs. K sighed, lifted Benjamin off his lap, and hoisted him at John. John took the cat and shook his head. "It was a lively group, huh?" said K.

"That fire," said John. "What are you doing about it?"

"Which fire?" asked K.

"The trailer fire. The one that killed Emma and Samuel Nakai."

"You knew them?"

"We are all family," said John tersely. "What are you doing about that fire?"

"We are looking at suspects."

"If it's Alice Nakai you have for a suspect, you are wrong," said John.

"The inquiry is ongoing."

"Everybody has seen those warrant posters."

"Everybody?"

"Cops always go for the easy target. Why don't you look at those developers that are taking away our land?"

"What has that to do with the trailer fire?

"That's the kind of land they like. In a couple of years there's gonna be another gated development. You need to go after those folks. Not Alice." Felix John's eyes bore into K's: "The times when we are taking all these things lying down are over."

CHAPTER TWENTY-EIGHT

K was toting up the day's sales and going hard at the Wite Out when the doorbells tinkled and Córdoba came in. He had quite forgotten Córdoba's intended visit.

"You look tired," said Córdoba. It was rare for her to make such a personal remark.

"Well, yeah ..." said K evasively.

"They say you took it hard, with that DUI lady ..."

"Who is 'they?'" K asked sharply. "Weren't you going to bring your fiancé?"

Córdoba looked at him intently and nodded: "Parking the car."

K wondered if she had issued her fiancé with instructions to give her a bit of time, until she had ferreted out K's state of mind. That's what unhappiness did to you. It made you suspicious, ungrateful, and ungracious.

"I'll make us some coffee," said K woodenly. "Why don't you have a browse? What kind of books do you like?"

"Feminist," Córdoba said crisply.

K had never heard the word uttered inside the confines of Milagro PD. It was as if she'd asked for the Meth-lab Instruction Manuals section. "We have a big section: feminist theory; history, fiction, politics, Marxist feminism, Latin American liberation feminism ..."

Córdoba laughed. "You got it all covered, huh?"

"It's a wide field," K said modestly.

It felt weird, to be here in his bookstore, off PD turf, with Córdoba.

While Córdoba browsed, K busied himself brewing coffee that would put hairs on Córdoba's fiancé's chest. Strange, anyway, that the usually so-private Córdoba was voluntarily seeking to introduce her fiancé to a fellow cop. Who was the lucky sod, who had managed to snare a prize like her? Did she go for hunky and dim? Weedy and bright? Dark and brooding? Light and sunny? Latinx? Anglo? Native? African? Asian? Rich and callow? Poor and idealistic? Arty? Pragmatic? Practical? Radical? Creative? NRA or Antifa? Over the years, K had realized that most competent, attractive women punched way below their weight. It was a truth yet to be universally acknowledged that many a strong woman's Achilles' heel was her weak man.

K put mugs, milk, and sugar on the tray that bore the words DAS KAPITAL—an ironic gift to Agnes Prohaska, surely. He carried the tray to the First Editions section, which almost looked respectable with its glass-fronted bookcases and the round table with vintage chairs grouped around it. Cuauhtémoc liked to do his homework there.

In the front of the store a tall, rangy woman in denim and cowboy boots was perusing the Regional History and Politics shelf. "Hi," said K. "If there's something particular you are looking for, just let me know."

The woman turned around. She had high cheekbones, hair the color of honey and golden skin with a dusting of freckles over her nose. Her eyes were a deep sapphire-blue, and she could have starred in one of those ads in which beautiful women rode on wild horses through a vast tableau of natural splendor. K was probably thinking of the cigarette ads of his youth, though the rider would have been some mustachioed guy, not a rangy cowgirl.

"Meet Dana," said a voice behind him.

Dana stretched out her hand. She had the iron grip of a cattle-wrangler. "Pleased to meet you, Dana," said K. "How about some coffee?"

He tore into the kitchen without waiting for an answer. Pity he had already made the coffee. Right now he could have used the chance to buy himself some time. He opened the faucet, held his hands under it, watched the water gurgle down the sink and waited for his surprise, or shock, or whatever it was, to settle. He carried the coffee pot to the First Editions room, where the two women had seated themselves.

Seen side by side, it was striking how well matched they were. One a dark-haired, olive-skinned, curvaceous regal beauty, the other a golden-colored Amazon: they were a feast for any old sexist lecher's eyes. K was aware of Córdoba watching him—or, rather, of Córdoba ostensibly not watching him. But Dana, Benjamin on her knees, *was* watching him, and she looked amused. The twitch of mirth around her Grecian lips got K's goat. There was nothing so potent as spite to determine his reaction.

"You probably noticed that you aren't what I expected," K said to Dana. Dana smiled. Her smile was slow and sexy, and damn ... a man's flesh was weak.

"Nita thought we should have a trial run." Her voice was deep and husky, carrying with it a timbre of amusement, like Lauren Bacall's in the "whistle and blow" thing.

So that's what he was, a trial run. A trial run for what? Lesser sexist among the pigsty of misogynists? Least red-blooded among the rednecks? Effete boy-wonder hailing from the land of pederasts?

"Dana!" said Córdoba, and there was admonishment and love, yes love, in her voice. K looked at Córdoba. There were laugh lines around her eyes, her cheeks were dimpled, and her usually reserved face was animated and beaming and glowing with warmth. He had never seen her like this.

"Wow," said K before he could stop himself, "I've never seen you like this."

Dana laughed. "How do you see her?"

"Formidable," said K. "Strong ... competent." He stopped. What a crock of bullshit. As if a person couldn't be formidable, strong, competent, and emotionally engaged. At the rate he was trotting out sexist tropes, they'd be gone before the coffee was poured. "I meant to say: *reserved*," K said. "Reserved." Maybe he had made it even worse now.

"She has to be," said Dana, and laid a strong, supple hand on Córdoba's arm. "Don't you?"

Córdoba covered Dana's hand with her own and smiled: "It feels good, though, to let somebody know." Apparently it took very little to make you feel good, when you had finally taken a baby-step out of the closet.

'Fiancée.' If Córdoba had written it down he would have known that he was a she, unless Córdoba didn't know about the French gendering of nouns, which was pretty likely, as Córdoba had received a proper American education which did not hold with foreign languages.

Dana grinned. He could see what she was thinking: *You are having a tough time with this, huh?* "No," he said to her unspoken question.

But this dame understood. This dame was solid. She winked, her nose crinkled, and she burst out laughing: "Nita was real worried."

K nodded.

"What do you think the other guys will say?" said Córdoba. She was beginning to look like her old self again, stern and forbidding.

"They won't say anything," K said. Not to her face, they wouldn't. But perhaps they wouldn't even say anything behind her back, either. Because if they didn't now, even when they thought she was straight and therefore presumably gagging for some horizontal rock n' roll with a real red-blooded man, they might not then. Except for those occasions when one good ol' boy had to prove his virility to another good ol' boy by running his mouth via some dirty talk.

"I really don't think they'll say anything," K repeated. "Have they ever said anything before?"

Córdoba shrugged: "Not to my face."

"Who cares anyway," said K jovially, before remembering that perhaps it wasn't for him to decide who was supposed to care or not.

"You were right, Nita," said Dana to Córdoba. "This guy really overthinks things."

Córdoba shrugged and bit her lip.

"At least we now know that everybody talks behind everybody else's back," said K.

"She didn't say anything bad. At all. You are her favorite," said Dana.

If she'd met the rest of the squad, she'd know this wasn't a great compliment. "I can see we are going to get on, you and me," said K waspishly. Dana grinned. Not a gal to take offense. All in all, Córdoba hadn't made such a bad choice.

"So, you are planning to marry?" said K.

Córdoba nodded, and Dana said: "That's why we're here. We need a witness." She studied K's face, and turned to her fiancée: "He's fixing to ask if we mean him." Córdoba shook her head at Dana the way one does at a wayward child.

"Either you are a very good reader of character, or I'm just very transparent," said K.

"Both," said Dana. "I work with horses." She studied his face. "It helps to understand humans."

"Ah," said K. It must be odd to be married to someone who always knew what you were thinking because they read you like a horse.

"Anyways," said Dana, "Nita and I wanted to ask you to be a witness at our wedding."

"Sure," said K.

"Great. We don't have a fixed date yet, and it isn't going to be a big thing, either. None of our folks are so hot on ... this." She made a sweeping gesture with a sinewy, tanned arm.

"Maybe they'll change their minds," said Córdoba.

"Whatever," Dana shrugged. "But we got you, right?"

There was something about her that reminded him of someone. Her easy capacity to put him on the back foot, both formidable and irritating, was familiar. Córdoba, on the other hand, seemed like a completely different person, someone he did not know. Love and fulfillment radiated from her, softened her beauty, transformed her entire persona. Fucking lucky Dana, to have such an effect.

Dana got up, stretched her long limbs and deposited Benjamin on K's lap. "We'll see you." She stretched out her hand to Córdoba, and pulled her up. The way their eyes locked gave K an electric jolt.

"You make great coffee," Dana called, and they were gone.

K washed up and walked through the store, putting back books and turning off lights. He stopped at the Kafka shelf. There were three copies of *Amerika*, one in German and two in English. K pulled out the German copy and carried it to the front desk. He opened the book and pondered the flysheet. Then he wrote, carefully, in the best hand he could manage:

Auf ein baldiges Wiedersehen, Ihr ergebener Freund Franz Kafka

He rummaged around in the desk drawers, found some packing paper, wrapped up the book, addressed it, and wrote a note to Cuauhtémoc that he stuck on the parcel. The lad was reliable. And if not, it was fate. Fate always had the final call.

He turned off the last light, locked up and stepped into the night.

CHAPTER TWENTY-NINE

The white thread of dawn was just about visible over the dark edge of the mesa when they took off in Francis's pickup. K spied a basket on the back seat of the truck's cabin.

"The snakes are in the back seat?" asked K.

"Yeah," said Francis.

"There's quite a lot of space on the loading bed ..." suggested K.

"They get cold out there."

Out in the high desert, cold nights followed warm days. They could see their breath rising in plumes.

At the intersection, Francis turned right. A deer stood by the roadside, its eyes iridescent in the dark. They drove along the silent empty road, Resting Warrior Mountain looming steeply in the dark. Francis swerved around the remains of a skunk. The truck's cabin filled with the characteristic skunk smell of acrid burnt rubber. K fancied he heard a faint rattling issue from the basket.

"Do rattlers eat skunk?" he asked K.

"What?"

"Somebody back there started rattling when the cabin started stinking of skunk ... I was just wondering if snakes fancy the taste of skunks."

"I don't even know that snakes have a sense of smell," said Francis. "I just think it was the swerving that woke them up."

"You sure you tied the basket down?" asked K.

"Tied it down? Don't worry. It's got a neat cover fitting right over it."

"Oh," said K. He started whistling through his teeth, then remembered that these snakes liked to party to music.

Dawn had broken, casting McKinnon Canyon in monochrome colors. "You take McKinnon Canyon Road to get to Quorum Valley?"

"Know the 5528? It cuts across Thunderbolt Creek and runs past Casita Ruins, then you take that ungraded road up to Latep Plain and you're in Desolation Valley."

K had thought he knew all the roads to Quorum Valley. "I wonder if they caught the cougar," he said. They were driving past McKinnon Canyon Community Center, the stone-hewn building looking cold and forbidding in the leaden light of dawn.

"They haven't so far," said Francis.

"You heard about the cougar?"

"Sure. Anytime these folks get ready to kill some poor critter, we get to hear about it. The cougar has got himself some good friends."

"That's good to know," said K.

"They're not all bad, those McKinnon folks, you know?" said Francis.

"I probably just haven't met the good ones yet."

Francis laughed. "They kinda got it right in what they say about you."

This was the point at which K would have liked to stick his fingers in his ears, singing *la la la* very loudly. It wasn't even so much what they might have said than the fact that they said anything at all. K preferred to imagine himself as a foggy specter, an éminence grise, a nowhere man. "I don't need to know what they say about me," he snapped.

"Can't remember, anyways," said Francis.

"What about the cougar?"

"You'll see," said Francis, and took a sharp right. The truck bounced down a stony road, barely more than a path, crossed a riverbed, and climbed up a steep incline. They found themselves on a plateau strewn with red boulders. At its far end, the promontory of McKinnon Canyon glowed crimson in the rising sun. Francis wove around boulders until they got to a rock formation that rose up steeply from the plateau. An old Jeep was parked at its foot.

"Don't mention the snakes," said Francis.

He reached into the cabin and retrieved a tote bag. He whistled softly. The morning air was chilly, and the sun's early rays did not yet provide much warmth. There was the sound of loose stones rolling, and two shadowy figures came sliding down the narrow path leading down from the boulder's top. They were wrapped in down jackets with woolen knitted caps on their heads. It wasn't immediately obvious if they were male or female, except that K assumed the bearded person was a man. The other one had a very red, dripping nose.

"Coffee time," said Francis. "Got you some bagels too."

The red-nosed person wiped their sleeve across their nose. "Gosh, this was one hell of a cold night." It was a woman.

Francis poured the coffee and passed it over to them. They held their faces over it and inhaled the hot steam. K turned away before the bead suspended from the woman's nose dropped into the coffee. He was probably developing some weird humoralist phobia.

"Wish you could have come at about 3 AM," the woman said through chattering teeth. "Man, it was cold. So cold." She slurped the coffee.

"Anything happen?" asked Francis.

The man shook his head "*Nada*. No cougar, no vigilantes. No shots. We're just going to hang in here another hour, and then go. Don't think anything's going to happen. It's too late for the cougar now, anyways."

"Who's on tonight?"

"Don't know," said the woman, "but there's going to be somebody. We got two people on watch every night."

"That's a great thing you are doing," said K, although he didn't really mean it. It was one of those well-meaning things that aging hippies did because they had been brought up with a sense of responsibility and couldn't bear seeing the world go the way it was going. As far as he could see, they wouldn't be able to do much, either for the cougar or against the McKinnon vigilantes, if the vigilantes happened to put their minds and guns to it and were seriously out to get the cougar.

Francis topped up their coffees and handed over the bagels, and they were on their way again. In the rear-view mirror the hooded cougar guardians bending over their steaming coffee mugs looked like witches hunching over churning cauldrons.

They bumped along for a while, their bouncing underscored by the occasional rattle.

"I'd feel better, if Curtis Malone was doing his job instead of these poor folks catching pneumonia," K said eventually.

"He ought to do his job," Francis agreed. "You're right. It is because he doesn't, that these folks are spending their nights in the freezing cold."

"What's up with him?" asked K.

"Oughtn't you to know?"

"I? I only know that he left me talking to those McKinnon guys on my own. They weren't exactly happy about it, and neither was I."

"Was he supposed to meet you?" asked Francis.

"He was. He didn't turn up. No call. No message. Doesn't answer his phone, either." All of a sudden K heard how that sounded. "Hey, you don't think ... I mean ... I don't know him that well. I just thought he's one of those guys who likes to do things by himself. Maybe he's following a moose trail up to Oregon?" He looked at Francis. No, this wasn't a time for jokes apparently. "Look—I don't really know him. I met him a couple of times, max. Should we worry?"

"Yes," said Francis, "I think so."

"You think something happened to him?"

"He's got a dangerous job. Also, he doesn't know his own limits real well. Maybe because he doesn't want to."

The truck bounced over potholes, while K kept a nervous eye on the back seat. The road lay deep in the shadow of Resting Warrior Mountain. At the crossroads, Francis took a right. To the left, the swollen river raged. The river always seemed full, no matter how dry the weather. It was as if it sprang from a secret plentiful well. At the weathered signpost, Francis took another right. This was the old road to Casita Ruins, along the high ridge of the plateau. To the north, the plain opened out onto a terrible, beautiful desolation that always gave K a lump in the throat and made it hard for him to breathe. The land unfolded before them in pleats of translucent ocher, delicate coral, earthy russet, and, where the hills cast their shadows on to the valleys, solid mahogany. The sky was the soft blue of a pigeon's egg.

To the north, the plain rose to a hillside where scattered trailers, corrals, and hogans indicated that this was Diné territory. On the plain, oil donkeys dipped and rose in perpetual motion, and flare stacks spat out red-hot flames.

"Surely it's not been that long since I was last here?" said K. "When did all these oil donkeys and flare stacks spring up?"

"When the federal government removed all the restrictions on energy companies and cut the price of land leases."

"But that was barely a few weeks ago."

"They were ready to take off as soon as the starting pistol was fired. And if you're gonna ask how do they know when the starting pistol gets fired: they know because they got their lobbyists over there in DC in relay."

To K appeared, like a vision, the old landscape, a sleeping beauty, languid, slumbering, serene, immaculate, waiting for the kiss of a prince. Now, she was trampled over by an infantry, raped by a thousand oil-donkey and gas-stake penetrations hammering and drilling into her depths, brown, sticky oil bubbling out of her torn-up, ravaged innards, while the eternal flames of gas flares hissed and spat and burned like the cinders of Hell.

The earth did not slumber. She lay comatose, mortally wounded, and no prince's gentle kiss could ever hope to revive her flayed and battered, insensible body. Oh, God. God have mercy.

"You want to pray some with those snakes?" asked Francis. He didn't even sound as if he was joking.

"Did I say something?" asked K. "Sometimes I say stuff out loud that should stay in my head."

"You just said, 'Oh God.' Can't say I blame you."

"I'm not religious," said K.

"It's bad, isn't it?" said Francis.

"Worse than that," said K.

The ungraded road led down a vertiginous rock face in steep hair-pin curves, barely wider than a mule track. There was an instant when K thought that Francis, as world-weary as himself, was pre-paring to drive off the cliff. A track had revealed itself at the last moment—a split second after K had decided that now was a good time to make peace with his Maker. Considering how little pain that resolution had cost him, he assumed that he was even less at-tached to life than he had guessed, which was something to ponder on, should he find himself in the mood to ponder on something.

The track was Pothole Central, and K's jaw ached from clenching. His knuckles shone white as he sought purchase on the truck's dashboard. A hail of gravel flew up and clattered on the windscreen. The track climbed up and descended the hill-ranges that K had so admired in their remote, serene, ocher, coral, and russet beauty. Close up and in the flesh, they were—as most other things—harsh, menacing, arid, and perilous. Precariously balanced boulders dotted the ridges, looking as if the slightest breeze, the gentle nose-nudge of a gopher, the jolly bounce of a tumbleweed, might dislocate them. K had quite forgotten to monitor the snakes.

"Fuck." K hoisted up his long legs and pressed his feet against the dashboard.

"What?" said Francis.

"I think the snakes got loose."

"They did? Uh-oh."

"I think there's one on the floor. At least one."

"Just stay very still, and we'll find a place to pull over."

K stared ahead. There was just track, leading up and up and disappearing into ridges, and beyond them higher ridges leading, presumably, to deeper valleys and some more higher ridges, and on and on.

The truck climbed the track and K wrapped his arms around his knees, to make himself as compact and rattlesnake-repellent as possible. They were now on top of the ridge, a plateau of sorts with enough space to park a modest-size pickup.

Francis stopped the truck.

"Keep still!"

He opened the vehicle door and jumped out. Great. Now K was all alone in a truck cabin with twelve rattling Apostles. Francis walked around the truck, opened the door on K's side, stretched his arm underneath K's legs, and grabbed something. Bare-handed snake wrangler.

"Is it safe to put my legs down?" asked K. He had a cramp in his calf.

"Always was," said Francis, holding up a rope. "I told you, that cover fits real well."

"It was just a rope? Would you do me a favor and make sure the basket is closed and none of the Apostles has gotten out?"

"The 'Apostles?'"

"That's what the pastor called them. The guy who was going to take them to his church service at Redwater. They are twelve, like the Apostles."

"Crap," said Francis.

"Why?"

"I'd planned to release them in smaller groups, like in pairs or something. Didn't want to swamp any place with loads of rattlers, you know?"

"There's nothing to stop you now, is there?" said K.

"Now it doesn't feel right, somehow," Francis said. "Apostles are supposed to be together. I don't know much about snake socialization, but maybe they're friends? They spent heaps of time cozying up in that basket. They might miss each other if we split them up."

There were another three ridges to traverse until the track finally dropped down, crossing the majestic void of Desolation Valley. At last Quorum Valley lay before them, a vast plain dotted with hamlets marked by clumps of oaks that spread their branches over homesteads and ranches. There was the red steeple of the community center, the corrugated metal roof of the school and library, the winding course of the Merced River, contoured by the soft green of the weeping willows bordering its banks.

"Pretty, huh?" said Francis.

"As long as you don't look too closely," said K. He braced himself for what was to come. "Where shall we take them?"

"I was thinking Goosewash Wilderness," said Francis.

"Goosewash Wilderness? How long has it been since you were last here?" asked K. They might as well have saved themselves a bumpy ride and dumped the rattlers right in front of XOX Big Energy HQ in Milagro town.

"Must be a couple of weeks," said Francis. On the hillside loomed an XOX billboard, gaudy neon letters flashing like a Bruce Nauman installation. They were ascending a road that bore so many bad memories. Here was the curve beyond which had once thrived abundant nature, a fertile spot teeming with life, a patch of verdant paradise, the likes of which was only found in arid and barren places. Maybe it was the contrast that made them seem so lush, so abundant. K remembered the ancient Gambel oak, heard its mandrake wail …

The truck came to a stop. K reluctantly opened his eyes. *Good morning, Mr. Ostrich, sir.* Francis was walking, basket in hand, toward Goosewash Wilderness. Yes, *wilderness*. Though nothing would ever restore the trees that had been razed by the energy company's bulldozers, here were brushes and bushes and shrubs and striplings, leafing, blossoming, flowering. Oh, but for this tenacious flora, which, over evolutionary millennia, had learned to avoid annihilation, to survive no matter what, returning again and again and again in a riot of blossoms, gloriously scented and pollen-heavy, swaying in the mountain breeze and covered by an iridescent halo of ecstatically humming bees. The old Gambel oak rose out of a meadow of Alpine flowers like a resting wanderer, its knotted branches casting filigree shadow patterns on the teeming ground.

K walked to the old oak and wrapped his arms around its trunk. The rough bark rubbed against his cheek, and he breathed in the warm, utterly live smell of the old tree's rising sap. "Last time I was here, it was chaos and destruction," K said. "I didn't think then that this place would ever heal." The last time he had been here, he had found a person hanging from this tree.

Francis nodded. If he thought that a grown man embracing a tree was weird, his face didn't show it. "A lot of negotiation and politics and pressure went into preserving this."

"Who did this?" asked K.

"It was the Merced River Alliance. Don't worry if you've never heard of them. They aren't that old. It's basically an alliance of all those environmental associations that had been fighting for their stuff separately, and when things got really bad, they realized that uniting makes us stronger."

"I never wanted to come here again," said K. "It was so awful."

"Well, they had to compromise a little," Francis said. He pointed to a sign, large and glossy and big, that K had somehow managed to overlook in the throes of his euphoria:

GOOSEWASH WILDERNESS SPONSORED BY
XOX BIG ENERGY
COMMUNITY UNIFYING NATURAL TREASURE SENSATION

"Ugh! Damn XOX. They had to get their name on here somehow, didn't they? 'Community Unifying Natural Treasure Sensation?' What does that even mean!" Such was the human psyche. Once again, he'd managed to negotiate the trajectory from ecstatic, damn-near tearful gratitude to disgusted outrage in record time.

"'The Community Unifying Natural Treasure Sensation,'" Francis enunciated carefully, "was the Alliance's idea. Specifically, that British gal's who works with them. Phoebe—you know her?"

"I don't think so. 'Community ... Unifying ... Natural ... Treasure ... Sensation' ... Oh! Oh, I see!" The sun was shining, and K almost felt at home "How did they get away with *that*?"

"Who knows?" said Francis, "XOX uses so many weird expressions in their promotions, it probably didn't seem strange to them. They're real used to seeing meaningless, pretty words strung together."

"Isn't it just beautiful?" said K. "I think I better take a photo, just in case XOX decide they aren't into strings of pretty words anymore."

They took all the necessary precautions, tiptoeing through the meadow, setting down the basket, stealthily lifting off the lid, and rapidly stepping back, Francis holding the snake stick. They watched the basket sitting amid swaying grasses and buzzing insects. Nothing moved. For an age. Francis seemed cool with this—cooler, at least, than K, who wondered if the snakes had suffocated, dined on each other or were indeed disporting themselves in the well of Francis's pickup truck at this very moment. An XOX truck came rumbling down the serpentine road.

"That's the guys we don't want to catch us," Francis said. He approached the basket, snake stick held aloft, and peered into it. "Hey, you gotta see this," he called to K.

"Can't wait," K said. Not wanting to be churlish, he followed Francis's summons. In the basket, the rattlers were sleeping like a litter of puppies.

"Did you tranquilize them?"

"Nope. Just fed them a big chicken dinner, just so that they got some reserves while they learn the ropes here. It's hard to know if they were brought up in captivity. If they were, it might take them a while to learn how to survive in the wild."

"Are they like elephants?" asked K.

"Like elephants?"

"Young elephants need to learn from the adults. Elephants growing up in a herd without elders miss out on their education. They start running wild and behaving badly."

"Really? Wow. Learned something. Don't know how rattlers learn. Anyways, too late now to worry." Francis carefully lowered the stick into the basket.

"They really seem very chilled," said K.

"Don't they just?" said Francis. From the hilltop, the rumbling of another truck could be heard. "Rise and shine!" Francis poked his stick into the basket with more emphasis. "Sorry, guys, but we need you to go."

"Why don't we just take the basket to the tree and turn it over?"

They carried the basket, lid on, to the oak tree, took the lid off, counted to three, and turned it over. The Apostles tumbled to the ground with a heavy plop. There they lay like a giant ball of gray wool, inert.

"They are trying to worry me," said K. "Why aren't they reacting?"

"These poor critters are used to being in that basket, and maybe an occasional church service." So K could put this down as yet another intervention of his that had made things worse. He wished he hadn't stopped the preacher man's car. "They'll be okay. It's like folks that have been in prison, and they get scared when they're about to be released. But after they get used to freedom again, they're fine with it." Francis separated the snakes with his snake stick and began to carry them, one by one, to different patches in the meadow.

"Couldn't you just leave them here to let them go how they want to?"

"What do you think is gonna happen if somebody happens to stop here and finds a whole load of rattlesnakes? Then we can kiss the Community Unifying Natural Treasure goodbye. Besides, I'm sure they can find each other, if they start missing each other. Look!"

The diminished heap of rattlers was starting to stir, and soon enough the snakes followed their brethren, singly, in pairs and small files, disappearing into the tall, swaying grass. The green canopy closed over their secret world; the grass swished, the insects buzzed, the birds sang, and it was Eden before the Fall.

CHAPTER THIRTY

"There's some people in the interview suite," said Becky, without lifting her head from whatever task she was frowning at. "Can you take their statement? No biggie. Just a vandalized vehicle."

Even though Francis had taken the fastest route back down to Milagro, they had not made it back anytime near as early as he had promised. The man and woman Becky had accommodated in the interrogation chamber had drawn their chairs right up to the table and sat, slumped, heads in hands. Maybe not as easy-peasy and straightforward as Becky had promised. To some people, their vehicle was all they possessed of value, and they spent more time in it than in their home.

Well, maybe they *did* live in it. With the way things were going, more and more people were being forced to live in their cars. K cleared his throat and drew up a chair.

The couple slowly lifted their heads from their hands and looked at him, bleary-eyed.

"Good morning," K said. "You'd like to report vandalism to a vehicle?"

"Hi!" said the man. "How's it going?"

"No complaints," said K disingenuously. For someone whose vehicle had been vandalized, this fellow was certainly jolly.

"Hi!" said the woman. "Great to see you again!"

Among the many faults and weaknesses that made K perhaps not the most suitable candidate for police work was his difficulty recognizing faces. Who was it who had given a dollar to the guy panhandling in front of City Market? The guy who had turned out to be the very person whom a certain Officer Kafka had booked into jail barely a couple of hours earlier, and who had promptly absconded because Young had forgotten to lock the cell?

"Well ..." said K. "Let's call it serendipity." On second thought, maybe he should have called it karma. These folks looked more as if they held with karma, emitting the mellowed-out, slightly disoriented-in-space-and-time, slightly irritating vibe of old hippies. Maybe this was the way his own parents would have eventually turned out, had they not expired before their use-by date, of carbon monoxide poisoning in their latest harebrained adventure: an inexpertly restored houseboat. "So, how can I help you?"

"It must've happened right after you brought us the coffee," said the man. "We sure appreciated that coffee!"

"Man, it was freezing!" said the woman.

"So, we were just going to stay another hour. So, we go up there with our binoculars, and there was nothing much going on. So, we stay the hour, and when we get back to our vehicle, that's what we found."

"What did you find?"

"Slashed tire and cracked windshield."

"Slashed, or flat?" asked K.

"Slashed."

"And the windshield—might it have been a crack that was there before?"

"No. It's more like a hole with loads of cracks running from it. Like someone just whacked a big stone on it, you know?"

They really did seem like mellow, good-natured folks. Unlike many customers who seemed to feel a keen need to pass on their misfortune by means of maxing out on ungracious behavior, this couple remained courteous, cooperative, and ever so slightly twinkly, too. None of his police manual-mandated questions seemed to make them angry, for which he was grateful.

"Are you here with the vehicle?" They nodded. "Why don't we go out and have a look at it?"

They trooped out into the midday sun. The car was the old Jeep that he had seen parked at the foot of the boulder earlier that morning.

"Where is the tire?"

The woman opened the back of the Jeep and K lifted out the tire. It was as flat as a yoga mat. He turned it until he found the slash marks, which he photographed while the woman held the tire. Somebody really had gone to town on it.

The windshield was as they had described. It looked as if an iron fist had smashed into the glass, which just about held together. K photographed this, too, and the Jeep from all angles, just in case, before leading the cougar-loving hippies back to the interview room.

"You said it must have happened right after we brought you the coffee?"

"Within that hour," said the man.

K certainly hadn't paid close enough attention to the Jeep to have noticed if its tires were slashed or its windscreen damaged. It had been too dark, anyway. But the woman had gotten another scarf out of the car, and she was adamant she would have noticed if the windscreen had already been smashed then. K, who'd once driven around for a couple of weeks without noticing that somebody had stolen his front license plate—before being stopped by the Gopher cops, of all people—obviously wasn't in their league.

"Did you hear any vehicles?"

"No," said the man.

"*Would* you have heard anything?"

"We hear everything," said the woman. "That's why we camp out up there. Sound carries real well there."

Evidently not this time, though. "So you didn't hear anything at all?"

"The only time we might not have heard is when the plane lands and takes off. That spot is right on the flight path, and it's where they fly real low."

Poor cougars. And poor deer. And poor whatever other wildlife was at its most active during the dawn hours. K had never considered aircraft noise being yet another stressor for these critters.

"The plane noise is very loud up there?"

"Real loud. There's the echo, too. Kind of doubles the noise."

Just wait and see how the fish-pedicure/goat-yoga-aficionados on whom Milagro's new economy hinged would like being woken up from their restorative detox slumber by aircraft engine noise at 4.45 AM.

He gave them each a statement form. Seeing them frowning at the small print, he hoped they had brought their reading glasses. These days forms seemed to get longer, and the print smaller. "Would you like me to get you some coffee?"

Their heads rose eagerly, and their wan countenances assumed some liveliness. K took precise instructions as to creamer and sugar. Happily, the breakroom was empty except for Córdoba, who greeted him soberly, as if her visit to the bookstore had never happened.

"How's it going?" asked K.

"It looks like they're letting that rapist go. They say there's no evidence."

"I'm sorry," said K. "No evidence?"

"We'll see about that," said Córdoba grimly. "We'll see."

"Fingers crossed," K said inappropriately, as if it was a game of chance. Which it seemed to be. But just because it was when it shouldn't be didn't mean it was alright if he treated it as such. Or something.

K poured coffee into two passably clean mugs. Of course, he had forgotten how those folks wanted their coffee. He could remember "black," "creamer," and "sugar," but not the constellation. Psychologically speaking, it was plausible that a body who wanted their coffee black would be a purist and therefore forego any additions, whereas a person who took creamer in their coffee ... well, there was nothing one could put past somebody like that. So he loaded the creamed coffee with three sugars, left the other mug black and carried both back to the interview room.

The hippie couple emerged simultaneously from their scribbling on statement forms, received the coffees, sipped, and winced.

"Did I get both wrong?" asked K.

"Not to worry," said the woman. "Rich likes sweet coffee."

She pushed her mug over to Rich, and Rich handed over his mug to her. K felt he had just witnessed one of those micro-scenes that defined a compatible partnership. These folks were growing on him.

"Oh," said the woman suddenly. The coffee, even if not to her specifications, seemed to have revived her somewhat. She put a hand in her jacket pocket and brought forth a crumpled-up Kleenex, a folded flyer, another crumpled tissue, the stump of a pencil, a withered apple core, a cough drop and, finally, a piece of paper. She smoothed out the paper and slid it across the table to K.

The paper had been roughly torn out of a yellow, lined ledger and folded in half; K guessed that somebody had run their fingernail along the ridge to perforate it. On the paper was written, in green ballpoint pen:

next Time we mean Busyness

The handwriting was less erratic than the spelling. It wasn't too bad, in fact.

"Where was this?" K asked.

"Wedged under the windshield wiper," Rich said. "We only saw it when we got home. That's why we came here. Vandalism is one thing. But a note …"

"It could be kids, too, right?" said the woman hopefully. "They might have seen it in a movie or something."

"We shall consider all possibilities," said K. Somehow, he felt even more ridiculous than usual, using that tired old trope on this kindly, easygoing couple. "Look," he added, "I know you really care about the cougar, but I can't help feeling you shouldn't be putting yourselves at risk."

"We need to protect the cougar," the well-synchronized pair said in unison.

"*We* need to protect the cougar," said K firmly. More precisely, bloody Fish & Wildlife or the Bureau of Land Management or whatever bloody well they were called now needed to protect the cougar. He looked at the man with his gray beard and Father Christmas apple cheeks, and the woman with her frizzy hair, mandala scarf and trusting eyes, and said: "I'm not asking you; I'm telling you. Stop the cougar watch until we find who did this." That'd be the Tuesday after Doomsday, then. "You're with Pet Rescue?" They nodded. "I'm going to let Martha know," K said.

"You know Martha?" asked the woman.

"I owe her a depth of gratitude," said K. "Thanks to Martha, I got Benjamin living in my bookstore, and it has made all the difference. Benjamin is a most handsome, mature cat, and my co-host." Actually, Benjamin was doing a rather better job of hosting than K; if only he'd learn to make coffee.

The couple's faces cleared. "Is it you who bought Agnes's bookstore?" the woman asked.

"I'm running it," said K.

"We had heard that a cop got the bookstore ... and we didn't know ..."

... If the pig wouldn't let dust settle on the shelves before turning a social and socialist haven into a fascist, gun-toting neo-lib emporium ...

"I intend to keep it much as it was," said K (bar occasional dusting and minus nicotine-poisoned air—which, actually, had accounted for a goodish proportion of the store's special atmosphere). "We also have room for meetings: the Water Alliance are meeting there; Native Networks are meeting there. It's free. So if you happen to hear of a group that fits, let them know."

"Neat!" said the woman. "We'll definitely visit!"

"Sure will," said the man.

On the way out, under Becky's withering gaze, K photocopied the piece of paper for them. "Keep hold of this," he said, "just for reference." He watched them trot toward their Jeep, hoping they were insured. Windshields didn't come cheap these days.

CHAPTER THIRTY-ONE

K retrieved the bunch of message slips that were sticking out of his pigeonhole and leafed through them. Either he was losing his ability to read cursive, or Becky's handwriting had deteriorated at an alarming rate.

"Jesus."

"Don't take the Lord's name in vain," said Becky.

"I have a feeling you wouldn't like my alternatives," said K. "Anyway, what's gotten into you? Last time we spoke you were Native American Church." To be honest, it had been a while since they *had* last spoken, properly spoken. Of late, they just seemed to snipe at each other.

"You're supposed to respect all religions," said Becky.

"You better tell the government that," said K. "So what's happened to your handwriting?"

Becky ripped the message slip out of his hand and frowned at it: "… Uh … call back … something … W? K?"

"I'm kind of relieved you can't read your own handwriting either," said K. "I was worried I'm losing the knack."

"What? I didn't write this. It was Myers. He covered for me because I had to go to the dentist. Oh, wait …" Becky traced letters with her finger. "I think it says 'McKinnon … Fights … Back …' Okay! Yeah. It's the McKinnon Fights Back Group called you."

"The McKinnon Fights Back Group? What the f—"

"I don't want to hear that," Becky said primly. "They must've called again." She shuffled a pile of message slips on her desk. "The first time they called, they said they are fed up with waiting for you to do something, and if that Wildlife guy doesn't do his job, they'll do it themselves. They are not going to … uh … sit on their hands and wait around until … uh … that darn animal has killed all their … uh … donkeys? Something ate a donkey?"

"The cougar killed a miniature horse."

"What's a miniature horse?"

"It is as described: a tiny horse," said K.

"Can you ride it?"

"I wouldn't have thought so. Unless you are three years old. It's about the size of a Labradoodle."

"What do they keep them for, then?"

"They're supposed to be cute."

"People have no business putting little-bitty animals in a cougar's way and then killing the cougars," said Becky heatedly.

"You try telling those McKinnon folk," said K.

"I will," said Becky. There was a glint in her eye.

"Go for it. You're probably the only person that might get away with telling them stuff. Just talk to them like you talk to me."

"What?"

"Did Curtis Malone happen to get in touch?" K said quickly.

"Who?"

"The Fish & Wildlife guy I asked you to phone a couple of days ago."

"Everybody here asks me to phone somebody all the time. You think I can remember? Phone him yourself!" said Becky.

"Sure," said K and walked off whistling, "Always Look at the Bright Side of Life."

In his office, he dialed Malone's cellphone. A robotic voice informed him that the number he was calling was switched off. That, at least, was a new development.

K dug out the number of the Department of Fish & Wildlife. The call got rerouted to the Bureau of Land Management, which ran the kind of message entirely unsuited to people with memory or concentration problems or ADHD: a wordy announcement that encompassed the department's entire history and inception, funding streams, vision statement, and mission statement, including an ingratiating message to the American people whom it strove to ceaselessly serve, *yadda yadda yadda*, plus an approximately forty-seven-option menu. After an inventory of available services lasting thirteen minutes (timed by K), there was, at last, an option for Fish & Wildlife. K pressed the requisite number key with hope in his foolish heart. The Department of Fish and Wildlife had taken it upon itself to repeat the mission statement/vision statement/funding streams and never-ending public commitment oath verbatim, and had added another menu of their own: "Press sixteen to speak to the Department for Traps and Fish Bait … Press seventeen to speak to the Department for Raccoon Droppings and Fox Scat." K pressed three, whatever department that was. He was hoping to land at the Department for Wayward Jackalopes and Feral Wolpertingers.

The department's holding music was Peggy Lee singing "Is That All There Is?," a somewhat confounding choice for a government agency entrusted with guardianship over the natural world.

"Bureau of Land Management," a sober, not to say abrasive, voice announced.

"Which department am I speaking to?" asked K.

"Bureau of Land Management." The voice had an edge to it.

K saw his theory confirmed again: that the willingness to cater to the public decreased in inverse proportion to the length and fervor of an outfit's mission statement.

"I would like to speak to Fish & Wildlife."

"Bureau of Land Management."

"How do I get hold of Fish & Wildlife?"

"The Department of Fish & Wildlife was incorporated into the Bureau of Land Management."

"So, I am speaking to Fish & Wildlife?"

"You are speaking to the Bureau of Land Management."

"I need to speak to the San Matteo Wildlife officer. This is the police."

"Name?"

"Mine, or the Wildlife officer's?"

"Officer."

"Curtis Malone," K said.

"Putting you through," the voice said.

Peggy Lee was still bemoaning her disappointment with life. Well, you couldn't say you hadn't been warned.

The phone rang, then a message played: "Hi! This is Curtis Malone's voicemail. I'm away from the office. Please leave a message, and I'll get back to you right away! Have a great day!" That chirpy ditty, blatantly, hadn't been recorded by Curtis Malone, but by some obsequious minion with scant regard for the Stanislavsky Method of voicemail message impersonation. God help those who had the misfortune to eventually speak to the real Curtis Malone, unprepared.

Then came elaborate instructions, another twenty-seven-point menu pertaining to replaying, editing, or erasing your message, then the instruction to speak after the tone, then a high-pitched beeping sound and then——the disconnect tone.

K redialed, endured the mission/vision and forty-seven-point menu, went for option seven and got another voice, not any friendlier, and relayed his problem.

"Putting you through," the voice said.

"I do not want to be put through," K implored.

"You don't want to speak to Officer Malone?"

K went through the whole spiel again: "I would like for someone to tell me where Officer Malone can be reached."

"Putting you through," the voice said, and in no time at all K had the pleasure of Peggy Lee's disappointments again.

Caught between the Devil and the deep blue sea, the fire and the frying pan, K rang the number for McKinnon Fights Back relayed in Myers's spider-on-acid handwriting, hoping that Myers had either gotten the number wrong, or—in the event that he hadn't—that there would be no answer, just as there was never any answer from Curtis Malone.

But there was, at the third ring. It was a youthful and slightly come-hither voice. To K's question as to whether or not whoever he was speaking to was connected to the McKinnon Fights Back group, the young person said that she did not know, but that Mr. Oppenheimer would be able to answer all his questions, and that she was putting him through right away. Oppenheimer spoke in surprisingly smooth cadences, sounding more like a broadband salesman than a backwoods cougar vigilante. K had a hard time fighting the temptation to use "nuclear option"-style puns, though it was likely that Oppenheimer had heard them all before. In the matter of McKinnon Fights Back, Mr. Oppenheimer had a slot in his diary. He could see K at 3 PM.

CHAPTER THIRTY-TWO

Oppenheimer, it turned out, was not *in situ* at McKinnon Canyon, but inhabited instead a suite in a shiny, new, glass-fronted, multistorey office building, which housed the economic brave new world of Milagro town. His suite was on the third floor, sporting on its bulletproof glass door a highly polished steel plate with abstract insignia that generated no associations whatsoever in K, subtitled with a similarly oblique word-jumble of which K only retained that the business was a consultancy of some sort or other.

The furniture was cubic and in primary colors, which was either very retro or very avant-garde, and made the eyeballs ache in either case. The tinted windows looked out on City Park, where young children and indigents competed with each other to vie for the attention of waterfowl by accustoming them to an entirely unsuitable diet of wheat-based refined carbohydrates.

"Isn't this too cute?" Oppenheimer, a perma-tanned man of below-average height with bouffant, sun-bleached hair, which possibly owed something to costly transplant procedures, approached K with an outstretched hand and an expansive smile, showing every one of his pearly-whites. So often had K been received in this exact same manner, these exact same gestures, this exact same smile, that he had begun to wonder if there was a "Suck Up to Suckers 101" course being run somewhere for these guys. Oppenheimer took K by the elbow, escorting him to the inner sanctum, where there were no primary colors at all and no cubic furniture either, but which was kitted out entirely in monochrome and unforgiving rigid lines, as if a bipolar interior designer had completed the project during respective critical episodes of their condition.

Oppenheimer lost some of his bonhomie as soon as he planted his ass on the other side of the desk. Out of his perma-tanned face, his preternaturally light eyes looked coldly at K. It was like having the privilege of a meet n' greet with the good cop and the bad cop in one. "I'm so glad you came, Officer ..." Oppenheimer said.

K nodded. If the guy wanted to know his name, he was welcome to look at his name badge. They eyeballed each other like incompatible species stuck together in a cage by an inept zookeeper. Oppenheimer broke the silence by expounding on the trials of the livestock holders of McKinnon Canyon, with particular reference to the trials of miniature-horse owners.

K cemented their newly established friendship by querying whether or not miniature horses counted as livestock. It turned out that the miniature horse had belonged to—*quelle surprise*—Oppenheimer himself. Oppenheimer wasn't having it. This was not why he had upped sticks from whichever pampered urban center he had inhabited before. Wild predatory animals tearing into rarity pets weren't part of the deal he had signed up for.

"What deal *did* you sign up for, sir?" asked K.

The deal Oppenheimer had signed up for was all the trimmings without the main dish. His vision was a bucolic mirage through a Disney lens, in which miniature horses stood about decoratively on impeccably manicured lawns that were maintained by grateful migrant workers, obsequiously complicit in their own exploitation through fear of deportation.

McKinnon Canyon was an as-yet undiscovered jewel in the American West's crown. Its potential for tourist trade was untold. Oppenheimer, it transpired, was the owner of the fish-pedicure-wellness-spa-to-be, though maybe K had gotten the thing with the fish pedicures wrong, because Oppenheimer just frowned and shook his head in the impatient, dismissive manner such people used with somebody they considered too much of a moron to bother arguing with.

"What are you planning to do with that cougar?" Oppenheimer eventually asked. "If you won't get rid of it, there are some folks who surely will."

"If you happen to see those folks, tell them they are committing a federal offense. For those you don't see, we'll put up some nice, shiny posters to remind them of that fact."

Oppenheimer spluttered. As far as he was concerned, the cougar had condemned itself to death when it had made the unforgivable mistake of slaying Princess Luna, his family's pet miniature horse.

How many domestic animals besides Princess Luna had been slain by the cougar, asked K.

Wasn't the death of Princess Luna enough, Oppenheimer retorted theatrically.

Animals small enough to tempt a cougar should be kept in stables overnight, said K. Cougars were opportunists, and would go wherever pickings were easiest. They also were careful and stealthy, and didn't really like humans—so it would take an exceptional temptation, as in this case the much-lamented Princess Luna, to lure them into the proximity of human settlements. After all, there was no record of the cougar attacking McKinnon sheep, even though sheep were of a convenient larder-size for such a predator.

What about all the brave burghers of McKinnon Canyon who were demanding the cougar be punished? Who were armed with pitchforks and rifles and semi-automatics?

So the whole McKinnon vigilante mob, the horny-handed sons of toil, were apparently in uproar on behalf of this leisure-tanned, hair-transplanted fop of an incomer who insisted on the right to waive his caretaker responsibilities vis-à-vis his preposterously named pony. How to explain to this soft bastard that McKinnon old-timers just liked to shoot at things. It was in their genes from way back, since their ancestors had first set foot in this hostile, alien environment populated by real and imaginary foes. K had a theory that the fight-or-flight impulse, if not furnished with proper purpose, degenerated into delinquency and psychopathological aggression. That's what had happened to the McKinnon folks. Any opportunity at all, and they started baying for blood.

"McKinnon people will not stand for this much longer," Oppenheimer repeated. "If you want to prevent bad things from happening, you better get on it and do something about this, pronto."

Roleplay wasn't necessary anymore. K felt scorn for this man pulsing through his veins. His cold fury must have hit his eyes, because Oppenheimer's coyly provocative smirk began to falter until it vanished altogether. Robbed of his Colgate dazzle, Oppenheimer looked older, worn, his tanned hide making him look like a weary thespian with too much foundation and no curtain calls.

"Should you be under a misapprehension regarding the purpose of my visit, let me tell you why I'm here … sir." K drew the mock-up warning poster out of his pocket, unfolded it, and pushed it at Oppenheimer. "Would you like to keep this … sir? And do remind your friends in McKinnon Canyon that any deliberate harm to the cougar constitutes a federal offense. Should anyone attempt to harm the cougar in any way, we shall hold you, Mr. Oppenheimer, as the spokesperson for McKinnon Fights Back, accountable."

Oppenheimer opened his mouth to protest, and K saw in his face alpha-male aspirations on a collision course with low cunning. He got up and stretched out his hand. Oppenheimer's paw was clammy, and lay in his own like a damp dishcloth. K used the technique that an old rogue cop past caring had taught him, of grasping the hand and squeezing the bones at the back of the hand together in a manner that hurt, but could not be called out as a cruel and unnecessarily firm handshake. Successful police work lay in the finer details. He smiled into Oppenheimer's rictus and left him massaging his knuckles.

Either Oppenheimer, left once more to the hothouse of his own delusions, would rediscover his momentarily oppressed alpha impulses and would be on the blower like a rat up a drain to complain to the sheriff, or he would opt for a pretense of "playing nice" until more opportune times. K guessed that the ingrained contempt of the urban slicker for hicks would win out, and Oppenheimer would decide that a future of finding himself and his Wellness Spa on the law's bad side on behalf of a bunch of braying rednecks wasn't worth it. Whichever way this shit-show went was copacetic. There was, after all, the bookstore, and Benjamin.

CHAPTER THIRTY-THREE

By the time K reached the station, his buoyancy had pretty much evaporated, and he had worked on his resentment toward Curtis Malone. All the energy that had been spent on the weaselly Oppenheimer could surely have been put to better use. It did not help that Alice Nakai's haunted eyes followed him across reception from the bulletin board. In his pigeonhole were no new messages, and he tried telling himself that no news was, indeed, good news.

He fired up ARGUS and produced an insipid entry for his encounter with Oppenheimer. Under ACTION TAKEN he wrote: CAUTIONED.

K's call to Pet Rescue was answered by a reedy-voiced person who sounded worryingly out of breath. Despite this, they offered to go look for Martha. K listened to the receiver being placed on a surface, and faltering steps moving away from the phone, the reedy voice calling, "Martha! Martha!"

"I'm not asking you; I'm telling ya: sit down. Take a break." Martha's voice was tender and exasperated in one. A chair scraped on the floor, and there was a thud and a sigh. "Here's your drink," said Martha. "Don't you dare move before you finish it, ya hear?" The wheezing chuckle that followed this admonishment made K realize what the fabric was that held society together.

"Yes!" said Martha, taking the phone. Not much tenderness in her voice now. This didn't make K's task of warning her motley bunch of idealists off their cougar watch any easier. "No," said Martha, after K had finished his spiel. "You can tell me and I can tell them, but these aren't the kind of folks that you can tell anything to. If they made up their minds that they are going to watch out for the cougar, that's what they are going to do."

"It could get quite dicey," said K.

"'Get?'" snorted Martha. "Where have you been? You think a bit of messing with a vehicle is a big deal?"

"A tire was slashed and the windscreen damaged, and there is that threatening note, too," K reminded her.

"It was just one tire. The windshield wasn't broken, and that note ain't a death threat."

"Some people would think that's plenty." K had wanted to say something to the effect of Wild West customs, but of course that's where they were, the new Wild West, ruled by a cabal of good ol' boys and Big Energy barons and land speculators whose sensibilities weren't any daintier than the old West's had been, but who had, over more than a century and a half of tricking Indians out of land and assets, honed their legalistic cunning.

"Chicken feed!" declared Martha.

"It almost sounds as if these kinds of attacks are routine to you," said K.

"You betcha," said Martha. K waited. What he had heard beneath Martha's bravura was the baseline of despair of the permanently hounded. "Ricin," she said eventually. "They're real partial to sending ricin in their letters. At least they say that's what it is. Could be baking soda, for all I know. I'm not going to try it, is what I do know."

"You get threatening letters with ricin?" K asked.

"Death-threat letters with ricin," said Martha.

"What do you do with them?"

"The ricin, I dissolve in bleach and flush down the commode. The letters, I burn. And don't tell me what to do or not to do with this crap. I'm not going to hand them in to you and your buddies, because it's not going to help any—besides slowing everything down because I gave you some more stuff to file reports on."

Always good to know what civilians thought of you. "Next time you get a letter like that, you bring it in," said K firmly. He added what he always said in such cases: "This isn't just about protecting you; it is about protecting everybody." He took Martha's silence as a grudging agreement. "Who do you think sends you those letters?"

"Try everybody that feels we're interfering with their right to do some killing. These guys want to kill everything, everything at all that gets in their way. They want to kill stray cats, dogs, prairie dogs, foxes, skunks, snakes, raccoons, bears, cougars, raptors, anything that kills what they feel is their right to kill. Deer! I forgot the deer, of course. And the elk." She sounded tired. "So, no. I'm not going to call anybody off the cougar watch. Besides, nobody would listen to me anyways. You got that? Gotta go."

On his way out of the station, K passed the sheriff's office. He hesitated, then knocked. He had a feeling he ought to cover his ass preemptively with regard to the pony-fetishist Oppenheimer. His type had a way with litigation.

"Come in." The sheriff seemed to have worked his way through some of the files. A couple of the precipitous towers had shrunk in height. Weismaker pushed his glasses down the bridge of his nose and looked at K over their rim. Judging by his squint, K guessed that it wasn't too comfortable. Probably Weismaker had mislaid his glasses one time too many, and had decided to keep them on all the time, just in case.

"I was just about to call you," said the sheriff.

"Sir?"

"Any news on Curtis Malone?"

"None."

"You didn't get to speak to him at all?"

"No, sir," K said. He remembered learning a long time ago to pay great attention when posing questions to Navajo, who would, inevitably and correctly, answer negative questions in the affirmative, which led many a zealous cop to assume a confession. "*So you didn't kill your grandmother?*" "*Yes.*" "*Suspect admits to killing his grandmother.*"

"He didn't call, either? Left no message?" insisted the sheriff.

"No, sir." Weismaker wasn't Navajo. So K answered in the inaccurate *bilagáana* way. Didn't the sheriff have better things to do than bother himself with Curtis Malone?

"That ain't right," said the sheriff. "What's your take on this?"

K's personal take on this was that Curtis Malone, forced to endure his organization's mission declaration one time too many, had turned his back on civilization and had run for the hills.

"I don't really know Curtis Malone that well."

"Well, I do," said Weismaker, "and there is something not right. We need to contact him."

"I've tried to get hold of this guy most days since he left me hanging out to dry out there at McKinnon Canyon," said K.

"Left you hanging out to dry, huh?"

"It certainly felt like that. But what's worse is that he didn't even think it necessary to let me know. Send me a message, you know? Using one of these." K held up his cellphone. "I'm not asking for an apology. It would just have been good to be kept in the loop. Regarding McKinnon, sir ..."

"That isn't like Malone at all. Sure, he's not a talker, and he's a bit of a lone wolf. But he's not a guy who would let somebody down," said Weismaker.

"He knows this land like the back of his hand. He's been around the block a few times. He likes to do his own thing," said K.

"Didn't you just say you don't know him real well?"

"I'm sure he is okay, sir," K said.

"I'm not," said Weismaker curtly.

"... Did BLM ask us to look into this, sir?"

"No."

"Shouldn't we let them worry first, before we do?"

"They got this whole new team in that don't know each other," said Weismaker. "They might not know when they ought to get worried."

K shivered.

"You okay, son?"

"Fine," K lied. That citizens' trust in official agencies should be fragile was no more than deserved. But where was a society headed, when its agencies didn't even trust one another? The country was rotting at its very core, and the raving psychopaths and chancers at the helm were busy drilling sinkholes into its foundations. "Does Malone have a family? Relatives? I suppose you could try to contact them," suggested K. It probably wasn't the time to discuss failing societal structures with the sheriff, even now with one of Agnes Prohaska's lectures on Gramsci fresh in his mind.

"Malone's wife died a couple of months ago," said Weismaker.

"Curtis Malone had a wife?"

"Clarita. Took a strong and wise woman to handle Curtis." The sheriff's eyes had a faraway look that made K turn away.

"Did you want me to do anything, sir?" said K.

"Why don't you go over to the Bureau of Land Management and talk to them?" said the sheriff. K should have remembered that Mennonites didn't do rhetorical questions.

CHAPTER THIRTY-FOUR

The Department of Fish & Wildlife incorporated into the Bureau of Land Management had relocated—or had been relocated—from a cozy homestead-like ramshackle building at the eastern foothills of the mesa to the other side of town, the edge of Milagro's "industrial zone," near the town's branch of the Department of Social Services. With its Social Services Agency building, Milagro's city planning department had opted for a postmodern "Hacienda" style; for the Bureau of Land Management, the municipality had gone for a provincial architect's idea of Bauhaus, all edges, gleaming white angles, and too much glass in the wrong places.

Outside the building, on a ledge, stood a sentry-like row of lead-gray glazed planters bearing unfeasibly green and perfectly spherical herbage; presumably a potted metaphor for the BLM's combative 'Man Against Nature' mission. K entered through sliding doors that glided open like unfolding angel's wings, and walked along gleaming marble floors that reflected the blinding whiteness of the walls and ceiling. Milagro, once a redneck town of miners and ranchers, sure was morphing into a white-collar ghetto.

For the umpteenth time, though not any more coherently, K relayed his concerns regarding the whereabouts of Curtis Malone to the receptionist perching on a barstool behind a desk entirely fashioned of glass. The receptionist, a middle-aged woman engrossed in stitching a quilt, presented a somewhat incongruous image in these polished surroundings. She was not familiar with Curtis Malone. But then this was a very large team. Could she think of anybody who might know of Malone? "Marjorie," according to her name tag, frowned, perused the screen and finally pressed keys on her switchboard.

"A police officer is here to see you." She listened. "Thank you." She turned to K and said: "Ms. Huffington has ten minutes for you now. Floor 5, Room 501."

K took his time strolling to the elevator, changed his mind upon seeing the polished steel door, and took the stairwell. The stairs presented a backstage look into the pristine Bauhaus front-of-house aesthetic. Maybe nobody who counted took the stairs. Evidently there were plenty of people who did not count, using the staircase as their smoking den. Cigarette butt-ends, scrunched-up candy and Slim Jim wrappers, and used tissues littered the corners on practically every floor; the fire alarms had been disabled, and on the fourth floor K spied a used condom in a corner.

He opened the door to Floor 5 and emerged into an even more surreal, shiny, light-flooded world. The corridor had floor-to-ceiling windows that afforded a view over the valley toward the San Matteo Mountains, soon to be fetchingly adorned by drill-towers as far as the eye could see, if the Department of Profit and Destruction had its way. K knocked on the door of Room 501.

"Come in," said a sharp voice. Sonia Huffington had been standing at the window. She looked pointedly at her watch. K flashed his badge and his teeth, and made himself comfortable on a white-leather-and-undulating-chrome affair with a good view of Resting Warrior Mountain.

"We have six minutes," said Sonia Huffington.

"We will have however long it takes," said K pleasantly.

Huffington's immaculately *maquillaged* face contorted briefly. It was like one of those moments in a horror movie when the beautiful heroine morphs into a twelve-foot, fang-bearing reptile. Sonia Huffington *was* something to look at. She looked eerily like one of Philip Marlowe's hot dames who, at the end, always would turn out to be the bad guy. She had straight platinum hair, green eyes, and a blood-red-painted mouth. She was dressed in a gray pencil skirt, white tailored blouse, and five-inch black stilettos. Huffington was leaning against the windowsill, one leg crossed over the other. K didn't mind her standing. From a safe distance she was pretty good to look at.

"Curtis Malone," he said.

"Who?"

"Curtis Malone. Your Wildlife officer."

"What department is he in?" Huffington worked her chin in the manner of someone trying to suppress a yawn and glanced at her watch.

"Shouldn't you know?"

Huffington trained her chemical-green eyes on him. Prize sociopath that she likely was, she didn't even attempt to justify herself, just kept staring at him with those reptilian eyes. Huffington opened her blood-red lips. The sunlight reflected on glacier-white teeth. She raised her wrist and narrowed her eyes at her watch.

"I gather you have no idea where Curtis Malone is? Or who he is?" said K.

Huffington shrugged. "This is a huge organization."

Seven puffy clouds drifted toward Resting Warrior Mountain like a flock of sheep trooping to pasture. A fire engine blared in the far distance. Sonia Huffington's red mouth was a thin line. She drummed her fingers on the windowsill. Her nails were the same color as her lipstick. The puffy clouds were all alone in the bright blue sky. Maybe they weren't clouds at all, but smoke from a spreading fire. K enjoyed the cloud-puffs' leisurely progress, biding his time until the arm on the wall clock had completed enough full circles to mark his fifteenth minute in Sonia Huffington's office.

"Well, I suppose it is a learning curve," he said heartily. "I really mustn't get in the way of your responsibilities any longer." A frown rippled across the smooth expanse of Huffington's forehead. K got up, walked toward Sonia Huffington, grasped her hand and pumped it up and down. "Thank you so much for agreeing to see me, despite the demands on your time." Huffington's eyes searched his, her frown now more pronounced.

K gave her hand another shake. His elbow collided with the rhomboid vase standing on the desk. The vase tumbled to the floor and exploded in a spectacular fountain of shards. The single red poppy that it had hosted was catapulted onto a Tree of Life rug, where it lay, broken-stemmed, bleeding spinach-green chlorophyll into the white wool. "Oh dear," said K, "I'm so, so sorry. If your insurance doesn't cover this, please don't hesitate to contact the Sheriff."

On his way out, K stopped at Marjorie's desk.

"Did you get some help with your problem?" asked Marjorie.

"Frankly, no," said K.

He saw her good-natured face fall. Then she brightened: "Hold on!" She opened an invisible drawer secreted in her transparent desk.

"Wow," said K. "You can hardly tell there is a drawer in there."

"Clever, huh?" said Marjorie. "You think it's transparent, but as a matter of fact it isn't."

"The BLM should have that as their motto," said K.

Marjorie drew out a dog-eared, leatherbound ledger that, in these environs, looked as appropriate as a slug on Marlene Dietrich's satin lapel: "Here! Look! Here!"

The ledger had columns and rows for the categories of DATE, NAME, DEPARTURE TIME, APPROX. DURATION, LOCATION, PURPOSE, and RETURN TIME. And there it was, Curtis Malone's entry, filled out in a precise, somewhat cramped hand. The intended location was the mesa; purpose of the visit to follow up reports of poaching; time of departure 3:30 AM; and approximate duration of the field trip 5-8 hours, on the day before the scheduled McKinnon meeting.

"So, usually the field officer would sign in when they come back?"

Marjorie looked uncertain. "I suppose so," she said.

"Is Curtis Malone the only person still using this ledger now?"

Marjorie nodded.

"Would you let me borrow it? There may be some clues in there to where he went." He could see that Marjorie liked the word *clues*. Just like in a real TV police show. From a higher floor, K could hear the pings of the elevator setting in motion. He grabbed the ledger and swiftly said goodbye. Marjorie resumed stitching a pink square with a teapot to a blue polka-dotted one bearing a goose, and barely looked up as K took his leave.

CHAPTER THIRTY-FIVE

At Milagro City Park, K stopped for a flock of geese crossing over to the playing fields. They made their way across the road in a neat row, keeping precisely one goose-length's distance between each other. In their pursuit of unsuitable snacks, the geese adhered to a fixed schedule whereby they spent mornings and noontimes patrolling the pond area populated by workers on lunch break and their sandwiches, and in the afternoons proceeded to the playing fields, where kids—laden down with chips and candy bars—hung out.

As K watched the last health-compromised goose climb the sidewalk, he remembered an old co-worker of Curtis Malone's who'd be sure to remember him: Jenny. Jenny Quillian.

If only everything in life was as easy as getting in touch with and arranging a meeting with Jenny Quillian. Jenny answered in person, on the fourth ring. She was on her way into town to run some errands, and would meet K at the library in ten minutes. And indeed, K had been perusing the library's bulletin board for no more than five minutes when he saw Jenny Quillian mount the steps, a couple of bulging tote bags weighing down her shoulders.

"Hi," said Jenny. "It's been a while. Three years?"

"More like eight," said K. It had been during his early days, when he still thought of his cop-job as a kind of summer job, a student work-experience placement that he could and would walk away from at any moment.

"That long! Yeah—I can see it now ... you have changed some."

"I have?"

"Somewhat," said Jenny.

Best not to go into details. Jenny herself hadn't changed as much as K was wishing on her right now. She was carrying a stack of posters for a wildlife fundraiser—or maybe they were for a meeting protesting the opening of public lands to ATVs. By the looks of it, there were enough posters in her tote bags to paper the entire town hall.

Apparently, K's principal use to Jenny was his height. "It's better up there," she instructed, waving an arm above her head. K doubted that many people would crane their necks like giraffes in order to read a boisterously verbose, indifferently designed flyer positioned at approximately ceiling level. He also began to question whether or not it was a good look for one of Milagro's Finest to be seen putting up protest posters under the instructions of an old hippie.

Jenny was right. He had changed.

"How about we grab a chair at the back?" he suggested eventually. They found a table in a corner with a panoramic view of the park and looked out at the pond, where a man on a bench surreptitiously swigged on something wrapped in a brown paper bag.

"Want me to wait while you go and arrest him?" Jenny asked.

He was The Man, alright. At least Jenny had desisted from making *oink oink* noises.

"Nobody forced you to choose that job," said Jenny pitilessly. "Just suck it up, dude."

"I'm taking some solace from the fact that you don't respect me at all," said K.

Jenny laughed. Her laughter wasn't particularly musical. K began to wonder if it was, in fact laughter, or if she was coughing.

"So what's up?" said Jenny.

"I just visited your new HQ."

"Not mine." Jenny wrinkled her nose. "Any particular reason?" K thought he heard hope in her voice. Her face was grim, and became grimmer while listening to his description of the headquarters. "Biggest sellout in history. Why didn't they just write Big Energy a big, blank check for all of our country? There's nothing now that can stop them."

"Is that why you left, Jenny?"

"I left way before. I thought it was bad way back then. Imagine that! If I'd known, I'd have fire-bombed the crap out of them." There was pure hatred in her eyes. Within K, counselor and policeman fought, and counselor won: "It must be hard to see a job you once must have thought worthwhile change like this?"

"Tell me about it," grumbled Jenny. "I was one of those that held out longest. One by one, everybody dropped off. Then there was that thing with Jedediah, and after that ... Except Curtis. Bless Curtis; he's the only one of us there, still holding out."

"I don't know exactly about holding out," said K. "Matter of fact, that's why I wanted to see you. Curtis has gone AWOL."

"*Curtis?*" Jenny shook her head. "Curtis wouldn't go AWOL."

In the course of his plodding life, K had learned that denial had many causes and many guises, ranging in scale from pure Freudian defense mechanism to wily, determined obfuscation; but here in Jenny's face, he could only see utter conviction.

"You seem pretty sure."

"I am. I worked with that guy for thirty years. We were both rookies together. Man, he was hot. We even had a thing together when we were out there, supposed to be checking on horned toads. My butt got chewed up by red ants—but, boy, was it worth it ..."

"So, Curtis wouldn't have gone AWOL," K interrupted hastily. There had once been a time when mature women had prided themselves on decorum and discretion ... "We were supposed to meet up at McKinnon Canyon to do a talk together—"

"McKinnon?" said Jenny. "Anything happening over there?" K told the tale of the mini-horse, the cougar, and the vigilantes. It occurred to him that '*The Mini-horse, the Cougar and the Vigilantes*' would make a great title for a picture book. "Lula Mae?"

"Well, it is only a tiny horse," said K.

"Who keeps a tiny horse out there? Why keep a tiny horse at all?"

"It's some Californians working on the Disneyland principle," said K. "It's kind of hard for them to accept the existence of wildlife, and that's what Curtis was supposed to help me with. Actually, it was Curtis who was supposed to do the work. I was supposed to just stand there, to make them take the issue seriously."

Jenny spluttered.

"There's a whole gang of folks who want to get that cougar, though I'm not exactly sure why, because they've got nothing to do with the horse." K estimated that trying to maintain his gravitas with Jenny was a pretty much a lost cause. "The horse belonged to a guy called Oppenheimer, who is going to open a spa in McKinnon, and apparently they all got his back."

"The only reason those McKinnon good ol' boys will have anyone's back is for money. Money and guns. Could be, though, that they're just standing up for their right to kill anything they have a mind to."

"That's what I was told," said K.

"I can't see them vandalizing vehicles though, and writing letters. Firstly, most of them can hardly write. Also, these guys aren't going to creep around to damage a vehicle. These folks will do what they've always done: point their gun at you, march you to your truck and tell you to be sure not to come back. And I betcha there's hardly a body that would *want* to come back."

"I spoke to somebody recently who gets letters with ricin and death threats," K said carefully.

"Sure," Jenny said dismissively. "I have a bunch of those for practically all the causes I'm active for. I figure it's retired ranchers who don't sleep well because their arthritis bothers them, and that gets them thinking about everything they're pissed at, and top of the list are liberals and socialists—and that gets them busy writing some letters. I don't believe it's ricin, either. I tried some, and I bet you it's baking soda."

"You tried something that you thought might be ricin?" K asked, horrified. "If this ever happens again, you hand in the letter in to us, right away, understand?"

"Why? So that you can file some reports on it?" K hadn't realized how widespread was the distrust of his profession. And, truth be told, it hurt. "Anyway, it's not McKinnon folk, 'cause they don't retire. They work until they drop. They don't have time to write letters and damage vehicles. That's kid stuff ... So, Curtis didn't turn up to your meeting?"

"He didn't. He didn't leave me a message, either. And he didn't answer or return any of the phone calls we made." Saying it like that made it seem not that casual anymore, but rather more ominous. "You don't feel he could just be taking some time out?"

"Not Curtis."

"Should we worry?" asked K.

"Yes," said Jenny.

"Somebody mentioned that Malone lost his wife a couple of months ago."

"So?"

"Well, might Curtis be depressed? Like ... depressed enough to ...?"

Jenny snorted. "Depressed? That guy loved his job. His job was his life. His whole life. I doubt he even notices that his wife has gone."

"That's pretty harsh," said K. It was getting to be his go-to phrase.

"It's the truth, that's all," said Jenny. "That's why he's the only one of us that survived all that mess."

"Let's hope he did," said K. As soon as he'd said it, he wished he could take it back. Up to now he'd regarded the random inquiry into the absence of Curtis Malone as a time-wasting *Hunting of the Snark*-type nuisance. The only good thing about it had been that it had kept K's mind off Alice Nakai, wherever she was now.

"Did you just say 'mess?'" asked K. Damn. He'd stopped listening, and had no way to find out whether he'd missed something of significance. Jenny Quillian, he now remembered, was a ranter. One question was all she needed to get her going. Another five sentences in, and K gave up trying to follow. One thing he did catch was that the dark forces had stealthily closed in on the Department of Fish & Wildlife, and there had been blood on the carpet.

"Jedediah Unruh?" he interrupted Jenny's diatribe. "The name seems familiar."

"Could be you met him," Jenny said dismissively. "He was great as long as everything was okay, you know. He was another one that loved his job. A real Edward Abbey type, that guy."

"What happened to him?"

"When it got bad, like the shit started hitting the fan, they had to get him some treatment."

"Treatment?"

"Like, *counseling*," said Jenny, as if talking about a frontal lobotomy.

"Oh."

"Yep. You heard that right. Jedediah went so batshit-crazy they had to get him counseling."

"That crazy, huh?" K asked. Jenny nodded. They contemplated the park outside. "It didn't affect you?"

"What didn't?" said Jenny.

"The 'shit hitting the fan.'"

"Naaah," said Jenny, "I got my cats and my weed. Oops. Shit. I forgot you're with The Man. But it's legal now, anyways."

"No worries," said K. "To recap: you think Curtis going AWOL is out of character, and we should be worried?"

"Yeah, I do," said Jenny. "Unless he finally got fed up with these sellout morons and decided to get on with doing his own thing."

"But that does sound as if he might have gone AWOL after all?"

"Uh … I guess. He could have. Because who likes to be controlled by assholes, right?"

"But didn't you just say that Curtis was really conscientious about his job? That he would care more about it than his wife dying?"

"Sure. But I didn't know how bad it had gotten until you told me just now. I've never even been to the new HQ. If it's that bad, even Curtis may have given up." Jenny frowned, rummaged in her pocket, retrieved a roll-up and lit it.

A powerful aroma of prime Acapulco Gold hit K's nostrils. "We are in a library, Jenny," he said.

"Shit, I forgot." Jenny spat on her fingers and pinched the smoldering reefer between calloused thumb and forefinger.

K was feeling a desperate need to get back to *terra firma*. "So, is it out of character for Curtis not to return calls, not to be in touch?"

Jenny nodded. "Yeah, it is."

"Even if he had started feeling really fed up and had decided to do his own thing?"

Jenny shrugged. "Maybe not. I mean, if you decide to walk out on something that you've been doing for about forty years because you're so pissed, you aren't going to bother keeping in touch and returning phone calls, are you?"

Great. As usual in K's life, an inquiry had started out in certainty and ended up at the deep end of befuddlement.

"Why would he fill in the logbook, though? In it, he put he'd be gone around five to eight hours."

"Maybe he was planning to come back, and then something happened that made him decide he didn't want to?"

"Now you are saying the complete opposite from 'Curtis would never go AWOL,'" K said, exasperated.

"So? I changed my mind. You want me to do your job for ya?"

"I don't even know what my job is," K mumbled.

"Why are you here then, talking to me?"

"The sheriff is worried," said K, and realized that this, at least, was true. He was here because he wanted to please Daddy.

Jenny draped her tie-dye shawl around her neck and ran nicotine-stained fingers through her gray curls. "Why don't you just go where he said he would be in his last entry and poke around some?" She got up and wriggled her fingers at him: "Love ya n' leave ya!"

K watched Jenny Quillian's somewhat unsteady progress toward the library exit before he, too, got up.

"Sad thing about Jenny," said an elderly gent who had been reading a newspaper at the other table.

K turned around to face him: "Pardon?"

The man coughed: "Sad thing about Jenny. She's not been the same."

K knew he shouldn't ask. "Since ...?"

"She got that disease ... MS? That's what she got: MS."

Maybe that's why she was on weed. K wondered if Emma Nakai had been on weed too, if MS was what she had had.

There seemed rather a lot of it about these days.

CHAPTER THIRTY-SIX

For more than four years, Curtis Malone had been the only member of the Fish & Wildlife team who had used the ledger that, with its yellowed paper and crinkling corners, felt damn close to a historic document. It was a hefty tome, weighing in at a good five hundred pages or so, bound in brown leather. Over decades of handling, the grain had been smoothed down and polished to a patent-leather patina.

The ledger did, in fact, go back to a time long before K had even been a twinkle in his daddy's eye. Its virgin pages had first been written on sometime during the Johnson administration, since when so much had changed that K's head hurt even trying to think about it. Most of the people whose handwriting he was looking at had long since been reborn as shrubs or trees, or been ingested by generations upon generations of whatever grubs and bugs populated the underworld; they would have metamorphosed into nutrient-rich humus, been ground down into fine dust and carried off by the wind. That's what K wished to happen to him eventually: being danced across the land contained within a joyous whirlwind.

The ledger had been in use for a good few years already when Malone wrote his first entry, in a precise hand and with meticulous wording that spoke of a reverence for the organization that employed him and of the determination of a starry-eyed young man starting out where he wanted to be and aiming for places to go to. Yes, gnarly old Curtis had taken his job seriously. He had been eager and motivated, apparently keen on transparency and perhaps also on making an impression, full of the joy of dedicated service to the Nation. *O tempora, o mores* and all that.

As he thumbed through the ledger and the years advanced, K began to recognize a name here and there. Here was Jenny Quillian, whose letters leaned right like a puppy straining on a leash, and whose bold *t*-strokes and prominent *i*-dots graphologists would know something about.

Tom Cruick ... Hadn't he been the one who chained himself to a tree up there by Lostboy Summit when the loggers moved in? Where was Tom now?

Here was Karl, whose job it had been to liaise with local ecologists and to keep track of wildlife. Had Karl persisted in his mission, or had his spirit been broken?

Sera, who'd apparently followed a calling to teach and whose every outing was logged as "training," "instruction," or "lecture." K hadn't known that there were so many folks in San Matteo County who wanted to be instructed. By and by, the names thinned out, and then there were three that remained: Curtis Malone, Jenny Quillian, and Jedediah Unruh.

Jedediah's handwriting over the years was a study in disintegration. Even if Jenny hadn't told him about Jedediah *going so batshit crazy he needed counseling*, K would have noticed. Well, he told himself he would have noticed, because let's face it, there wasn't a lot in his track record that established that he noticed anything much; but *this*, he would have noticed. Just hazarding a guess, K would have said that Jedediah had gone a ways beyond where counseling would help. His letters tumbled across the lines like maimed dervishes, mediating a disquiet that was palpable across the pages and the ages.

Malone's writing stood out as the neatest. It wasn't handwriting K would have necessarily associated with the man, but what did he know except that Malone alone had endured in that organization, and had made the transition to the Bauhaus Burg of Corruption. Of all the old guard, only he remained.

K leafed back through the ledger. All those people patrolling, studying, protecting the land. At least K thought that was what they were supposed to do. It was like seeing Ten Green Bottles performed on a ledger—or like one of those Agatha Christie mysteries where people dropped off like flies, one by one, while the guests to the party went on partying, unaffected, changing for dinner and drinking sherry until their number came up.

"Sir," said K, "I got this ledger with Curtis Malone's last entry, and there's nobody that could tell me where he could have gone, just that last entry … Am I supposed to file him as a Missing Person? There seems to be nobody who is missing him, though."

"I am," said the sheriff, polishing his glasses.

"But how do we know if he's gone missing or just AWOL? How do we know he wants to be found?"

"It's a risk you're gonna have to take, I guess," said Weismaker.

"You are saying I should try to find him? Sir?"

"I guess."

Woe betide the missing of San Matteo County, who were doomed to have K work on their case. Unless they did not want to be found.

Sir? "We could use a track reader, couldn't we? Somebody who really knows how to search? Somebody who is specialized in finding people? You know Robbie Begay? He's done a lot of work for us. Anytime we hired him on a case, it got solved." For better or worse.

"Does he still work out of Redwater?" asked the sheriff.

"Uh, no. He's doing some cultural education up here, actually."

"Cultural education? Sounds like a great gig." The sheriff regarded K over the rims of his glasses.

"Well, it's not going to go on forever," said K. "Begay is one of the best. We'd be lucky to have him."

"Will he want to work with us?"

"Needs must," said K.

Weismaker took off his glasses and rubbed them on his sleeve: "Did Begay ask you to put in a word for him, by chance?"

"Did he—? No, sir. Really. He didn't," stammered K.

"So you're job-hunting for him?"

"I guess," mumbled K. "I don't want him to waste his talents."

"I'll think about it," said the sheriff.

Myers was on desk duty, Smithson and Dilger on traffic; Young was roaming the corridors itching to make mischief, and K was fed up with having to avert his eyes every time he passed that warrant in reception.

"Where are you going?" said Becky.

"Ongoing investigation," said K.

Becky snorted, but did not try to dissuade him. Spare Wheels R Us.

K drove east on Main, then took a left and drove north until he came to the cross section, where he took a right onto an ungraded road. He passed a small trailer with a hand-painted sign advertising sewing and alterations; a dog kennel where half a dozen dogs howled, yelped, threw themselves against the bars, or snoozed in their cages; a medical-grade marijuana plantation behind a barbed wire fence; and an orchard in the shade of which a group of does and their kids were having a siesta. He followed the road as it climbed a hill, descended, climbed again, descended, and finally ended in a narrow path that wound around the foothills. He parked the patrol car next to the irrigation ditch and walked along the stony path. The house was what passed for "historic" in these parts. It had been built a hundred and thirty years or so ago, by one of the early Anglo settlers who, by the looks of it, had not planned on an extended family. Why an early settler should have chosen to build his home here was something of a riddle. It was one of those places where there was plenty of nothing and nothing of anything. It was a place well suited to a man like Curtis Malone—austere, arid, remote and not exactly conducive to joie de vivre. Except for a bird of prey's high-pitched call somewhere up in the sky, all was silent.

K, having learned that things lost will often be found at the very place they belonged, had managed to convince himself that he would find Curtis Malone here, at his homestead, doing whatever tough old boots like Malone did to pass the time, tanning a bear hide say, or forging tools in a furnace, or breaking a wild horse. K opened the gate. A splinter the size of a toothpick embedded itself in his thumb.

He walked along the brick path that led past neglected vegetable beds to the house. K knocked on the solid wooden door and waited. He knocked again. He put his ear to the door and rapped his knuckles on the wood. He walked around the house. All windows were shut. Here, too, were vegetable beds that looked as if they had lain fallow for months. K made a full circle of the house and knocked on the door once more. He tried the door handle. It creaked, but didn't give. The house had the melancholy aura of a deserted place, but that probably was his imagination. He opened the rusty mailbox, and drew out a fistful of mail. It was all junk mail and K stuffed it back into the mailbox.

Outside K looked at the winding footpath disappearing into the landscape. That's where missing people were often found; having fallen and broken a leg, they starved to death just yards from home. In the Australian Outback, anyway. There was a pretty good view of the footpath here, and there was nothing on it or next to it as far as the eye could see.

K took out his phone and scrolled through past calls.

Predictably, there was no signal. He returned to the car, drove back along the ungraded road, parked opposite the dog kennel, and dialed.

"*¿Qué pasa?*"

"It's K. Kafka. Franz. The cop."

"You again? I'm gonna start charging you … No, wait. Don't want to be working for The Man. What is it now?"

The line crackled as K spoke into it. "Can you hear me?"

"Sure … uh … best way to get there's to take that turn-off to Gopher Lake, up on Merced Main, and then keep on driving … uh. No … maybe it's better taking County Road … damn … you know the one with the cider folks? No? Or you could, uh, hey, why dontcha just pick me up and I show you where it is?"

"This is a patrol car," said K.

"So what? I need to concentrate. Besides, you owe me." Jenny Quillian drew a papery tongue over a King Size Rizla, kneaded the reefer between her fingers, rummaged in her pockets, drew out a box of matches, picked out a match, and drew it over K's dashboard.

"Hey!" K protested. Jenny leaned back in her seat and inhaled deeply. K shot her a sideways glance. She had her eyes closed and her nostrils were dilated, holding in the magic vapor as long as possible. Given that she'd misdirected him twice already, K wasn't too pleased that she had her eyes closed. "Hey, can't you at least open your eyes?"

The reefer smell was sweet and overpowering, and, truth be told, tempting. K was starting to feel a bit lightheaded, because he was driving with the windows closed. He knew some of those Merced cops wouldn't pass up a chance to get him into the shit.

"I need to concentrate." Jenny hummed what sounded like an incantation. It was starting to feel like one of those supernatural ghost-hunting things that Meyers was so fond of watching on night shift.

"Jenny ..."

"Yeah! Dude! Relax! It's all copacetic!"

"What do I do now? Turn right, left, or straight ahead?"

Jenny opened her eyes. "Turn right."

"That's where we've just been."

"If you know that, why did you ask me? Huh? Huh? To test me?"

K nodded. "Straight ahead, or left?"

Jenny hummed. "Straight ahead, then left," she decided.

That left after this left was a narrow road that climbed the side of the canyon almost vertically, and could be taken only in the lowest gear.

"This must be a bunch of fun in winter," said K.

Jenny drew on her joint so that the weed crackled, and held her breath. At the top of the hill, she motioned ahead. This was another road that K had never been on. It led through a stretch of open grassland. To the far east, he could see the snow-covered peaks of the Rockies' outcrops glistening through the haze. Then the canopy closed over the road, and now they were in the forest. They drove for what seemed like miles, Jenny humming and smoking.

"No!" K said sharply, as she let down the window and made to throw out what remained of her reefer.

"What's the matter with you? This tiny butt isn't gonna start a fire!"

"That's what they all say," said K. "Give it to me."

Jenny dumped the reefer remains into K's palm. He squeezed it between thumb and finger, and felt the burning heat. Of course, it had still been smoldering. He dropped it into the ashtray, which held two revoltingly pink globs of chewing gum. Must be Young's.

"Right here! Make a right here!" Jenny said.

There was no 'here' here, no road, no path, no visible markers. "How do you know?"

"Coz of this," Jenny slurred. She pointed at the charred remains of what once must have been a gigantic tree.

"Are you sure?"

"Sure I'm sure," said Jenny. "That tree's got some memories for me, I tell ya ..."

"Great," said K hastily. "If you're really sure."

He couldn't remember ever having driven through a forest, over the soft, springy forest floor, over crunching conifers, bunny-hopping over protruding roots. He let down all windows. Somewhere in the distance, a woodpecker drummed on bark. A couple of chipmunks had a loud argument atop a tree. A blue jay came sailing down somewhere out of the green yonder and settled on a branch, eyeing them curiously. Jenny motioned for K to drive on.

"I hope you'll find our way out of here," said K.

"Haven't you got one of those whatsits?" asked Jenny.

"GPS? There's no signal here."

"Uh ..." She hummed some more, and drummed both hands on the dashboard as if it were a tabla. Ravi Shankar, eat your heart out.

In lucid moments—of which he had few—K sometimes saw himself through external eyes: shambolic cop, reefer smoldering in ashtray, carts spaced-out hippie through the outer boondocks. Or:

shambolic cop and spaced-out hippie get lost in the wilderness and last three weeks before they kill and eat each other. Or: a bear and a cougar come upon a buffet in the forest ... Or—

"Here," said Jenny. "Take a right here." They came upon a clearing in the forest, and there, lo and behold, was ... *something*. "I'm gonna stay here ... There's some stuff gone down between us, you know ..." said Jenny vaguely.

"Sure. Just don't blow up the car, okay?" said K, and pulled the key out of the ignition.

What if you came unprepared upon such a place? What if you came, unprepared and high on psychedelic substances, upon such a place? As it was, K could hardly believe that he was seeing this sober. His first impression was of a humongous caterpillar creeping out of the trees into the clearing. It was, on closer inspection, a three-segmented caterpillar, its middle section being most easily identified as part of a reappropriated trailer. The front segment looked like a shack in a *favela*, for which new arrivals would use any materials found in dumps and landfills to hurriedly build their shelter. K spied discarded plywood panels, the roof of a truck, wooden crates, a refrigerator door, a tarpaulin, heavy-duty trash bags, and pieces of corrugated iron, all girdled by a kind of corset fashioned out of heavy tree branches and rope.

It was the last segment, though, which sat halfway between the trees, that was the most remarkable. There was something of a Gaudí work-in-progress about it. The outer shell had been hewn, carved, and assembled from wood—salvaged, not harvested, K guessed. In contrast to the utilitarian haste evidenced by the front segment, this one sang of a labor of love. It was as if someone had fashioned a giant, habitable puzzle out of pieces of wood. There were branches stripped of bark and polished to the sheen of bones, trunks that served as pillars, a domed roof constructed out of bark tiles, twigs and woven grass, an arch made of innumerable pinecones ...

K walked to the end of the caterpillar. Behind it was parked an old school bus. Here, too, someone had once tilled the land and appeared to have given up. As at an archaeological excavation site, there was rudimentary evidence of cultivation that had long since fallen prey to the forest's appetites.

K contemplated the wisps of smoke rising through the caterpillar's midsection. He walked up to the trailer door—though he would have preferred to explore the caterpillar's fantastic rear instead—and knocked. There was a thump, as if somebody had dropped something. K knocked again. He heard steps approaching, and the door opened in the manner of a fairytale witch's house: creakily, and by increments. K beheld a pointed nose on which perched gold-rimmed spectacles. This was not what he had expected.

"Yes?" The voice was tense but contained, as if the person was making an effort to keep calm.

"Police," K said jovially. He would have to work on his tone, because he saw the man's face—which had been apprehensive to start with—fall. His pale eyes darted to and fro, and he stepped back from the door. "May I come in?" asked K. The man stepped toward the door and wedged himself into the entrance. "I guess that's a no, then," K said. This guy didn't look anything like the way he had imagined him. There were the specs, the sober dress, old, brown corduroys, and a blue sweatshirt. There was the short hair, and the stubble that was barely three days old. Of course, imagination was just conjecture, but even K didn't like to be wrong all the time. "Who are you?" he asked.

"Why do you want to know?" said the man tersely.

"A missing-persons case." He saw the man flinch and blink rapidly. "Your name, sir?"

"Do you have a warrant?" asked the man.

"Usually," K said, "I do not anticipate needing a warrant when asking somebody's name."

"I don't have to give you my name," said the man, and swallowed hard.

"No, indeed, you do not," said K. He turned around and walked away. Twenty strides across the clearing equaled one jump across the trailer, one grab for the gun, one loading, one positioning at the door …

By the aroma that assailed him when K opened the car door, Jenny was at the very least on her third reefer. "Are you hallucinating yet?" he asked her. Jenny coughed expansively and flipped him the bird. "I need you to help me out here, Jenny. Come on out, the fresh air will do you good."

Jenny slid out of the car. He had to catch her and prop her against the car. "Deep breath," he said. "Okay now? Let's go." He put a hand under Jenny's elbow, and she gamely zig-zagged along. In the clearing, she looked at the caterpillar.

"Yikes, he's done some stuff here."

"Has it changed since you were last here?"

"You betcha," said Jenny, and freed her elbow from K's grasp, gamboling toward the trailer like a filly, apparently having forgotten the stuff that had gone down before, which had kept her in the car.

"Jenny!" K called. He didn't think it would look too good on his record if yet another citizen came to grief while in his company, but Jenny was already knocking on the door. K followed her, hand on holster. The door opened a bare two inches.

"Hey!" said Jenny.

The door opened. "Jenny? What are you doing here?" Sunlight caught in the man's spectacles and made them gleam like beacons. *Shine on, you crazy diamond.*

"What are *you* doing here? You were living down there by the river, weren't you?"

The man shrugged.

"Would you mind introducing us, Jenny?" said K, as if they were about to have tea at the Savoy.

"Sure," said Jenny, "Karl this is K, like the KKK; he's The Man. K, this is Karl."

"Pleased to meet you Karl," said K, though this was not the case. Karl, perhaps having more integrity than K, said nothing.

"We came to see Jed," said Jenny. K took note of the "we."

Karl adjusted his spectacles. He put his hand on the doorknob as if to pull the door shut. K put a foot in the door, pushed it wide open, and squeezed past Karl. All that training had to be good for something. Jenny, apparently not woke enough to boycott his methods, followed in his wake. Karl remained standing at the open door. Inside, it looked like somebody had worked on creating a clearing. Crates, stacks, piles, and bundles had been pushed against the wall. In the middle of the room stood a rough-hewn wooden table and bench; in one corner was a wood-burning stove with a kettle on it.

Jenny walked over to the table and plumped down on the bench. She began drumming her fingers on the table—*dum-dum-dumdum-dum dum*: "Hey Karl! Good to see ya! How you been?"

"Okay, I guess." Karl shrugged. He'd remained standing at the door like a wary, half-tamed fox.

"This is Karl!" Jenny said to K.

"Uh-huh," K said. He cleared his throat. "So you aren't Jedediah?"

Karl had another spasm. Whatever he was, he wasn't great at concealing his preoccupations, which was why K started to warm to him some. "Why don't you join us at the table, Karl, so we can have a little chat?" There was a lot of truth in the trope that one eventually became what one particularly loathed. The "little chat" thing had traveled across decades, courtesy of a particularly repugnant headmaster who had made K's life a misery for a while.

Karl dragged a tree trunk across the room and set it down a yard from the table. He sat down gingerly. His hands were bunched into tight fists. He rubbed his fists up and down his knees. The corduroy made a peculiar crackling sound, as if it was about to ignite.

"You didn't kill him, did you?" asked K.

"Wha— what?!" Karl actually jumped. Shot up from his trunk like a rocket, and came thudding down again. There were beads of sweat on his forehead.

"Where is Jedediah Unruh?" K asked. Trust him to pursue a crackpot idea on a whim and get into another one of those unforeseen and most probably totally time-wasting messes.

Karl grasped both his knees with his hands and pressed down on them. "I don't know," he whispered.

"This *is* Jedediah's place, is it?" asked K.

"Jed," said Jenny. "We always called him Jed."

"Waste of a good name," said K. Americans liked to ruin stuff with their obsessive time-saving. Anything above one syllable was too much trouble for them.

"Why don't you tell us how come you're here, and where Jedediah might be?"

"Just tell him, Karl," said Jenny. "I want to go home."

"I don't know," said Karl. "I really don't … I came by to visit with him. He wasn't here, so I waited around some … and he didn't show."

"When was that?" asked K.

Karl chewed his lip. "About three years ago?" he said eventually.

"You've been here, waiting for Jedediah, for three years?"

Karl chewed his lip some more. He took off his spectacles and began polishing them on his pants. "Not exactly. See …" He held the spectacles toward the light. "They made me move my bus. So I came up here to ask Jed if I could stay here for a while—I converted a school bus to live in."

"The bus over there in the clearing?"

"Yeah," said Karl. "So I wait for Jed, and a couple of months pass, and then it gets cold, and I say to myself … well … Jed won't mind me staying in his place while it is so cold, just until he comes back … and then some more months pass, and it's spring, and Jed still isn't back. I actually waited a year before I started moving his stuff around just a little bit …" He pointed to the walls. "I didn't change anything or take anything; I just moved things around a little bit."

"Uh," said K, because he couldn't think of what to say. He wasn't sure where he was supposed to stand in terms of defending property against squatters. "So, you don't know where Jedediah is?"

"No."

"Or could be?"

Karl shrugged. "No. I knew he had some trouble. That he had taken some time out …"

Jenny whinnied: "Some *trouble*? He went batshit crazy! They had to get him counseling."

"Counseling?" said Karl, round-eyed and startled, looking as if about to rehearse Munch's *Scream*.

"Yeah!" said Jenny.

"You worked for Fish & Wildlife too," said K, now remembering meeting a "Karl" in the ledger.

"Got out while the going was good," said Karl. *Which, presumably, was why he was here occupying a vanished man's fantasy caterpillar.* "Are you still there, Jenny?"

"You betcher sweet ass I'm not," said Jenny.

"Any of the old crew still there?"

"Curtis," said Jenny with a sensuous sigh.

"That's actually why we are here," said K. "Curtis seems to have disappeared."

"Curtis? That ain't like him at all," said Karl.

"Conscientious, was he?"

Karl moved his head from side to side as he considered. "'Conscientious' ... I don't know. That guy just really loves his job. He believes in it."

"You didn't?"

"Not like he does," said Karl. "After a while of so much BS ..."

Jenny whinnied again: "BS! Yeah! *So* much BS!"

"... It gets you down, you know ... everything was changing, and there was getting to be more paperwork than real work; and the guys further up, the administration, were having some weird ideas ... It got so that there was practically nothing left that had made the job great, you know? Nothing." He looked at the floor and rubbed his knees.

"So you got out before Jedediah?"

"And me!" said Jenny.

"The last folks left were Jed and Curtis," said Karl. "And then I guess Jed left. And Curtis was all alone."

"How did Jedediah and Curtis get on?"

"They got on great," said Karl. "They used to get on great."

"Used to?" asked K.

"I don't know," said Karl. "I just know they used to get on great, like blood brothers or something. Jed joined after Curtis, and

Curtis kind of taught him the ropes, you know? Curtis knew everything about the job there is to know."

"Why did you say 'used to,' though?" asked K. Sometimes
even an unconscious choice of words could harbor a clue. Or maybe that was just another trope he had absorbed from the Annoying
Counselor.

"It's just ... I don't rightly know Curtis's attitude about that
counseling. Can't picture Curtis liking Jed getting counseling."

"No?" said K testily.

"Curtis believed that everything we need to get better, we can
find right out there in Nature."

Maybe Curtis had changed his mind when his wife died. Who
knew?

"Can we go now?" asked Jenny, like a child.

"I guess," said K and got up.

Karl followed them to the door. "What ...?" he said, and made
a sweeping motion toward the interior of the trailer.

"That's between you and your conscience," said K. "When
Jedediah returns, you must leave, of course."

"Of course," said Karl.

"Unless he wants you to stay."

The way back was easier than K had anticipated, because the
tracks the patrol car had left on the forest floor were still visible—
which was just as well, because Jenny had fallen asleep as soon
as he had forced her to snap the seatbelt on, and was now snoring
softly, a little bubble of saliva at the corner of her mouth inflating
and deflating with the rhythm of her breathing.

CHAPTER THIRTY-SEVEN

Apart from a monochrome photograph taken approximately at the time of Watergate, and a perfunctory entry in a list of Fish & Wildlife staff, Jedediah Unruh had left no digital imprint. Nowadays, such scarcity was unusual, and surprising.

Privacy wasn't a privilege granted to a majority. Here, for instance, was Curtis Malone. There wasn't much on him; but there was a heap more than on Jedediah. K sensed that most of what there was on Malone had been put out there without his knowledge or consent. There was a medley of images of Curtis, looking lean and mean and resilient in the way of those desiccated desert-fiends who habitually took on, and survived, the great outdoors. The photos had probably been taken when Malone guided hiking tours of the back country—a task, K guessed, he would have performed reluctantly. In no image was there a hint of a smile. Except in one. It had been taken not too long ago, in a yard, perhaps a restaurant garden, and Malone and the woman beside him were looking up at the camera. His face was relaxed, his eyes wide and sparkling in the sunlight, his arm draped around the woman's shoulder. The woman wasn't smiling. Her face was closed and harrowed and in such contrast to Malone's expression that K looked away. He hoped that Malone had not and wouldn't ever see this picture.

K went back to Jedediah Unruh's photo. It was of another age and time, when center partings ruled. The young man in the photo had light hair, cut short. He wore a white shirt, possibly starched and bleached. Considering that those were the days when photos entailed excursions to a photographer's studio, Jedediah's smile seemed reasonably easy and unaffected. His wasn't an "all the world's my oyster," "hail thee fair conqueror" or "future you'll be mine" kind of smile. It wasn't a conceited smile, or contrived;

neither was it shy. It was … a natural smile. K would have called it wholesome, if the word weren't routinely applied to so many things that patently weren't.

Whenever that photo had been taken, K was fairly sure that Jedediah Unruh hadn't been rolling with the times even then, hadn't been a hip cat, or cool, or with it, or whatever the term then used to be. What sort of name was "Jedediah," anyway? A rural boy from a small, God-fearing farming community, working the land somewhere in Nebraska or the Dakotas. A country boy who maybe had never known that he loved Nature until he got into the big city and saw the havoc that people created, who had gone to work for The Man to stop The Man from driving even more of God's fair bounty into wrack and ruin, who had been *broken* by The Man. At least K assumed that this was what Jenny meant by "batshit crazy." K looked at Jedediah's innocent face, open smile, and large eyes fringed with long, dark lashes that might have served him well with the lasses during those barn-raising dances they would have had over there—wherever "there" was.

Counseling seemed a very Man-like solution to a Man-made problem. Counseling was the carrot of the establishment; psychiatry was its stick. Old anti-establishmentarians like Jenny didn't see much difference between the two. Whatever it was, it must have been one hell of a long way that had led Jedediah Unruh from whomever he had been then to whomever he was now. Wherever he was now.

The woman's voice was soft and creaky in the way of old people's voices who lived alone and only spoke to other people once in a blue moon. Her inflection sounded like that of the Amish in a movie K had seen a long time ago, elongated vowels and a melodic rise to the end of her sentences. She spoke quietly, with long pauses that might arise out of memory lapses, or perhaps were merely due to thoughtfulness. She came from frugal, taciturn people who *did* rather than *talked*; or maybe she had dropped a stitch in her lacemaking. Or was playing Killer Cheese Curds on her cellphone. K had learned the hard way about the letdowns harbored by conjecture.

"There is nobody left here," said the old woman. "Just I ... Just I," she repeated, as if astonished. As if it had only occurred to her now. Then she said it again: "Just I." Her voice sank to a whisper, and K's heart sank like a stone.

What had he expected? Wasn't that what always happened when he showed some initiative and tried to do what he thought was his job? A karmic harbinger of death and loss and gloom. All that he had achieved now was to remind an old woman how alone she was. All his thanking her, the warmth that he hadn't had to struggle to put into his voice, the pity that choked him, wouldn't have helped her. He rang off, promising her to let her know when he had found Cousin Jedediah: Cousin Jedediah, who had left his family a long, long time ago, and whom she hadn't heard from for many years. Yet this did not seem to impede the family ties that were there, and which lasted all this life and possibly into the next. Now K had gifted her a "lost" cousin instead of a cousin who had merely left. And yes, there was a difference. A big difference. It had been there in her voice.

Mazel tov.

"What is it now!" Jenny screeched into the phone.

"Do you know who this is?" K faltered.

"'KKK—The Man!' That's what comes up for you. Sure I know who you are!"

"I come up on your contacts as 'KKK—The Man?'" Hark the overflowing cups...

"Yeah, KKK! Suck it up! Were you gonna ask me out on a date?"

"What did Jedediah look like?"

"What did ...? Oh sweet Jesus! You're asking me to identify him!"

"No, no," said K quickly, "nothing like that. I was just wondering what he looks like."

"You said 'looked!'" Jenny's voice was very loud. Maybe they'd been giving out freebies over at the dope dispensary.

"I did," said K. "I misspoke. I just wanted to know—"

"Are you fixing to ask *him* for a date when you find him?" Jenny asked.

"I'm keeping my options open until I find him," said K.

"You're phoning me to ask what Jed looks like?"

"Yep," said K. "You got it."

The line went silent. Either Jenny had hung up, or passed out, or was practicing levitation.

"... Not cute. Or hunky, like Curtis," she said after a while. "I guess he could've been cute, if he, I dunno ... What do you mean 'looks like?'"

"He's missing, and there's only one photo of him, and that's from his high school days. I want to know what he looks like now ... in case we happen to cross paths in Walmart."

"No way you're gonna catch Jed in Evilmart," snorted Jenny. "I haven't seen the guy in years. People change, you know."

"There's nothing you can tell me about him?"

"His eyes are the color of an emu's egg," said Jenny, and hung up.

You just had to look at the Missing Persons database to understand that this was a big, merciless land, and its cloak of civilization gossamer thin.

K wished he hadn't spoken to Jenny. There was something about faceless Jedediah Unruh that wouldn't let go. Maybe it was his fantastic caterpillar home out there in the forest, or that looking at the image of his young face, so long ago, had made K feel the drag of the currents of time, its waves crashing on rocky, inhospitable shores.

The Missing Persons database was organized into greentick files, red-cross files and blue-cross files. Green-tick files denoted that a missing person had been located, alive or dead. To the bureaucratic Moloch, the quality of outcome made no difference; it was the solving that counted. Red-X files denoted active cases. Blue-X files signified open cold cases. Even K, with his long-sustained phobia of stats, could see that the majority of missing-persons cases staying unsolved wasn't a good thing—and these were all people who had been missed by somebody who then had gone through the trouble of reporting them missing.

What about the day-tripper who had been dropped off at lunchtime by his wife at the Mesa Museum, to walk three hundred yards down to the Fir-Tree Cave Dwellings? There was a photo of him, red baseball cap on his head, holding a water bottle and grinning into the sun, taken by his wife just before he set off. This was the last photo of the guy. It was just three hundred yards, for chrisssakes, on a paved path churning with visitors. Everybody and their grandma with her walker was on that path, most of which was fully viewable from the parking lot.

By evening, the wife was still waiting. K had never quite understood why she hadn't walked the three hundred yards of path and looked for her husband herself, but she hadn't. She had waited and waited and waited, until almost dusk. Then she had told the rangers, who searched that path as well as the slightly more rustic path to the petroglyphs, which went up to the top of the mesa. The rangers also searched the hiking trail that led down through the valley. By then, night had fallen. The following day, they called in the search team, which didn't find anything, either. The day after that, they brought in dogs. The dogs briefly yipped in a couple of places, but failed to pick up scent. The following day, they called in helicopters, and a couple more search teams. They combed through every inch of brush and undergrowth. They looked behind and under every rock and boulder. This went on for weeks, the wife waiting in a small fleapit motel the municipality was paying for. The weather broke. Winter set in. The mesa was covered with a fine blanket of snow. The temperature dropped to 10° F, at which point some brave body told the wife that it was not at all likely now that her husband would be found alive. That was three years ago.

Here were two brothers, strapping, healthy lads, gone hiking to Winston's View. The hike was rated "moderate" in guidebooks. They were never seen again. A hiker, some weeks later, found a lunchbox on a rock, lid missing. The brothers' roommate identified the lunchbox as theirs. He even recalled the sandwiches they had taken along: peanut butter and jelly for energy, and because they didn't go soggy. Two years ago this spring.

The young girl gone out walking the dog on the old Orchard Road. The dog returned. The girl didn't.

The guy who had set off to hike the mesa to celebrate a year of sobriety. He had backpacked with a bivouac sack. His image had been captured at the park entrance, and in the visitor's center. There were a couple of possible sightings by visitors driving by a man with a blue-and-orange backpack. His partner did not raise the alarm until three months after his leaving; three months minus two days after his last sighting. They had agreed that he should take as much time as possible; she took that to mean two weeks, maybe three. But she had been with him for such a long time. They had been through so much together. Was it possible that he had gone back to his habits? She had hoped that this time, he had beaten his demons, that his sobriety might last. She was prepared to give him all the time he needed. Yes, she would take him back. She wanted them to tell him that as soon as they found him. She would take him back.

That had been two years ago. His file was open and cold.

"So many people are going missing, sir."

"Let me guess," said Weismaker. "You're gonna ask me if we need a track reader. Again."

"Yes, sir," said K. He found he hadn't the energy to beat about the bush. "I've been looking at the missing-persons database, and 59 percent are cold cases. That's not good."

"Fifty-nine percent, eh?"

"Yes, sir. You're welcome to check." *And just like that, you were back in primary school. Luckily, computers had calculators.*

"Life's too short," said the sheriff.

"Not for those who are waiting for their loved ones to be found," said K.

The sheriff sighed: "By the way, you've been scheduled for a drug test."

"Why me?" said K.

Becky did not look as happy as she might have: "I don't know. Did you do something silly?"

"Don't I always?"

"What you always do is *dumb*," said Becky, somewhat recovering her spirit, "but you know what I mean ... somebody must have called you in."

"Somebody called me in? You mean somebody grassed me up?" Becky frowned and chewed her lip. "You know who it is, don't you?"

She shrugged and looked away. "You didn't do anything silly, though, did you?"

That Becky was worried compensated somewhat for the indignity of having to piss into a container within eyeshot of some municipal busybody, who was deriving maximum job satisfaction from subjecting a cop to a drug test. The guy had taken one look at K and behaved as if indefinite suspension was already a foregone conclusion:

Never mind. You're gonna have loads of time to go fishing, huh? had been his parting shot.

It had been a while since K had committed any sort of chemical indiscretion, so unless the lab had been instructed to tamper with his sample, he wasn't too worried. Besides, he now knew that Becky, despite practically all her behavior toward him demonstrating the contrary, did not really hate him, was worried about him, even. So he had his old friend back—in theory, at least.

"Did we move the older files out of the annex?" What better strategy to disperse hurt and ire than to dive headlong into the tragedies of others' lives? The annex housed the county jail and the case archive, a not particularly auspicious combination, as they had found out when a prisoner whom Young had been too lazy to search had set his blanket on fire and had nearly succeeded burning both jail and archive down.

"Were supposed to," said Becky, "but didn't."

"Is there anybody down there now?"

"Don't think so," said Becky.

"In that case, may I have the keys?" asked K. Some people had been issued their own keys to the annex, but K wasn't one of them.

"Don't lose them like last time, okay?"

"I didn't *lose* them. I temporarily mislaid them."

"Whatever," said Becky and rolled her eyes.

The annex was dark and silent. The wall-mounted CCTV showed empty corridors, dipped in flickering shadows. K hated the annex; he had not been there more than half a dozen times since that terrible night. Despite all that time spent with the Annoying Counselor and his preposterous takes on PTSD and trauma, despite the purification ceremony that Lorinda had insisted upon to banish vengeful spirits, K still felt the boy haunt the building. Even the purification ceremony conducted by a solemn Native American Church medicine man hadn't brought Lorinda back to the annex. It was Clara, native of Ciudad Juárez, who now cleaned the building. According to her, people in Juárez were more used to living among the dead than the living anyways.

The smell of bleach in the annex was so strong that it served as a paradoxical reminder of what it was meant to make one forget. As K walked along the corridor in the dim light, he thought he could see, as then, the boy's outline, walking so determinedly into the dark.

K shivered and opened the door to the archive. Light pooled at the bottom of the gap of the door to the evidence room. K's hand twitched to his holster. He stood and listened. In the silence, the building seemed to have a life of its own. It creaked and rustled and shifted and moaned. Desert sand borne by a gust of wind smattered against the barred windows; a truck rumbling by made the windows vibrate.

Just structure and cladding antagonizing each other. Enough of the foolishness. Buildings had no souls, and the dead did not leave their ghosts behind.

But it had been like this: K standing in a dark, empty space. It had been exactly like this, his hand on his holster, waiting, listening outside a closed door that he never should have opened—

K rapped on the door and opened it. He heard a drawer slam close. "Oh! Are you working?" he asked. "Sorry! I'm looking for a file."

Córdoba turned. She rested her back against the storage lockers. "All yours," she said.

"I'm not getting in your way, am I?"

Córdoba shook her head, pulled off her latex gloves and pushed a crumpled plastic bag into her pocket. "See you later."

K tore through the filing cabinets. As usual, there was no method to the madness. There seemed to be no designated place for missing files, open files, closed files, or cold files. They weren't filed alphabetically. Nor chronologically. Nor causally. In the end, K found his files stacked in boxes in a corner cabinet that he had taken for Clara's cleaning-supplies cupboard. Each box held five years of missing-persons files, and as they were heavy, a couple of trips would be needed to haul them up.

By now K had forgotten why he was going after the files, if he had ever known. He lifted the topmost box and set it down on the table. Better make sure to leave all filing cabinets locked and in good order: these days, Becky needed hardly any excuse to chew his ass. He went around checking every cabinet. There were quite a few that weren't locked, which he hadn't been near. K made up his mind to tell that to Becky at an opportune moment. It was quite a drag to always be made whipping boy for the whole department.

For good measure, he tried the evidence lockers too, and lo! He found one that hadn't been locked either. Police stations were much like restaurant kitchens—once you were privy to their machinations, you had a hard time ever trusting them again.

At the reception, Becky was on the phone. A frown grooved her forehead, and she was scribbling furiously. The bunch of keys clattered when K deposited them on the counter, and Becky's frown deepened. She shook her head.

"Thank you," K said with warmth and volume. Of late, he was discovering that ham-acted joviality provided greater catharsis than the seething fury that was his default.

In his office, smugness quickly evaporated. He remembered now why he was tearing after those missing-persons files. It wasn't a particular mission to find random folks he'd never met and wasn't particularly interested in. That included Curtis Malone, who, K was willing to bet, was doing just fine and dandy. Malone, hanging out in the wilderness he knew so well, was probably right now roasting a squirrel or some other unsuspecting critter for his lunch, at peace and far away from the aggro of everyday "civilized" life. Had K not been a vegetarian, he would have contemplated that kind of life for himself.

K had remembered the reason for all this frantic displacement activity in the reception area, when he'd forgotten to avert his eyes and had looked up and straight into the anguished face of Alice Nakai.

"Why me?" asked K.

"Coz you're doing nothing right now," said Becky.

"Nothing?"

"Nothing that's important anyways." Becky was undeterred. "I got the stuff ready for you here."

There were worse things than being roped in for courier duty, thought K, as he drove east on the mountain road climbing up to Delgado. The valley opened and widened, verdant and fertile, its foliage green and fresh and thrusting; traces of snow glittering on mountain crests and the cloudless sky so blue, oh-so blue. Cattle grazed ruminatively by the side of the road. A bird of prey swooped, arrow straight, into the brush and rose, carrying a limp, furry bundle in its talons.

One creature's loss was another's gain. There was no morality to it, no justice or injustice. It was simply the way of the world, one providing fuel for the other in an endless cycle, an ever-widening spiral. That was all there was to it, all there was to everyone. Just fuel to keep the world running. It was the whole that counted, not its parts.

Contemplating one's value reduced to the number of calories one provided for anther organism, which in turn would provide calories for another organism, which in turn would provide calories for another, had a curiously Zen effect on K—momentarily, at least, before he started wondering about the effect that cells laden with sorrow, misery, uncertainty, and doubt would have on the cycle of life and level of the universal mood.

"Hey, Franz. Got some new evidence on the trailer?"

"I don't know," said K. "I don't think so." If they'd sent him up here with evidence on a case he was working on, without telling him, then he would hand in his resignation and do what he ought to do anyway, and concentrate on making Agnes Prohaska's bookstore into the beating heart of the community.

Grimes pushed the sealed evidence bag back into the satchel and drew out an envelope, which he proceeded to open. "Ah. Some more evidence." He looked up. "Tell me why you guys are always in such a darn hurry? How am I supposed to get this done in a day? You expecting me to do overtime?"

"I don't know what you are talking about," said K.

"I'll do it. But this is the last time, okay?"

"Sure," said K.

"I'll do it because it's for Juanita. I won't do it for any of you guys, okay?"

"Got it," said K.

"She's stand-up," said Grimes, gooseberry eyes gleaming behind bottle-glass lenses. "If all cops were like her, the world would be a better place."

"Thank you," said K.

"Before I forget," said Grimes, handing over an envelope, "give this to Weismaker."

CHAPTER THIRTY-EIGHT

Weismaker was sitting behind his desk, obscured by precariously towering piles of files, the coffee machine hissing and gurgling like an exorcised demon, fumes rising ceilingward like emissions from Beelzebub's trapdoor.

K handed over Grimes's envelope. The sheriff slid a ruler under its edge, and the envelope opened along a razor-straight crease. Weismaker drew out a sheet of paper and began to read. K remembered Grandpapa opening letters like that. It had seemed like a magic trick, then.

"Coffee!" boomed the sheriff.

"Sir?"

"Get yourself a coffee!"

"What have I done?" asked K, before he could check himself.

"Get yourself a coffee, and I'll be telling ya," said the sheriff, thereby confirming K's long-held suspicion that coffee was a mainstay of Weismaker's inventory of ruthless chastisements. K took his time accordingly, ripping open eleven packets of sugar and sprinkling them, one by one, into a cup he had half-filled with coffee. He sat down opposite the sheriff and began stirring the foul brew.

Weismaker slapped his hand on the envelope. "Why didn't you pass this on to the folks at Creosote Canyon, huh? Why not?"

"Why did I have to take a drug test?"

"Read your contract. You take a drug test anytime you're asked to, and that can be *any time*."

"But why now? Who ...?"

Weismaker sighed, reached into a drawer, brought forth a matchbox, and opened it. "That was found in the ashtray of the patrol car."

K looked at the flattened reefer stubs. "I see," he said. "Just so you know, if the test isn't clear, somebody's tampered with it. Probably the same person who called me in. I don't ride around smoking weed. I'd be much happier if I did."

"Anyways," said the sheriff, holding up the sheet of paper, "anything like this, you just pass it on straight away—if there's any other agency at all that is supposed to deal with this stuff, or that could deal with this stuff, you pass it on to them."

"Sir?"

"You pass it on!" roared the sheriff. "You pass it on, dammit!"

"Sir!" It was pretty disconcerting to hear Weismaker use profanity.

The sheriff stabbed a finger at the envelope and held up a sheet of paper: "You remember that skull? The skull that little boy brought in? What I got here is Delgado's report, and what it says is that this skull is *fresh*, and that there's even a piece of ear hanging from it, and that the skull was ... uh ... severed from the neck with a sharpened flint—which is a historic method alright, but it was done not that long ago, so it's likely we got ourselves some pretty sick killer out there. And thanks to you, it's our case now, and no getting out of it."

K took a gulp of his coffee and spluttered. Sickly-sweet and rancid at the same time, it tasted just like life.

"Now I need you to search wherever the skull came from. We need to find the rest of the body."

"There's a couple of folks here that need to speak to an officer," said Becky.

"I'm supposed to organize a search ..."

"You got no chance of that happening today, anyways. Tomorrow, neither. Use the interview suite, and hurry! The dude is kind of mean-looking."

"Thanks a bunch," said K, turning his back on Becky's smirk.

The folks waiting for K were a beetle-browed, scowling man and an anxious-looking teenager.

"Hi," said K. "You wanted to speak to an officer?" K took the man's growl as an affirmative. "Follow me please." The man hauled the teenager up by the scruff of his T-shirt and gave him a shove. The boy stumbled against the wall. "Let's see how this goes before we get angry, shall we?" K said evenly. He wondered if Córdoba was around, in case he had to file a child-abuse case.

He held the interrogation room door open. The man shoved the boy toward a chair and issued a phlegmy "Sit!" He pulled up a chair next to the boy and sat down, glowering at K from under knitted brows. The man sported an impressive mustache and a chinful of afternoon stubble, and wore heavy-duty work pants stuffed into rubber boots, and a stained white T-shirt. His hands were enormous and calloused.

The boy, who looked anything from a prematurely developed twelve-year-old to a young sixteen, sat with his head bowed. The man slapped the boy on the back of the head. The boy did not wince.

"Please, sir," said K sharply, "there is no need for that."

"My son," said the man, "has done something very bad." The man spoke with a very strong accent that K found hard to place.

"I see. Would your son like to tell me what he did?" It was always preferable to get your info straight from the horse's mouth. The man raised his shovel of a hand. K raised his, and said: "Please. We don't need this. Let's just see how we go without smacking, shall we? What is your name?"

"Afrim. A-F-R-I-M," the kid spelled.

"And your name, sir?"

"Abdyl."

"A-B-D-Y-L," spelled the kid. "Our surname is Hoxha. H-O-X-H-A." The boy spoke without an accent, unless you counted "rural badlands" as accent.

"Thank you," said K. "Hoxha? Like Enver Hoxha?"

"You know Enver Hoxha?" The man unknitted his brows. There was a shadow of a smile on his face. "You know Albania?"

"I know of Albania," said K. "Do you come from Albania?"

The man nodded. "Green Card."

"A beautiful country," K said, although, truth be told, he did not know. The boy was looking at him with large, liquid, brown eyes. "So. What have you come here to tell me?" Abdyl Hoxha raised his hand. "Please, Mr. Hoxha; even good kids sometimes do something bad."

"They all bad," growled Hoxha, "because father don't beat them enough."

If K had wanted to get into the dialectics of corporal punishment, he would have asked how come young Afrim—who, by the looks of it, got licked plenty—nevertheless had still done something bad. "Would you like to tell me what you did, Afrim?" he asked. The boy hunched his shoulders, and his father raised his hand again. "Mr. Hoxha!" said K. "This is witness intimidation!"

"I broke a windshield," the boy whispered.

"You broke the windscreen of a car? Was it an accident? Were you playing football?" The boy shook his head. "So you deliberately broke the windscreen?" The boy nodded. "Did you know the people the car belonged to?" The boy shook his head.

Usually, K's strategy was to sit and wait things out; but with Abdyl Hoxha's massive hands itching for a cuff, this didn't seem advisable.

"He did something else bad, too! Tell to the Mister Police!" Hoxha growled something to the boy that K did not understand.

"I slashed a tire," the boy said.

"Was that the same car or another car?"

"Same car."

"So you didn't know the people the car belonged to? And you slashed a tire and smashed the windscreen?"

The boy nodded. "I took a rock and smashed it on the glass."

"He put a note," said Abdyl Hoxha.

"You slashed a tire, smashed a windscreen, and put a note on the car? What did you write on the note?"

"They were supposed to be frightened," mumbled the boy. Something dawned on K. "Where was this car, Afrim?"

"Near Crowhurst Vineyard. On the hill."

"Crowhust Vineyard in McKinnon Canyon?" asked K. Sometimes cases really did solve themselves, without much input. "So you just found that car and felt like doing some damage and frightening the owner?"

What normal teenager crept around at dawn to damage cars? Unless, of course, there was something very wrong at home, in which case he would need to speak to Córdoba pronto.

Abdyl Hoxha produced from of his pants pocket a sandwich bag, and held it up. In the bag was a twenty-dollar note.

"I find. I ask, 'how you get this?' He don't want give answer." Hoxha clenched his fist. "I make him give answer! He sell drugs? He say no. He steal? He say no. Very bad children in school, you know? Can learn bad things from other children."

The boy's head hung below his shoulders, and he stared at the floor. "We all do stupid things sometimes," K said lamely.

"No, we no do. We want, but father beat us and we learn what is bad thing." Hoxha slapped the bag with the twenty dollars on the table. "You take."

"Are you saying somebody paid your son to damage the car?"

Hoxha nodded: "Give twenty dollars, break glass, put knife in tire, and write paper."

"Is that true, Afrim?"

The boy nodded. He looked up. His eyes were large and anxious: "He told me not to tell anyone. He said if I say something, we will be sent to Mexico."

"You will be sent to Mexico? Why should you be sent to Mexico?"

"He said we will be deported."

Abdyl Hoxha dug into his pocket, produced a frayed wallet, opened it, and retrieved a card: "Green Card! Can no deport!"

"Indeed," said K. "Afrim, are you saying that this person threatened you with deportation if you didn't do what they told you?"

The boy dipped his head.

"I need you to make a statement. Write down everything that happened, how it happened and who told you to do this. How about you sit at that desk at the window?"

"But ..."

"You don't need to worry, Afrim. Not as much as the person who paid you to do this."

Statement signed, K issued a receipt for twenty dollars, and for the sandwich bag. He stood at the window watching father and son traverse the parking lot and then climb into an old truck that looked as if it was being held together by string. The exhaust backfired and the truck drove out, a plume of black smoke obscuring the vehicle. K sat down and read the boy's statement.

"Well, well, well," he said when he got to the end. "You made my day, punk."

Sometimes K almost relished his job. This was such a time. Rarely had he seen someone deflate so quickly, seen arrogance, bravado, and confidence drain in record time as right now, from this captoothed, perma-tanned, mini-horse-fetishizing, entitled human vacuum. For a man presumably making a mint by consulting gullible souls on whatever it was that he was a consultant of, Oppenheimer did not seem to possess even the most rudimentary knowledge of how encounters with the po-po worked. Here was a guy who'd apparently never watched *Law and Order*, never read crime fiction, never had had the benefit of legal counsel. It hadn't taken any more than K presenting his case and reading Oppenheimer his Carmen Miranda to get him to churn out his confession as if a pack of famished cougars were on his trail. And maybe they were. Which was a bit of luck for K, but also a trifle odd; had Oppenheimer not spilled, K would have had to beat it with plenty of nothing in his hands. Surely the guy knew that?

"We shall have to see whether or not the injured parties wish to pursue a course of prosecution," K pronounced weightily.

Oppenheimer whimpered.

K continued: "You do know that 'incitement to imminent illegal acts' is a serious offense?"

Oppenheimer fumbled in his pocket.

"The incited party may, of course, cite undue pressure ..."

Oppenheimer drew out a handkerchief and dabbed it at his brow with a shaking hand.

K went on: "… and attempted blackmail."

Oppenheimer issued a strangulated wail.

K had had more equanimous reactions from impulse killers apprehended shortly after embedding an ax in their old mother's skull. Oppenheimer's distress fanned in him sadistic impulses that K hadn't known he possessed: "It could go down as a federal offense, even."

Oppenheimer made another sound. It was the sound that K imagined Lili Marlen had made when the cougar got her. Poor little pony.

Oppenheimer loosened his tie, frantically tearing at the silky knot. Who went to their office in the Southwestern boondocks wearing a silk tie, really? Oppenheimer's face had gone from brick-red to waxen pale. He grasped at his throat and made a gurgling noise.

"Mr Oppenheimer …" K said.

Oppenheimer gasped, open mouthed, flecks of foaming spittle bubbling at the corners of his mouth. Slowly, he slid off the chair and fell to the floor.

K watched the paramedics load Oppenheimer—oxygen-mask clamped over his mouth—into the ambulance.

"What did you do to him?" the ambulance driver asked.

"Not enough to get him into this state," K said without thinking.

"We'll need your details, Officer," the ambulance driver said coldly.

"Sure," K mumbled. Soon he would have built up a nice little reputation for himself as the Milagro Angel of Death, bringing misery and destruction wherever he went, like a transatlantic Typhoid Mary. He sensed the sheriff wouldn't be impressed.

CHAPTER THIRTY-NINE

For some time now, days had started bright, blue and innocent, like a babe in arms carried forth into the light. The sun would climb the sky and begin its westward surf through the azure expanse. Then came the clouds—first, a gossamer trail of wispy cirri, by and by thickening into a veil; then, a shroud of altostrati; finally, great big towers of cumulonimbi, heralding a much-needed rain ... which never came. The sun would set on a cadmium-tinted sky, ending yet another day when something that should have happened had not happened, and so bringing with the darkness a sense of foreboding. But maybe that was just K.

The veil of cirri was just beginning its invasion of the bright-blue sky when K arrived at the Mesa Ranger Station. On the way, he had pulled over for a freshly hit doe lying on the stony verge, her neck bent back so that he could see the blood pulsing in her veins, her flanks juddering, her breathing fast and labored and becoming faster as he bent over her to try to determine the extent of her injuries. Then her breathing stopped and her eyes went glassy, and just like that she was gone.

Maybe it was better that something bad happened at the beginning of the day; maybe it would spare him from anticipating a crisis or catastrophe—unless, of course, the doe was an omen foreshadowing worse things to come.

The line of vehicles at the entrance to the park was twenty deep, and progress was slow. Maybe this purgatory of exhaust fumes, sunscreen, and frayed tempers was why the sheriff had packed him off on a mesa excursion. K had assumed that Weismaker wanted to avoid the soul-searching and self-incrimination in which he presumably thought K was going to indulge, in the matter of Oppenheimer.

Although technically, K's interrogation of Oppenheimer had been a success, the further development of the interview had arguably not been one. But go figure: the only thing K now worried about was that he *didn't* worry about Oppenheimer. At all. Had he at last acquired the carapace of sociopathy required by his profession?

Every time K got to the mesa, the National Park assumed more of an air of an amusement park. At the foot of the mesa sat the brand-new sandstone, steel, and glass Visitors' Center, surrounded by an artfully designed high desert landscape. The inside of the center was taken over by its shop, which sold an eat-your-heart-out variety of stuffed toys of Magic Dollar quality at 1,500 percent markup, on account of their classification as "educational toys." Fluffy marmots, candy-colored teddy bears, and rubber snakes were what people took away from the mesa.

If the Ancient Ones were ever to visit these environs—as the blossoming cottage industry of mediums specializing in communicating with the spirits of Native ghosts assured the spiritually inclined that they surely and momentarily would—then the Ancient Ones' spirits were in for a real humdinger of an eye-opener.

As to locating Curtis Malone here of all places, K wasn't holding his breath. To even encounter an old-timer like Malone in this ambience would feel like sharing a ski-lift with the Yeti. K would have preferred to get that other wild goose chase over with: the search for the body belonging to little Vernon's skull. But the county jail chain-gang was picking trash by the roadside, so the excursion to Hawksmoor Creek had been put on hold until the following day.

K joined the row of vehicles creeping up the serpentine road to the mesa. It took him nearly half an hour to the Ranger's Station. He found a space in the visitors' overflow parking lot, in the full-frontal glare of the sun, under the lightning-struck and burnt-out carcass of an old Douglas fir. The vicinity of the tree stank of ammonia-saturated vulture piss, and the soil was corrugated with vulture droppings.

The Ranger's Station was a wood-shuttered squat brick building that hadn't seen much change since its establishment in the

1920s or thereabouts. Inside, the station looked much as it would have around a century ago. Walls and ceilings were cured to a uniform nicotine yellow, and smelled accordingly. The row of metal filing cabinets that lined the walls wore a vintage patina, otherwise known as the grime of ages.

Gabe Lockhead, feet in mud-caked hiking boots pressed against the edge of his desk, was rocking to and fro, chewing on a matchstick and contemplating the ceiling.

"Hey Gabe."

Lockhead drew his eyes away from the ceiling and settled them on K. His face was without expression, and K started to wonder if it would be necessary to re-introduce himself.

"Hey, Franz," Lockhead said eventually. "Coffee?"

"Sure," said K.

Lockhead got up and walked, stiff-legged, to the back room and returned with a thermos bottle and two thermos-bottle tops that looked roughly the same vintage as the filing cabinets. He poured the coffee with no offer of sugar, milk, or creamer. The coffee tasted of a mixture of disintegrating rubber, tobacco, and tar, making it loads more palatable than Weismaker's.

"Long time no see," Lockhead rumbled. His voice was indistinct and deep, like distant thunder.

"How are you?" K asked.

"Calculating my retirement."

"Was that what you were doing just now when you were looking at the ceiling?"

"It's what I do every day, the whole day," said Lockhead.

"That bad, huh?"

The grizzled old-timer shrugged. "Who says it's bad? It's something to do."

"But ..." said K. He remembered Gabe Lockhead not that many years ago, still in his prime then, a colossus of a man who looked like some kind of mountain spirit or Green Man, with his wild mane and beard. Gabe had been forever in this job, relished every minute of it, and knew the mesa as few did. "What happened?" K asked. Too late, it occurred to him that he might have overstepped the mark. Gabe Lockhead drew back his lips, exposing fanglike, yellowing teeth. The noise he made was something between a bellow and a howl. It was an unearthly and pretty chilling sound. K took a couple of beats to process that Lockhead was laughing.

"Out with the old, in with the new—ain't that what they say? You saw what they been doing?"

"The Visitors' Center? The 'glamping?'"

"That ain't the half of it," said Gabe Lockhead. "All those kids that come in that want to be rangers? They're working for The Man."

"The Man?" said K.

"Their spirits are corrupted," said Lockhead, and showed more of his nicotine-stained gnashers.

"Doesn't sound a happy place to be."

"There's plenty that want this chair. And they ain't gonna get it." Lockhead issued another bellowing howl.

K cleared his throat: "So, what are you going to do, Gabe?"

"Echechechhwaaawhahaaaaghhh … Nothing. I'm just going to go on sitting here in their way, and know that they are hurting because there's no way they can get rid of me before I'm ready to go. Echechechaaaaghhhh … You just visiting?"

"Well," said K. "Kind of. Visiting and … Do you know Curtis Malone?"

"Curtis? Sure."

"You haven't heard from him, by chance?"

Lockhead spat out the soggy matchstick. He drew up one leg and laid it on the table, using one foot to tilt his chair until it met the wall.

"Did you happen to hear from Curtis in the last couple of weeks?"

Lockhead rocked his chair, forth and back, back and forth. The chair creaked.

"… Did you?"

Lockhead flicked at a match with his thumb. It ignited, and he shoved it flame-first into his mouth. "Any reason you want to know?" he asked, through clamped teeth.

"We were supposed to meet up in McKinnon Canyon, and he didn't show."

"Meet up for what?" asked Lockhead. Pretty nosy, considering his issues with Big Brother or The Man or whoever it was that bothered him.

"For some cougar thing."

"Some 'cougar thing,' eh?"

"Yeah. Some cougar's eating miniature horses down McKinnon Canyon, and the ranchers formed a vigilante group."

"Miniature horses? What's that supposed to be?"

"They are these tiny little horses ..." K began.

"These folks get themselves tiny little horses and they get mad at the cougar for thinking they're trying to feed him? What's a cougar supposed to think?"

"Precisely," said K. An idea occurred to him: "How'd you like to come along and help me educate those McKinnon folks on cougars?"

"Wouldn't like it any," said Lockhead.

"Just thought I'd ask. So you haven't heard from Curtis Malone?"

"Who says I haven't?"

"I thought you ... So you *have* heard from him?"

"Yeah. Must've been last week he asked about some poaching."

"He did? Poaching?"

"Must have been one of those new kids. They like to monitor everything. There been some animals killed and the kids are freaking."

"You're not?"

Lockhead shrugged. "Nobody out there's shooting them. Not using a crossbow, neither. Somebody out there knows how to kill the old way. You gotta be smart and fast. It's a fair fight."

"So Malone was going to follow up the poaching report ... where? Up here?" Lockhead spat the matchstick out in a perfect arc.

"Did he turn up?"

"He was fixing to have a look around. When he was done, he was going to drop in." Lockhead flicked his thumb at another match. The sulfur crackled and burnt bright yellow. Lockhead flicked the match away. It landed on the pockmarked linoleum floor, where it glimmered, smoked, and eventually expired.

"Did he?" Back and forth rocked Gabe Lockhead's chair. *Creak ... creak*, it went. "When was he fixing to visit?" The look in Lockhead's eyes made K glad that this conversation was taking place in a reasonably public place. "I'm trying to do my job, Gabe."

"Eckeckeckwhaahahahahahaawwww ..."

"When was Malone planning to have a look around, Gabe?"

"That day." He pointed a yellowed talon at a calendar on the wall.

"That's the day you spoke to him?"

"Is what I said."

"He hasn't been seen since, as far as I know. He hasn't been back at his office. His cellphone's switched off, and his voicemail box is full."

"Maybe needed some space. Eckeckeckwhaahaww ..."

"You think so?"

Lockhead stuck another match between his teeth. "Possible. How's Weismaker doing?"

"Okay, I guess," K said. "Well ... it's been good seeing you."

"Sure thing," said Gabe. He'd propped his boots back on the desk, and had resumed staring at the ceiling.

At the door K paused. "You said 'the old way.'"

"Huh?"

"You said the animals that were killed here were killed the 'old way.' What way is that?"

"The way they used to hunt eight hundred years ago," said Lockhead, "bow, arrow, snare, and flintstone."

"Bow, arrow, snare, and flintstone? That's *seriously* old school, isn't it?"

"Maybe the spirit of an Ancient One," said Gabe Lockhead, "Eckeckeckwahahaaaghhhh ..."

Outside, the cumulonimbi had been gathering. The parking lot had emptied. K walked toward the skeletal tree under which his vehicle stood, covered an inch deep in vulture crap.

"For fuck's sake," he said. Then he saw that it wasn't his vehicle. His was on the other side of the parking lot, under an identically dead tree. And this vehicle wasn't a patrol car. Nor was it a ranger's vehicle. It was a BLM vehicle. "Holy shit," said K.

"Gabe?"

"What?" Gabe Lockhead didn't even bother moving his eyes from the ceiling.

"I just found Malone's vehicle."

"Whoop-dee-do," said Lockhead. "Let me guess: it was parked out there under that dead fir."

"No, I found it in the ravine," said K spitefully.

"Uh. Somebody must have moved it," said Lockhead.

"You really don't care, do you?" said K. His rage was taking over.

"Care for what? Some car that's parked under a tree? No, you betcha, I don't."

"You know that I am looking for him," said K. Fury had him by the throat, and he could barely speak.

"You think because a vehicle is there, you found something? You looking for a vehicle, or a body? That's what's wrong with all you morons. You can't tell one from the other. That's not how it rolls, brother."

Lockhead took his eyes off the ceiling and fixed them on K. His eyes were approximately the same color as his teeth. He chewed on the matchstick and looked at K with those yellow eyes, which did not blink or falter; he stared in the way that wild animals do: remote, detached, looking through him, beyond him, looking at him as something that might make a good dinner. He bared his teeth; K could see now Lockhead's canines were indeed as sharp as fangs, and he remembered all those stories that he had been told of shapeshifters and skinwalkers, creatures who could switch between animal and human forms, and who should never be met by ordinary humans—because meeting them meant death.

Gabe Lockhead spat, and his matchstick flew past K's ear like a tiny arrow. His eyes lost their remoteness, as if by spitting out the matchstick he had rid himself of some kind of possession. Slowly, he assumed the unkempt, slightly eccentric demeanor of an old-time codger of the type that ran rampant in these parts.

"Well, let me know if you happen to hear anything," said K. Gabe turned his face to the ceiling again, and K left quickly. He peered through the BLM vehicle's stained windows. The smell of ammonia was so strong he had to hold his nose. The car was empty.

He walked along the edge of the precipice to where the canyon narrowed and formed a sharp right bend. The cliffs fell off steeply into a bottomless ravine.

Mesa, the Spanish word for *table*, was a misnomer, only speaking to a superficial first impression that conceived of the promontory as a continuous stretch of high plain. In reality, it was a maze of a thousand gorges and ravines, plateaus and promontories, runoffs and tributaries, caves and sheer rock face, inaccessible cliff palaces and petroglyphs that would never be discovered, would never fall prey to the forensic gaze of archaeologists, would never find their way into guidebooks.

In the east, storm clouds were gathering. Towers of dense cumuli advanced like determined warriors.

A kettle of turkey vultures rode the currents over the chasm.

CHAPTER FORTY

Cuauhtémoc's head was bent deep over the sales ledger. K remembered again his resolution to improve the bookstore's lighting.

"Did you have a good day?"

Cuauhtémoc looked up nervously. "There was this man who wanted to buy a first edition. But there was no price on it. He got kind of mean when I said I had to find out the price first."

"You did great," said K. "The first editions belong to Agnes Prohaska. She's the one who gets to decide if she wants to sell them, and at what price."

"He got pretty mean," repeated Cuauhtémoc. He closed the ledger and began putting on his coat.

"I'm sorry," K said. He put the little box on the table. "This is probably bad timing."

"What is it?" asked Cuauhtémoc.

"It's for you … I mean, it's for the shop. But I'm starting to think it could be a double-edged sword."

Cuauhtémoc opened the box. He took out a card and held it under the mellow beam of the desk lamp: "Oh!" he said, and turned bright eyes on K. His face shone with pure delight. "Can I take one to show my uncle?"

"You can take as many as you like. They are yours. Yours and the store's."

"Thank you! Thank you!" said Cuauhtémoc. He beamed, and was gone.

K made a round through the store. Everything was neat and tidy, the kitchen spotless, Benjamin's bowls washed and filled, the kitty litter tray clean, all books reshelved. Benjamin, his legs twitching in some feline adventure dream, was sleeping on his favorite chair. Cuauhtémoc had made some sales, too.

Time to lock up and go home.

The doorbells tinkled.

A burly figure in hooded top entered the shop.

"We are about to close, I'm afraid," said K.

The figure took no heed, and advanced into the store.

Better lighting would really be an advantage right now, K thought. The NRA brethren would argue that open-carry would be the better advantage right now—or, as a matter of fact, any kind of carry; but K never carried arms anywhere, unless on duty.

"So, you really need to get some books, huh?" he asked amicably.

"Yáadilá, digiis!"

"It's you!" K said.

"*You* need to get your eyes tested!" growled Robbie Begay.

"Better lighting," said K. "Fancy seeing you here! How about some coffee? Or soda water? I got nice cold soda water in the fridge. Or orange juice?"

"How 'bout some carrot juice, huh? If you're going to fuss around like *shimá sání,* I'm gonna leave right now."

"I'm not going to ask you how you are," said K, "but I'm really happy to see you."

"Let's see how long that's gonna last," said Begay.

"Wowzer," said K. "You really are in a mood."

Begay picked up the box from the desk and took out a card. He turned it into the light and read aloud: "THE MILAGRO BOOKSTORE, CUAUHTÉMOC ARRABAL, MANAGER." He flipped the card onto the desk. "I guess I can leave now."

"Robbie," said K, "Don't be like that. What's going on? Why don't I make us coffee and you tell me what's the matter?" He put his hand on Begay's shoulder. "But first, I need to introduce you to somebody." He guided Begay to the nook and tickled Benjamin's ears. Benjamin opened one eye, stretched and yawned. "This is Benjamin."

Begay frowned. "Where is WeeWeeSteen? Did he die? You should have told me!"

During time spent convalescing from a gunshot wound at K's house, Robbie had made a great friend of Wittgenstein, despite his persistence in addressing the formidable tom as "Puddy tat."

"Wittgenstein is alive and well. He's at home catching birds. Benjamin is the store cat."

"Does WeeWeeSteen know you have another cat?" demanded Begay.

"Perhaps," said K, and looked away. "Benjamin was a stray, and I took him in to return a favor." He scratched Benjamin's head. "But now I'm very happy to host him."

"WeeWeeSteen isn't gonna be happy," said Begay gloomily. Coming from a serial adulterer such as Robbie Begay had been in his not-too-long-past heyday, this was rich.

Sitting in the nook with steaming cups of coffee, K said: "You didn't come to talk about cats, did you?" He'd been somewhat relieved to see a slight improvement in his old friend's looks. The shadows underneath Robbie's eyes weren't quite as deep, his cheeks not quite as hollow, and his complexion not quite as puce as the last time he had seen him.

Begay sighed. "I came to ask you for a job. But you already got yourself a manager, huh?"

"I wanted to do something for this kid. He's great. He works really hard—for practically nothing."

"So you're just trying to keep him sweet by giving him some job title that doesn't mean anything?" Put like this, K's grand idea of an honorary promotion and getting cards printed for Cuauhtémoc as a gesture of appreciation sounded like the most avaricious and manipulative of self-serving capitalist ruses. He could think of nothing to say, and shook his head.

"How are your sweat lodges for the Anglo woman going?" he asked eventually.

"They're not," said Begay. "They shut us down."

"They shut you down?" said K.

"Yeah. Don't know if it's gonna be just for a little while, or for good."

"Is she leaving, your Anglo woman?" asked K.

"Don't know. Business was good. But she got this letter about some health-and-safety crap, and some city guy came and shut us down until they investigate it."

"The clients complained?" asked K.

"Don't know who complained." Begay looked up, and the light of the lamp reflected in his glasses. "Bet it was an anonymous complaint, and betcha it was one of those other outfits trying to cash in on sweat lodges—or maybe one of those sour old medicine men that don't like us to share our culture."

"So you are looking for a job. Long-term or short-term?"

"Depends what it is," said Begay.

"Whatever it is, it is bound to be better than running nine sweat lodges a week."

"Well, you ought to be happy that I lost that job." Begay squinted at K and bent forward: "Hey! Did *you* call in a complaint?"

"Me?" stammered K. "No. No, I didn't."

"You wanna swear?"

"Swear what?"

"That you didn't call in a complaint."

K raised his hands. "I didn't call in a complaint. Look, I'm holding up both hands, so you can see I'm not crossing any fingers behind my back."

"Okay," said Begay, and leaned back in his chair. "I know you're too dumb to lie." He watched Benjamin nudging his head against his knees, sighed, and lifted the cat on his lap: "What's this one called?"

"Benjamin," said K.

"Why can't you give your cats proper cats' names?" asked Begay.

"What's a proper cat's name?"

"Django. Or Growler," said Begay.

"I think you should go back to what you are best at," said K.

"Naming cats? Eating fry bread?"

"Track reading," said K. "Finding people. There is a heap of missing persons hereabouts who haven't been found. As a matter of fact, I'm working on a few cases right now."

"You?" Begay whinnied.

"That's why they are not getting found. I was talking to the sheriff the other day, about hiring a track reader ..."

"You talked to the sheriff about hiring a track reader?"

"Did I say that? No. No! The sheriff talked to *me* about hiring a track reader. I think he might have been thinking of you. There's this guy he really wants found ..."

"Well, Milagro ain't gonna be worse than Redwater, is it?"

"Somebody grassed me up and they made me take a drug test," said K.

"Uh. So maybe I can get your job, huh?"

"It came back clear," said K coldly.

"What are the chances, eh?" said Begay.

"Maybe you should apply to the drug-testing outfit. They're always looking for fieldworkers to take the piss. And don't you dare call Benjamin Growler."

CHAPTER FORTY-ONE

It was promising to be a scorcher of a day: not quite 9 AM, and the thermometer was already nudging 80° F.

"I reckon the sheriff is fixing you up for a disciplinary." Dilger stood, legs wide-spread and thumbs hooked into his belt, surveying the orange-jumpsuit-clad chain gang huddling in the shade of the transport van. *So it had been Dilger.*

The drug test had come back clear, and according to the hospital Oppenheimer had suffered a panic attack, not a heart attack; K figured that Dilger was having a go at another opportunity to fit him up. How about assault on a fellow officer?

"How about taking off those leg chains?" said K.

"You want them to run away?" snarled Dilger.

"Why not?" said K.

The night before, he'd taken some time reading through the files of the County Jail's current incumbents. If proof was needed that 'Doing Anything While Brown' was considered a crime in these parts, here were the stats. The majority of the eight-strong chain gang were Native—two Ute, four Diné, one Jicarilla Apache—along with one Latino. Their misdemeanors ranged from public intoxication; domestic disturbance (a trashcan emptied in a neighbor's yard during a dispute); shoplifting (one carton of doughnuts; toothpaste; a 24-pack of Advil); fleeing the scene of an accident (damaging a fence while reversing). There wasn't even a DUI among them. K recognized a couple of indigent street drinkers whom he had been obliged by municipal edict to cite due to contravention of the open-container laws, *aka* drinking in public.

Shuffling in leg chains, wretchedly squinting skyward, the men already knew that the sun wasn't going to be their friend on this long day.

Little Vernon's father, whose name K either hadn't got or had forgotten, was waiting outside the gate of his property. A steep and stony path descended from the roadside down to Hawksmoor Creek. Vernon's dad wasn't sure where his son had found the skull—could be east, could be west, could be on the northern bank or the southern bank of Hawksmoor Creek—and the kid was in school now. Also, Vernon's dad Whateverhisnamewas prayed that the kid would forget about the darn skull, because he had talked of nothing else for the past week, and how he wanted to be an "arcologist." He hoped they would be out of the creek and gone by the time Vernon returned from school, because otherwise there'd be no darn peace for any of them for weeks to come.

Vernon's dad apparently was a hands-off-type of father, or perhaps just a rural-badlands type, who seemed to think nothing of letting his small son explore the creek on his own, with all its dangers big and small, its spellbinding wonders and its blood-curdling terrors.

K took the leg chains off the prisoners while Dilger skulked in the shade. He had cut himself a switch off a bush, which he now slapped against his thigh like a plantation overseer in a movie about the old South. Already the prisoners were wilting in the heat, eyes glazed and foreheads beaded with sweat. None of them had a head-covering, and none of them seemed in robust health. A couple were of retirement age. Each had been issued a broom handle with which to part the undergrowth. None seemed overly curious about what they were supposed to be looking for. K wasn't sure, either.

In view of the fact that four of his courtesy-of-the-Thirteenth-Amendment crew were Diné and therefore probably not too keen on looking for human remains, it had seemed prudent to merely instruct them to watch out for anything that looked unusual. K divided the crew into four teams: down-creek, up-creek, north-bank, and south-bank. Dilger, flicking the switch at his boots, blew his whistle at eardrum-bursting decibels, recalling the men shuffling out of view.

"Y'all think we were born yesterday?" Under Dilger's malevolent glare, the men wilted some more. "You!" said Dilger, "and you! You go together! And you! And you there—No! You! Damn it! You! You go together! What are you saying?"

One of the men had muttered something. Dilger raised his switch and pointed it at the man's chest: "You wanna be here all week? It's gonna hit 110° tomorrow. You like that?"

Dilger had separated the men according to ye olde divide-'n-rule ruse: three teams were made up of Ute/Diné; the fourth team consisted of the oldest person—the Hispanic man—and the youngest, the Diné shoplifter. Perhaps Dilger was less dumb than K had given him credit for, or, as they said, it took one to know one. K, however, knew that at least two of the Ute were on bottle-sharing terms with a couple of the Diné. He called after the teams disappearing listlessly into the undergrowth: "When you hear the whistle, it's lunchtime."

"Lunchtime?" said Dilger. "There ain't no lunchtime. They each got a bottle of water. That's gonna be it."

"You know that's illegal, right?" said K.

"Yeah? Who's going to complain?"

"I am, if they don't," said K.

"You serious?"

"I would hope that my jokes are slightly funnier than that," said K.

"Well, we ain't got nothing to give them. How about that?" K saw the flicker of an idea ignite in Dilger's eyes. Well, it was not so much whatever happened in that empty window to Dilger's hollow soul than that his squint was accompanied by a slowly widening smirk. "How about I drive over there to City Market and get them some lunch? Or to Subway? How 'bout that? You got any cash?"

"No need," said K, "I got their lunch in a cooler in the van."

"*You* got their lunch? Why'd you get their lunch?"

Because I know what a creep you are, K thought. Supervising chain gangs was mainly Dilger's domain, and if K, yesterday on his way home, hadn't stopped to chat with Lorinda, who had been cleaning reception, he wouldn't have known that the food budget for County Jail chain gangs never reached the prisoners. Lorinda had a cousin who was one of the jail's revolving door customers, and he had told her what everyone out in the community knew: when you were called up for chain-gang duty, a bottle of water for the day was about all you got. As usual, people did not complain, because they did not know their rights. They did not know that the jail, besides having the pleasure of their free labor under the Thirteenth Amendment—a handy exemption clause to the abolition of slavery, permitting "involuntary servitude" for the purposes of criminal punishment—was also supposed to have a duty of care. As it was, and this spoke to the strength of *k'é*, Lorinda and Roberta, the station's cleaner and the jail's cook, and their assorted kin clubbed together on work-days to provide food for the prisoners to take along. K was hoping that Lorinda and Roberta, as advised, were working right now on their relatives to write anonymous letters of complaint addressed to the sheriff.

Dilger flicked his switch at low-hanging branches and said, "Gotta do the paperwork." K watched him haul his ass up the incline, his heavy tread setting loose minor avalanches of gravel and rock.

Up and down the creek, there was a rustling of undergrowth, murmured conversation, and the occasional exclamation. K walked a ways downstream, where a Ute/Diné team was wrestling with a jute sack. K was pretty sure what was in there. So was the Ute man: "It's gonna be puppies," he said, lifting the sack. "Too heavy for kittens. It's gonna be puppies. Big puppies." He didn't seem particularly fazed. He opened into the sack. "Told you so." The Diné man held his face averted.

"Are you okay?" K asked him, because he himself wasn't. The man shook his head. He was saying something; K had to bend near him to understand.

What he was saying was: "That's why I started drinking."

"You started drinking because of drowned puppies?" K asked. The man was now talking softly; it wasn't clear whether it was just to himself, or if he wanted to be heard. Whichever it was, it would have been rude to walk away in mid-sentence. Eventually, K got the gist of the man's story. As a kid, he had been designated to dispose of unwanted puppies and kittens, of which there had been many, many litters. He hadn't liked doing it, but he hadn't thought much about it, either.

Then, during a stint of mandated rehab at Redwater Treatment Facility, a caseworker had arranged a traditional diagnostic ceremony for him. And this was where he had learned the cause for his lifelong behavioral track record of being "out of balance."

The Diné didn't hold with messing with Nature, and with senseless killing. After the diagnosis, a healing ceremony had been scheduled.

"They organized a ceremony for you?" Sometimes those ceremonies did in a few, intense hours what took Alcoholics Anonymous a person's whole lifetime.

The man shook his head: "They cut the budget for the medicine man," he said.

"That's a pity," said K. The man stared at the ground, tracing circles into the dust with the tip of his sneaker. "Is there somebody else to organize a ceremony for you?"

Nobody. The man had been disowned by his family. There were no relatives looking out for him. K left the man contemplating the sack full of dead puppies with drooping shoulders and a face harrowed by pain. He wasn't clear about the procedure for handling quantities of massacred baby animals. It felt wrong to leave them here, their tiny, tortured bodies decomposing in the sack—them, and all the others that would be found before the day was over.

"Put anything that you find over there," K said. The men lumbered toward the undergrowth. K was pretty sure that the south-side team had gotten the easier section. Most of the litters were dumped on the north side, where it was just a few steps from curb to a sheer drop.

K crossed the creek to the north side and saw that he had been right. The north-side downstream team had a pile with four sacks, and they had barely been searching for more than half an hour. K didn't have the heart to make them open the sacks, so he had to do it himself. What he found made him hate humankind even more than he already did, and he hadn't thought that was possible. He walked some ways away from the search party and rang the number for Pet Rescue.

"I know," said the woman on the other end of the line. "That's why we offer that free neutering service." She sounded close to tears. Pet Rescue was mainly staffed by volunteers, and the kind of people who volunteered for such outfits were usually those least equipped in terms of mentality to deal with cruelty to animals.

"I'm sorry to bother you," K said, "but I was wondering what to do with the animals."

"There's the pet crematorium," she said. "Do you want me to phone them?" Her voice sounded somewhat brighter. K thanked her profusely. He felt somewhat lighter. How awful to imagine that little Vernon, instead of his not-so-arcological skull, might have come across one of these gruesome finds.

And with perfect timing from upstream, there came a scream— no, a roar—that filled the creek, bounced off the walls and rose as a sound-cloud skyward, making the turkey vultures scatter.

CHAPTER FORTY-TWO

"We are your favorite people, huh?" said Grimes. K smiled weakly. You had to have a pretty strong stomach to be able to make jokes in a situation as this. "You can send these guys home," Grimes continued. "We got everything we need from them."

"I'm taking them." Dilger was green around the gills.

"Need a mask?" asked Grimes.

"Please," K gasped.

"Look, boys," said Grimes. "Why don't you go back to the station?"

"But ..." choked K.

"There's nothing you can do here, I promise you. To be truthful, y'all are more of a hazard right now. With scenes like these you need to be real careful about cross-contamination. The smell's gonna get a lot worse when we open the vehicle. Just go, and we'll keep you posted, okay?"

K drove. The prisoners in the back of the van looked stunned. K had to stop twice for somebody to get out and retch into the ditch. Lucky that they had had their leg-chains taken off. There would have to be a ceremony. Or two, depending whether or not folks decided to go pan-tribal in the face of horror.

The old Latino man alone sat immobile, regarding his fellow prisoners with an inscrutable expression through rheumy eyes. "Are you okay?" K asked while helping the old man out of the van when they arrived at the jail.

"I seen it before," said the old man, "when they found my wife."

"How long is it going to take until they know?" asked Córdoba.

"Depends if there's any ID on the body. They can be pretty quick with preliminary results, if there is."

"Great," said Córdoba, which seemed a rather callous and somewhat out-of-character remark.

"I suppose that's one way of looking at it," said K. "You're looking happy today. Have you fixed your wedding date?"

Córdoba frowned and shook her head. K had a horrible feeling that perhaps he had dreamed up Córdoba visiting the bookstore with Dana. He looked out the window of the break room and drummed his fingers on the table.

"Here," said Córdoba, "have a coffee. You've been through something today."

"I haven't, really," said K. "It was those poor guys who found … it. Anyway, Dilger rang the sheriff and the sheriff asked us to stay away from the scene and called in Delgado right away. So I haven't really been through anything."

"I once found this woman. She'd been there weeks. It was summer. You never forget the smell."

"She died alone?"

"Her husband murdered her. And left," said Córdoba grimly. "And then he drove into a ravine, and by the time he was found he smelled just like his wife."

K looked at Córdoba: "That's quite …" he said weakly.

"He got what he deserved," said Córdoba. "His wife didn't."

K sipped. "Good coffee," he said.

"That guy," said Córdoba, "you know that psycho, who assaults Native women? I think we got him now."

"The guy with the creepy lawyer who was scaring off witnesses? That's great news! How did you get him?"

"There was some evidence they had overlooked," said Córdoba.

"Great!" said K. "That's lucky, that they found the evidence!" He remembered his drive to Delgado. "Is it the stuff Becky made me take to Forensics?"

Córdoba looked past his head at the wall clock and got up. "Got to hurry." She took her cup to the sink, adjusted her holster, and left. K slurped his coffee and tried to shake off the troublesome imp inside him, which insisted on digging up and inspecting discordant memories. "All's fair in love and war," he said loudly, just as Young entered the break room. Young sucked air through his teeth and barely budged when K squeezed past him and out the door.

CHAPTER FORTY-THREE

"There's no sugar," said the sheriff. "Some things you just can't sweeten, son."

K clenched his hands around the coffee mug while Weismaker let him have it straight. Then he did as bidden, and installed himself on traffic duty on the bypass, a couple of miles from the Kachina Village Development. After a scant hour he'd bagged himself four speeding tickets from the kind of folks who could afford them without losing a night's sleep—which was as good an outcome as there could be for this type of task. The sheriff had been adamant that the only way for somebody who'd survived drowning in the high seas to swim again was to be pushed into rough waters, so that's what that was about. That still didn't help K any on how to deal with that whole heap of mess after work was over, and he didn't want to taint the bookstore, his refuge and benign space, with the state he was currently in.

So he went to Barbie's, where Magnusson was nowhere to be seen; a raucous crowd was misusing the juke box, and Bella the barmaid kept rolling her eyes at him in mock exasperation. At least for the first few beers, she did. Then she took to asking, "Are you sure?" when he ordered the next one. Eventually, a woman joined him at the bar, and after a couple more beers they went back to her motel. She was Estonian or Latvian, but they didn't talk much anyway.

In the early dawn, K pulled on his clothes, left the motel room, and walked the mile along Main to Barbie's, where he picked up his car.

He managed to banish his terrible thoughts until he had fed Wittgenstein, put on a load of washing, and taken a hot shower.

Then the awful realization washed over him like a tsunami and he sat, head in hands at the kitchen table, whispering, "Oh God, oh God," while Wittgenstein nudged his legs making little mewling sounds, as if trying out a new language.

Over Resting Warrior Mountain, a high wind whipped dense clouds across the horizon. From here, the clouds looked like the Four Horsemen of the Apocalypse deliriously hastening toward calamity.

Hawksmoor Creek appeared harsh and unwelcoming in the leaden light. At the spot where it had happened, yellow police tape whirred in the wind.

"She started accelerating over there, where the road straightens," said Grimes. "She worked up some speed ... It's like a runway, that stretch, you know?" K cleared his throat. "... And then she just sailed over the edge." Grimes looked at K. "She wouldn't have felt anything. Her truck hit that boulder at a ferocious speed. The impact was devastating." He gestured at the road: "Over there she must've gotten that little old truck up to 90 miles per hour. See ..." Grimes made as if to trace some kind of speed-acceleration-velocity diagram into the air. His gooseberry eyes sparkled with forensic zest. He looked at K's face and lowered his arm: "She didn't feel anything. At all. Honest. The last thing she would have known is flying through the air." He raised one elbow like a fledgling bird raises a wing and held it there for a moment, looking at K. His eyes had lost their sparkle and were dark with concern. K grasped that Grimes had been about to nudge him with his elbow. From Grimes, that intended gesture was what a bear hug followed by a bloodletting bonding ritual would have been from another man. K tried to smile, and nodded. They stood side by side staring into the abyss, until the last sliver of sun had been swallowed by clouds and left the creek lying in a sulfurous hue.

The warrant poster had gone from the bulletin board in reception, and Becky was looking at him with a worried face: "Are you okay?" *Why did people only show they cared when you were too low to appreciate it?* He nodded and walked past Becky's desk into his office, which seemed dark and dank and dusty even when he pulled up the blinds and opened the windows.

He tugged at the lemon verbena plant—the gift of a grateful wife for locking away her violent husband—and pulled off a leaf, rubbing it between his fingers. Its bittersweet scent mingled with the smell of dust, and did little to lift his mood. A truck loaded with sheep rumbled past. One of the sheep looked straight at K. He looked away. Then he picked up his phone, chewed his lip, gazed after a low-rider motorcycle roaring past, scrolled down, and dialed. The phone rang. And rang. He would let it ring until the call was cut off. At least he would know he had really tried.

There was a click in the line. Somebody had picked up. There was no other sound.

"Mrs. Yazzie?" said K. He thought he heard an intake of breath. But he wasn't sure. He listened to the silence, covered the phone with his hand, and drew a ragged breath. "Mrs. Yazzie? I'm so sorry. So very sorry." His voice was shaking. There was a sound that could have been a stifled sob. He wasn't sure. He stayed on the line, silent, until he heard a soft click, and the call disconnected.

CHAPTER FORTY-FOUR

"No!" said Begay. "We been through all that crap before—remember? I said everything I had to say then. Get real, dude! It's just life. It's life, man! Shit happens! What you need to get is that what you are doing right now is unloading your crap. On me! All that's gonna do is make us both feel bad. You think the same stuff hasn't happened to me? I'm a cop too, remember? It's probably happened *more* to me than to you, coz I'm better at my job … Keep it shut!" he advised, when K opened his mouth. He tossed his daypack into the back of the truck and motioned for K to get in: "Got all the stuff we're gonna need?"

K nodded.

"It's a new dawn and a new day and we're feeling fine!" declared Begay. He turned the key in the ignition, and the truck sputtered to life. Then he accelerated out of the parking lot and barreled up Main while whistling tunelessly. About five miles into the drive, he began to intersperse his whistling with hissed incantations: *It's a new dawn, it's a new day, it's a new dawn, it's a new day, it's a new dawn, it's a new day, it's a new dawn, it's a new day, it's a new dawn, it's a new day, it's a new dawn, it's a new day, it's a new dawn, it's a new day, it's a new dawn, it's a new day...*

K watched the stony outliers of the mesa fly past; the shrubby plain stretching to the San Matteo Mountains; the ghostly pallor of the new dawn languidly taking on the faintest of blushes; the mesa's jagged contour looming steeply before them. They drove past the shuttered ticket huts. The transmission groaned as Begay shifted into low gear.

"Don't worry. We're all legit," said Begay.

"Why do you want me to play lookout, then?"

"In case anybody gets the wrong idea and makes us waste time we ain't got. Anyways, get over yourself. It's all done."

"That was quick."

Begay wrenched open the vulture-waste encrusted passenger door, opened the glove compartment, and retrieved a service manual. He clicked his tongue and replaced the manual. "Anything in the back seats?"

K looked over his shoulder before he opened the door. "Nothing."

"Sure?"

"Pretty much."

"Anything on the floor?" asked Begay.

"Nothing."

Begay walked around the vehicle and opened the back: "All clean."

"How did you open the back?" asked K.

"It was open," said Begay. "Just like the driver's door. And the passenger door, too."

"The car was open? Why'd you let me stand there, then, watching your back?"

"Didn't want you to get bored," said Begay.

"Curtis cleaned out the vehicle and dumped it here?" asked K. "I don't understand."

"Maybe he did, maybe he didn't," said Begay. He circled the car, peering at the locks, shading his eyes, and squinting at the windows. It was still early; the parking lot lay deserted, and the early-morning air retained the night's cold bite. Begay walked to the balustrade overlooking the precipice. "Is he a climber?" asked Begay.

"I don't know," said K. "He's an outdoorsy type. I imagine he would know how to climb if he had to." He joined Begay and peered over the balustrade. The rock face fell away steeply and relentlessly. "You'd have to be pretty desperate to climb here, wouldn't you?"

"Some people like this kind of thing. Mostly, *bílagáana* like this sort of thing. *Bílagáana* like to make trouble for themselves when there's no need to," said Begay. "That's why it's harder to figure out *bílagáana*, coz they don't always use common sense."

"I don't know if Curtis Malone would just climb into a ravine for the hell of it," said K. "I'm sure he would, if there was an eagle's nest or something he had to rescue."

"Could be he tried to climb to an eagle's nest and the eagle didn't like it," said Begay. He began walking along the precipice until the balustrade ended and there was just the path winding along the cliff-side. Behind them the sun's first rays tickled their necks. Before them the path vanished behind a curve. The terrain descended gradually. After a few hundred yards the path got lost in undergrowth.

"You got water and a jacket?" asked Begay.

"Yes, right here in my backpack."

"Let's get going."

"But where? Why are we taking this way and not the other side?"

"We got to start somewhere. Could be we are here for weeks. Or months."

"Like that guy who went missing on the footpath and never was found?"

"What guy? Where?"

"Some guy who went missing a couple of years ago. He just walked down that paved path over there to the ruins. His wife was waiting for him and he never showed up…"

"Where?"

"Over there, just a couple of miles from here."

"This must be the most thoroughly searched place on the whole Mesa," said K, as they trotted down the wide, paved path to the ruins. "Shall we have a look in there?"

Begay looked at the ruins nestling cozily in the rock cavern and shook his head. "There's nothing there."

That's when K saw a shadow moving at the far side of the recess. "There is. Up there," he whispered.

"Hey! You! Come on down or we'll come and get you!" boomed Begay.

"Are you crazy?"

Begay raised an eyebrow, scratched his ear and crossed his arms over his chest. "Come on down! We ain't got all day! And bring your stuff along!"

Out of the shadows crept one, then a second figure carrying bundles. Slowly they made their way across the cavern and down the stone steps.

"Did you clean up after yourselves?" asked Begay.

"Yessir," muttered the teenagers.

"Good," said Begay. "Now you go home." The boy and girl loped up the path. "Don't forget to book in for an exorcism!" Begay called after them. "Plenty of evil spirits around!"

"How did you know?" asked K.

"Why do you think your sheriff needs me?" asked Begay. "I'm the greatest."

"So you are," said K.

"You sure are easily impressed," said Begay. "Didn't you see their car over there?"

"Their car? No."

Begay snorted and cast his eyes at the sky. "That old low-rider with the graffiti? Practically screams 'teenagers making out.'"

Begay walked ahead until he came to a fork in the path. The sign to the left read "Petroglyphs" and the sign to the right said "Staff Only" hung on a pole barrier.

Begay contemplated the petroglyph path that meandered up and down the rock face, disappearing behind a boulder and further on reappearing near the top of the mesa.

"That path just loops back to the parking lot," K said.

"You don't say!" said Begay. "Come on!" He squeezed past the barrier. It was an unpaved road on which they were walking, used by rangers and maintenance crews and occasionally, fire fighters. After a couple of miles they came upon another fork in the road. The unpaved road continued to the left, and a stony path led to the right. Begay beckoned to the right. They walked on the stony path descending in undulating serpentines. High above them, the mesa crest sparkled in the sun's early rays.

Even if they did not find anything, and K didn't hold his breath that they would, this was a pleasant hike at least. A ladder-backed woodpecker tap-tapped his way up a tree. A chipmunk high-tailed it out of the undergrowth and took sentry position atop a boulder and a blue jay seemed to be shadowing their walk.

"I think we got a companion," said K, pointing at the bird regarding them curiously from a nearby branch.

"Where do we go?" Begay asked. The jay rose from its branch, flew a leisurely circle and disappeared into the ravine.

"What are you waiting for?" said Begay and began sliding over the rubble down the slope.

"We are following a bird?"

In the course of his life K had learned that just thinking a positive thought would lead to its instant reversal. Served him right. The rubble moved and rolled beneath his boots and he became aware that he was not so much walking down, as being carried by the momentum of rolling stones. Before him he saw Begay sprinting down the decline in great leaps. So K did the same. The clacking on stone propelling stone became a roar, as K flew over the scree that now moved under him like a tsunami wave. He saw Begay taking a wide jump to the left and did too. Begay was clinging to a lop-sided tree that was growing out of the mountainside with one hand and gripped K by the arm with the other. An avalanche of rubble whooshed past them and thundered into the chasm below. K made to free himself from Begay's grasp, but Begay tightened his grip. From high up there came a clanging sound and a man-sized boulder came thundering down the decline, bounced over the edge of the slope and crashed into the abyss.

Begay kept listening long after the boulder had smashed into the ground, somewhere deep below them. Eventually he nodded, let go of K's arm and began picking his way along the edge of the ravine. K copied the way Begay used brush and undergrowth to gain foothold on the steep slope. The slope went on for another hundred yards or so, and then abruptly dropped off. It took all his discipline and concentration to set foot before foot with infinite caution.

"Do you have any idea where we are going?"

Begay continued working his way across the brush and made no answer. Above them the canyon walls seemed to be growing taller and extending skyward. They were so tall that the sun, even at its zenith, would do little to relieve the shadows. K looked up, stepped on a loose rock that literally jumped under his step and set in motion a minor avalanche.

"I'm okay!" he called out.

No. He didn't hold out any hopes of finding Curtis Malone. And truth be told, Robbie's tracking methods seemed pretty erratic so far. K didn't mind, because the one thing he had hoped to get from this trip was some time out from his tormenting thoughts, the dreadful regrets that haunted him yet again, the what ifs and buts that crowded out every other thought. This trek was turning out awful enough to almost count as penitence. Negotiating undergrowth vis-á-vis abyss took enough concentration not to leave much space for lament and sorrow. K kept his head down, his eyes fixed on brush and shrub, trying to avoid thorny tentacles, treacherous rootwork and fatal missteps. After a while his mind emptied of thought and he felt like a machine, an unstoppable machine advancing relentlessly, annihilating obstacles.

The top of the mesa glowed in psychedelic purple and the sun stood in the sky like an unseeing eye that would not reach. This was the view from Hades, from so far down that the shadows never lifted and the rocks were never warmed by the sun's rays. It was the netherworld. It was Ni'hodiłhił, the First World of the Diné, the World of Darkness, before the Emergence, before Black Cloud met White Cloud; before beings were shaped; before they were given form and gender. They were the Mist People. Here they were: The Mist People. The Diné knew much about where they had come from and where they were supposed to be and how they were supposed to be, but not where they were going. As far as K knew the Diné didn't give much thought to where they would go to after being in this, the Fourth World. In matters of the after-world, if there was one, the only edict was to keep clear of the dead, who had lost all chances of getting things right, and their places of dying.

Maybe that's why Robbie Begay was being so erratic: Robbie wasn't supposed to be here. Robbie knew that he wasn't supposed to be here. And Robbie didn't trust his old buddy K enough to share his misgivings. K realized now, too late as ever, what Begay had meant, when he had chewed him out for *unloading his crap* on others. K had taken this as a purely pedagogic rebuke, the kind of character-forming thing a parent would say to a child. As usual K had not looked beyond his own nose, had not understood that Begay was not rebuking him so much as pleading with him not to burden him with his crap, because he had some crap of his own to deal with too. Shame made his ears burn and remorse twisted his gut.

"Robbie!" he called out and looked up and ahead. There was no Robbie. There was nothing here that he recognized. This was another place entirely. It was a place of towering, jagged rocks separated by rifts and chasms, stark and arid and forbidding like a fortressed city of ghosts and spirits. No scree, no slopes, no brush, no undergrowth, just towering rocks pointing skyward like skeletal fingers.

"Robbie!" he called and listened to his voice traveling along the canyon, rebounding off cliffs and returning as polyphonic reverberations that filled the gorge and rose upward as so many pleading cries: "Robbie."

CHAPTER FORTY-FIVE

He did not know where he was. He did not know how long he'd been walking. He did not know where he was going. He was all alone.

The landscape around him was alien and menacing, and the sun was beginning to vanish behind one of those pinnacles way over there. He was walking on a ledge halfway between bedrock and pinnacle, with no way up or down: a kind of purgatory, which was just okay with him. He walked along the narrow ledge, which was slightly wider than a tightrope.

He had given up calling for Robbie some time earlier, when he began to question whether or not Robbie had ever been there with him. He had called and listened to the sonic boomerang of his voice, and had had the thought that it would not be so unlike Robbie Begay to play K's echo, to be sitting behind some boulder laughing his ass off as he watched K calling into the void. That was what K had anticipated: a little prank played on an old buddy to teach him something about Nature.

But there had been no answer, no laughter, and no boulder with anybody hiding behind it. In fact, there hadn't been anything to establish that Robbie had ever been here—except for K's daypack, which contained a water bottle, a windbreaker, and four apples. Two of those apples had probably been meant for Robbie. K hadn't yet drunk any of the water. In the gorge's cool shade, there was no great need for water. It was a *bílagáana* obsession to carry water bottles everywhere, like weaning toddlers. Robbie Begay conducted nine sweat lodges a week, and K had never ever seen him with a bottle of water. But maybe that was why he had looked so ill?

K called out Robbie's name once more, and listened to the echo amplifying the anxious kink in his voice. And then he stopped call-

ing, because a person doing a thing all alone out there and not getting
a reaction would be stripped very rapidly of the capacity to think in
the way that the person had been able to when surrounded by other
people. Maybe that was what they meant by that question about a tree
making a noise or not when falling alone in a forest. It had taken no
more than however long he had been on his own to question whether
or not Robbie had ever been here with him, to whether Robbie existed at all, to whether Robbie Begay was just a secret friend construed
by K in the manner of a child in need of congenial company. This
hypothesis seemed as plausible as any other; for why had he found
himself in this place, where there was no going back, and going on
seemed to lead nowhere? Would Robbie Begay, had he been here—
and if he existed at all—really have been so reckless as to tumble
down a slope after a jaybird to lead them into this neverland?

K balanced along the ledge. The shadows deepened, and he
didn't feel anything; maybe he was a machine, or maybe it was *he*
who did not exist, and Robbie was looking for him or wondering if
he had imagined him, if K had existed at all; but Robbie—if indeed
Robbie, or the projection of K's needy imagination that might be
Robbie, existed—was too solid, too grounded in whatever it was
that people called reality, for such wondering. In Robbie, K had
created exactly what he needed, a *yin* to his *yang*, or was it *yang*
to his *yin*: his opposite, his composite other. So Robbie Begay was
indeed an altogether too complementary persona, hence, too good
to be true or to have been true.

But perhaps all this was one of K's waxing-moon dreams, those
dreams in which he tended to get lost, dreams that led him through
apocalyptic landscapes and into menacing labyrinths without ex-
its. Usually these dreams had to do with Grandpapa, and for some
time K had believed that these pockets of terror that he visited in
the night, or which visited him, were a small tribute that he paid to
Grandpapa and all he had gone through. *Lest we forget,* and all that.

Maybe he was just asleep. Not sleepwalking, but dreaming of
walking. One way to find out was to step off that ledge and into
the void.

Step off that ledge.

CHAPTER FORTY-SIX

His shins were raw and his hands were bleeding and cold sweat was pooling on his neck, and every single one of his bones hurt; so presumably he was alive, and not dreaming. He was back on the ledge. He didn't know how he had gotten back there. Everything hurt; lightning-sharp stabs of pain coursed through his body with every move.

It was dark. A full moon rose, vast and cruel, behind a pinnacle that looked like an osseous digit. From the top of the mesa came the high-pitched yipping of coyotes. The moonlight played tricks with shadows, throwing shapes onto canyon walls and creating recesses and alcoves on the rock face that had looked smooth in the dank light of day.

What had looked forbidding hours earlier looked downright hostile now. K struggled to control his ragged breath. The shrill yipping of the coyotes, like eerie, demented sirens, was closer now. The pinnacles shone in a cold, viscous light that made the shadowy ledge seem even darker. He shuffled along without lifting his feet, terrified that the ledge would end and he would step once again into the void. As long as he kept his feet on that precarious path he would be alright, just setting one foot before the other, never losing touch, never losing contact with the ground.

His legs hurt, as if the ground was holding onto him and trying to drag him down. Shuffling along was becoming harder, taking a lot more strength. He went on setting foot before foot, his breath rattling deep in his chest, his body fighting him with every step; he felt as a tree might, trying to extract its roots that had merged with the dirt over so many years, just to go on … to go on. But why go on. Why not step off that ledge again and be done.

Why not fly off that ledge, as Alice Nakai had done some thousand feet below, in Hawksmoor Creek. Maybe this was his fate, and his penitence: to end here, in the place of the Ancient Enemies, extracting their due for the life of Alice Nakai. An eye for an eye, a life for a life. He felt, briefly, all the spirits that had ever walked the land and were earthly no more, whirring about him, pulling at him, beckoning, teasing, and oh, how close their world was to this.

Then they were gone, and he was all alone again.

The moon now stood straight above, looking near enough to lasso it with a rope-ladder and to climb up to its pockmarked luminescence. And so he dragged on, every sinew and bone in his body flaring, suspended in a dream-time of pain, for wasn't pain what made you human, what made you alive. By dint of which he surely was very human and very alive right now.

Like the Little Mermaid, who had left her element for love and who had doomed herself to a life of pain, K heaved along the torturous path as the moon shone brighter and brighter and the shadows around him shrank away; the moonlight was blinding now; maybe he had climbed up to the moon's surface. Maybe he was dead. Maybe he had been snatched up by aliens.

Around him, all was bathed in a glaring light. Below him darkness yawned. And he was three steps away from the top of the mesa: three small steps for mankind, a giant feat for K. He sank on his raw and bleeding knees, crawled those last yards on all fours, and pulled himself up on the mesa that lay like a silver platter in the moonlight; he crawled along on all fours away from the abyss, and collapsed under a gnarled piñon.

"Fancy meeting you here," said Walter Benjamin. He was wearing a houndstooth tweed jacket with leather patches on the elbows, and was smoking a pipe.

"Sir," stammered K.

"Call me Walter," said Walter Benjamin.

"I don't think you ought to smoke here," said K. "It is very dangerous."

"Why not?" said Walter Benjamin. "We are dead, after all."

"Are we? Oh ... I know you are dead, sir ... Walter ..."

"As a matter of fact, I died somewhere just like here." Walter Benjamin traced a sweeping circle with his pipe. "Well, maybe not just like here, but close enough."

"Did it hurt?" asked K. "Dying?"

"Hurt? Not so much," said Walter Benjamin. "Although, had I known I would have saved myself that schlep up that blasted mountain with that bloody suitcase."

"I thought you ..." said K, and stopped; for who was he to re-mind a loquacious dead philosopher that he had died by suicide in a dingy hotel room, and not on a mountaintop? "Did you come to fetch me?" K asked.

"I came because I'm here. And to tell you to make sure you enjoy the selenelion. It's the moon you want to keep your eye on."

CHAPTER FORTY-SEVEN

The ground was cold. K hugged his legs to his chest and pressed his back against the tree bark. The tree cast a bell jar-shadow on the moonlit plateau. His body hurt like hell, but in his soul burned a small flame, kindled by that magic visitation. He should have asked Walter Benjamin about the Arcades Project; he should at least have told him that it was one of his favorite philosophical treatises.

"Don't worry, Master," he could have said. "It is such a great work, because it is unfinished. Because it is fragmented. Because that collection of thoughts and quotes and explorations feels exactly like walking through that place and its labyrinthine history, with enough oxygen to fan one's own thoughts. It is a meditation, that's what it is. And it always makes me feel enlivened when I read it."

What was the "selenelion?" An ethereal beauty, high up in her turret, serenaded by a troubadour, yearning for another place, that's who K imagined Selenelion to be.

The plateau lay glittering in the waning moonlight. K leaned against the tree, did as the Master had bidden, and kept his eyes on the moon. If he was dead like Walter Benjamin, why did his back hurt so much? And his legs? And his arms? And why was he so cold? Perhaps death was merely an amplified version of all the sensations that people took to be exclusive to life? Maybe death wasn't the great void, but the petty irksome?

Had Walter Benjamin really been a messenger from the afterlife? Truth be told, had K not known right away who he was, Walter Benjamin would have seemed more like a Walmart greeter than an illustrious herald from the Great Beyond. If K was dead, shouldn't it have been Alice Nakai visiting him? Or Robbie? *Oh God, Robbie* ... He set his palms on the ground, trying to push himself upright. It hurt so much he felt sick. He leaned back against the tree. His body convulsed in the cold. In the west, the moon was sinking. In the east, the dawn's first light drew a red line along the horizon.

K kept his eyes on the sinking moon withdrawing its light from the plateau, like an outgoing ocean tide. The promontories on the western edge cast solid and substantial shadows on the plateau, shadows within shadows that seemed to move and crowd together. Were they the shadows of the thickets and misshapen trees that swayed in the breeze? Over there, that tall tree … surely it was moving?

It wasn't a tree. It was a bear, upright, its pelt hanging loosely about its body; a bear striding out on two legs. K folded into himself, rammed his knuckles into his mouth to stifle a moan of pain, made himself as small as possible. Was that what you were supposed to do when meeting a bear in the wild? Make yourself small and play dead? Or was that how you were supposed to act with cougars? It was make-yourself-small with one, and big-yourself-up with the other. He couldn't remember which was which. But he knew that bears had a very fine sense of smell. Mostly they weren't carnivores, preferring the scent of honey to the smell of blood. Unless the bears were grizzlies.

But no, this wasn't a grizzly. This was no bear at all, but a human with preternaturally elongated, skeletal extremities clad in pelts. Human or humanlike: for the creature pranced in a circle, threw up its arms, faced the moon, bowed, crouched, and broke into a demented Rumpelstiltskin dance—an eerie, obscene, sensual, downing-moon dance, bowing, scraping, twirling dervish-like, then striding away and snatching from somewhere in the shade a kind of makeshift broom made of branches and drawing it over the ground while strutting, leaping, and twirling in gleeful abandon, and sweeping, sweeping.

K's eyes burnt and his lips bled from biting them; the bark was cutting into his bruised back; and yet he felt like a spectator at the theater, certain that the main act was still to come.

There was a mighty swooshing and bounding, and here he was again, this Caliban of the high plateau, sighing and groaning, dragging something across the ground: a substantial shape trussed in a wrap of woven grass. He dragged the shape with enormous effort, panting and gasping and murmuring, into the middle of the space he had swept. Dancing around the shape, he mouthed and mumbled spells, prayers, incantations, holding high a flint that flashed jagged in the moonlight. Diving down and running the flint along the woven wrap, he opened it, laying bare what lay within: the shape of a man, naked and immobile. *The shape of a man ...*

K gasped. The cry that had just begun to form was never born. A hand clamped over his mouth. The iron hand kept him pinned against the tree, and a hoarse voice whispered: "Be quiet. For Christ's sake, be quiet and don't move. Don't move, whatever happens!"

It wasn't the menace, it was the terror in that person's raw whisper that kept K quiet, even after the hand was removed from his mouth. Caliban was prancing around Robbie Begay's still body, still praying, with that terrible jagged flint held high over his head. The figure stopped, held the flint up at the sinking moon in the west, turned, and then held it up at the sun rising in the east. Maybe this was the final standoff between the moon and sun, facing each other across the horizon. Maybe this was the end of the world.

Caliban bowed before the aligned Father Sun and Mother Moon, proffering the flint, tracing an ellipse over Robbie's prone body.

"Oh, God—he's going to sacrifice Robbie!" The hand clamped on his shoulder, but K tore away. Nothing hurt now. On bleeding feet, he loped toward the man with a terrible, inhuman scream that he did not think had come from him; it carried through the mesa and set the coyotes howling as if answering to their master. K threw himself at the man and felt the flint digging into his arm. He got hold of Caliban's wrist, saw the flint glinting above him, felt the warm blood running down his arm, and swooped his elbow under the man's chin. Then his feet were pulled from underneath him, and he tumbled to the ground.

"Jed! It's me, Jed! Jedediah!"

Caliban stood still, arm raised, the flint pointing downward like a butcher's knife.

"Where have you been, my friend? I've been missing you," said Curtis Malone. "Things haven't been the same since you left." He spoke softly, hypnotically, repeating tender phrases, while the pelt-draped Caliban—Jedediah Unruh—changed into an emaciated, confused man with sloping shoulders, arms hanging by his side, fingers curled loosely around the flint.

Malone took Jedediah Unruh by the hand and plucked the flint from his fingers.

"I liberate their souls," said Jedediah Unruh. His voice was unsteady.

"Souls?" said Malone.

"I catch them and free their souls." Jedediah Unruh stretched his hand toward the flint, pointed at Begay and made a slashing motion: "I free their souls and let them fly into the sky."

K crawled to Robbie Begay, who lay pale and still. He put his ear to his chest. He heard it: he heard Begay's heart beating, evenly and steadily. He put his hand on Begay's forehead and smoothed away his hair, and then laid his cheek against Begay's face. "Wake up, *shik'is*. Wake up. You're okay. We are okay." Tears coursed down his cheeks and landed as great salty beads on Begay's face. "Did you just pull a face?" said K to his still friend, stroking his hair and his face. "Don't worry, *shik'is*. Don't worry. You are okay."

"Come along, Jed," said Malone. "We can get you some help."

"It is all of *you* who need help," said Jedediah Unruh. He now looked tall again, and not quite human—more like a desiccated tree, or the spirit of one. He held up an arm as if still holding the flint. On the horizon, the waning moon's beams and the rising sun's rays crossed daggers.

"Come with me," said Malone. "All's going to be okay. Everything's going to be good, Jed. I'm looking out for you. I'm always going to look out for you, Jed."

The dawn breeze ruffled Jedediah's pelts. He looked down at Begay and K. His eyes were pure turquoise. He threw back his head, turned his ravaged, bearded face toward the sky, and spread his arms wide. The sun's rays framed his body in a flame-red aureole against the lead-gray horizon.

Jedediah Unruh took one step back. And another. And stepped over the edge, into the void.

CHAPTER FORTY-EIGHT

"He had himself a regular bone house here," said Grimes, shrouded in billowing protective gear. Delgado Forensics had helicoptered in several crates in which to transport the bones.

"How many are there?" asked K.

"We got three skulls, but more bones. Four people, I'm guessing. Maybe five. That skull you sent us probably belongs to one of them."

The cave was cool and dark, and the bones had been stacked carefully and according to some method that was only apparent to those of a particular mindset.

"Look how clean these bones are!" said Grimes, a femur in his gloved hand. "He knew his stuff. You put the bodies out in the sun and it takes the vultures barely a couple of days to pick them clean. Neat, huh?" K felt that he would never look at turkey vultures the same way again. "So, you lost Begay and you came up here and you found that guy?" Grimes continued.

"More or less," said K.

"How did you know it was Jedediah Unruh?"

"Just a guess," said K.

"Damn good guess," said Grimes. "I'm serious, though, how did you know it wasn't somebody else? One of those guys that went missing? Or that Fish & Wildlife guy that Weismaker is so worried about? That's what your sheriff asked me right away, you know? He asked if the guy who fell was Curtis Malone. Are they buddies?"

"I think they might have been," said K. "I don't know."

"Maybe Malone's bones are here?" said Grimes.

"Maybe they are."

"You had a shock, huh?" Grimes said sympathetically. "You've gone through pretty bad stuff." Behind his glasses, his gooseberry eyes were wide and sorrowful. "You're not going to blame yourself for this one too, are you?"

"No," said K. "I'm not blaming myself for this." He met Grimes's eyes and did his best not to look away: "It's better that way. They would have put him into some secure unit. Can you imagine—after living out here for so many years, ending your days in some fluorescent-lighted cell with barred windows? Jedediah's better off dead."

"You didn't push him, did you?" asked Grimes. "Sorry! I was joking. My bad!"

"If he had killed Robbie, I might have."

"Begay's going to be alright. It's just concussion. And probably exhaustion and shock," said Grimes. "He's going to be your main witness. He's our sole survivor. You better treat him good."

"Better than he treats himself," promised K. Robbie Begay had been airlifted to the hospital, where he was hopefully slumbering his way into convalescence.

Squeezed in between four cooling boxes stuffed with human remains, K did not enjoy the helicopter ride down to the valley as much as he might have. From above, he could see yellow police tape marking the spot where Jedediah Unruh had hit the ground. From here, he could also see the burnt patch that had been Emma and Samuel Nakai's trailer.

"He didn't suffer, did he?" asked K.

"Not at all," said Grimes. "Falling's not such a bad way to die. Falling backward is even better. There's no faster, surer way of dying, I guarantee you that."

CHAPTER FORTY-NINE

"I'm getting bored of visiting you in hospitals," said K.

Begay nodded. His skin was papery, and there were purple shadows under his eyes. He looked at K as if from far away, or through fog. K had a hard time holding Begay's gaze. He had a hard time breathing. He couldn't think of anything to say.

"I'm gonna be okay," said Begay, and patted K's arm. His hand was cold and clammy.

"Sure you are," said K.

"I don't want to talk about what happened up there," said Begay.

"You don't have to. Really, you don't."

"Just one thing—was there another person there?"

"Jedediah Unruh," said K, "the guy who abducted you."

"I know about that guy," said Begay. "I'm talking about another guy. Was there another guy?" K shrugged. "Was there another guy?" insisted Begay.

"Time to leave now," said a nurse, poking her head through the door. "This patient needs a lot of sleep."

"Dom Benally will run a sweat for us when I'm out of here. A real sweat lodge," Begay called after him.

"I send you to look for one man, and you go and find another?" The sheriff cleared a stack of files from a chair and motioned for K to sit down. "How are you, son?"

"Okay," said K. "I don't need any more counseling, if that's what you mean."

The sheriff raised his eyebrows. "How are you?" he repeated.

So K ran through his whole spiel again. It had gotten to the stage that he pretty much believed what he was saying. "I'll be just fine when Robbie Begay gets out of hospital."

The sheriff nodded. "How did you find Jedediah Unruh?"

"He just appeared. Like on a stage."

"Like on a stage, eh?" Weismaker clicked the nub of the ballpoint pen. *Click-click-clickety-click.* The sound had a finger-nails-on-blackboard quality. "What are we going to do about Curtis Malone?"

"Delgado Forensics took away the remains. They are going to go through the missing files and contact relatives of people gone missing over the past five years for DNA samples, and they are going to check those against the remains. There are at least four, maybe five, but only three skulls—Grimes thinks that skull the kid found in Hawksmoor Creek is one of them. He thinks it was prob-ably washed down, and then got carried along downstream after a heavy rainfall—"

"Hold your horses, son. I was asking about Curtis Malone. You think one of them could be him?"

"Malone? No. Oh no, sir, I don't think that."

"What *do* you think?"

K kept his eyes fixed on a spot between Weismaker's eyes. "I don't know."

"I'm not asking you what you know, I'm asking you what you *think.*"

"That's what I'm saying: I don't know what I'm thinking."

"I see," said the sheriff. *Click-click-clickety-click.* "What do you think we should do?"

"There are people who don't want to be found."

"Jedediah didn't want to get found, I bet," said the sheriff.

"Not everyone who doesn't want to be found is going to act like Jedediah." Though K could think of some who might. But it seemed okay: an antidote to what they were doing out there on the plain, all the slashing and drilling and burning and pillaging. The more this went on, the more the number of guys like Jededi-ah—liberators of souls—was bound to grow. There was a beautiful symmetry to that. Maybe K would join them one day.

"You sure?"

K nodded, though he didn't know what he was supposed to be sure about. He could think of several things, and he could be sure about none of them. Sometimes you just had to let be.

Let be.

"You had a close shave, eh? Glad to have you back, friend." Magnusson was carrying a cake box.

"I can smell cinnamon," said K. "Did your friend visit again?"

Magnusson smiled bashfully. "*I* baked them for you."

"You did? I didn't know you could bake!"

Truth be told, he couldn't. Magnusson's *kanelbullar* were as compact as cannonballs, and only randomly more palatable. Under the big Swede's tender gaze, K nodded enthusiastically, took a second bite, and swallowed hard.

"How are you?" asked Magnusson.

"Allergic to concerned frowns," K snapped.

"Was I frowning?" said Magnusson. "I didn't mean to."

"What happens on the mesa, stays on the mesa," said K.

"I don't know what that means, and I'm not going to ask," said Magnusson.

They sipped their coffees. The silence hung thick. K bit into the *kanelbullar*, just to hear a sound.

Benjamin came into the nook and looked from K to Magnusson, and from Magnusson to K. If Benjamin sat on Magnusson's lap, K would take that as a sign and keep silent. If Benjamin came to sit on his lap, though, he might speak of it. Benjamin continued to sit between their chairs, a contingency for which K hadn't planned. K scratched his knee. His shins were still hurting. Basically, everything was still hurting.

Benjamin crouched, tensed his muscles, and jumped on K's lap.

"He would have come to me if you hadn't scratched your leg," said the perceptive Swede.

"He loves me," said K. He had meant to say it jokingly, but it came out sounding way too serious.

They sipped their coffees and stared at nothing in particular. Benjamin pushed his head hard against K's sore ribs, and purred.

"What do you think of dreams?" K asked Magnusson.

"Did we not have this conversation before?" said Magnusson.

"Did we?"

"Yes, I think it was about dreams and predictions. But I can't remember the conclusion we came to."

"When I was up there ..." K began. "... It's easy to lose touch with reality, you know? But maybe that's just me."

"Well, it is scary to get lost," said Magnusson.

"I wasn't talking about being scared," said K. "It was more like finding myself on another plane, you know?"

"I *don't* know," said Magnusson. "Why don't you tell me what you need to tell me?"

"I dreamed that Walter Benjamin visited me."

"Walter Benjamin! One could have worse visitors. What did he say?"

"Quite a lot. He seemed to think that he had died on a mountain, and that we were both dead. And then he told me to enjoy the selenelion, and to keep my eyes on the moon."

"Seems as good advice as any," said Magnusson. "And did you?"

"Yes," said K. "I did. But that's not the point. The thing is that I didn't know what a selenelion was. As far as I know, I had never heard the word. I just looked it up today. The point is, there *was* a selenelion that morning, just as he said. It's not a frequent occurrence."

Benjamin yawned widely and kneaded his paws on K's shirt. Magnusson sneezed, smiled at Benjamin, and sipped his coffee.

"So ...?" K eventually said.

"So what?" said Magnusson.

"Do I need to spell it out?" K felt both foolish and irritated.

"No," said Magnusson patiently. "That was my comment: so what?"

"Walter Benjamin teaches me about selenelions, and you say 'so what?'"

"No," said Magnusson. "For that, I envy you. I wish Walter Benjamin would visit *me* and tell me about lunar eclipses. About anything, as a matter of fact. I would be honored even if *this* Benjamin came and sat on my lap ... Apropos laps, your enchanting schoolteacher came to see me. She wanted a translation of your dedication in the book you sent her." Then the big Swede's clear blue eyes held K's, and he said: "Grasp life with both hands. Live. Marvel. Suffer. Forget. And repeat."

"What about Walter Benjamin's selenelion?"

"Accept your visions as a gift."

"A gift from the other side?"

"There are no sides, my friend."

EPILOGUE

The air was crisp and cool. An unseasonable wind was blowing in from the east, over a cloudless, pale blue sky. The river had shrunk to a trickle, making its leisurely way down the riverbed. The raging fire had died down to glowing embers some time earlier.

They entered the sweat lodge crouching, pushing aside the heavy, black felt draped over the entrance, moving clockwise through the pitch-dark cocoon, lowering themselves on the dry, sweet-smelling earth, and feeling the heat radiating from the nine rocks in the pit at the center.

They listened to Dom Benally's high-pitched call to the spirits before he drew the felt tight over the entrance, banishing the last sliver of daylight. And then there was a complete absence of light, a darkness so dense it wrapped itself around the body like a cloak, made the eyes forget they had ever seen. The darkness opened up all other senses wide to make up for the lost one.

Water hissed and crackled as it hit the stones and rose, reborn as a mighty cloud of scorching steam that mingled with the pure, bitter scent of smoldering sage. Skin burned, blossomed in the heat; pores opened; sweat beaded, dripped, coated the body, cooled and cleansed and purified.

Each spoke a welcome, an incantation, an invocation of the ancestral spirits, hunkering in that dark and comforting space all made of fire and water and earth, here now, side by side, zygotes as then, before being; as then, before this world; before the emergence. And the spirits gathered, drew close, unquiet no more, in this place of fire and water and earth, this place before time and in time and after time. This place for all.

There are no sides.

ACKNOWLEDGMENTS

Soon it will be twenty years since my first association with the Four Corners. I never thought then that one day I would convert my experiences, real and imaginary, into mystery novels. That I have done is not least due to the many people who hosted, helped and supported me; who shared their stories generously, who contributed their thoughts and opinions, and those who have held my hand through hard times and good.

Thank you:

Nancy and Bruce Maness and the 'village' at South Forty; Judy Wolfe and Mike Duncan; Kathryn and Rod Eckart.

Beta readers Andreas 'Eagle-eye' Diebold, Petra Villinger. Tania M.

Authors and mentors Chuck Greaves (aka Joseph K Greaves: *Church of the Graveyard Saints*), and Mark Stevens (*Alison Coill Mystery* series); Sara Pritchard (*Crackpots*) 2016 Leapfrog Fiction Prize Judge; Dr Robert Snell ('Portraits of the Insane').

Anita Pete and 'grandbabies;' Fernando Nakai and the Nakai family; Sharon Keating, Aidan, Gracie Mae and Louis (who has a special place in this book); Dorothee Shinoda; Gabriele and Haschem Lindner; Karin Hwezda and family; Lilian Umar-Bell, Tim Bell and family.

Amoo Jamshid Medhat and family; Kip and Tebby Wafer and the Polk family. Laura (for the story of the mini-horse and the cougar), and Steven Maness (for his story of the skull in the creek).

Staff of Cortez Public Library; Mary Fuller and students and staff of Cortez Adult Education Center; Montezuma Moms Demand Action; Marian Rohman and For Pets' Sake Humane Society; The Rural Utah Project, advocating for and empowering overlooked communities in rural Utah; Four Corners Vegetarians and Vegans.

My publishers Leapfrog Press (USA) and TSB | Can of Worms Press (UK): Rebecca Cuthbert; Tobias Steed; Lisa Graziano; Mitch Albert; Mary Bisbee-Beek.

In gratitude and loving memory of Jeanne Fitzgerald, who helped me in more ways than she ever knew, and in memory of Rosemarie Sauermilch who fought for a just and better world.

ALSO BY THIS AUTHOR

The Quality of Mercy – The First Milagro Mystery

"The quality of mercy is not strained; It droppeth as the gentle rain from heaven Upon the place beneath."
William Shakespeare; The Merchant of Venice

Franz Kafka, aka K, is pretty much settled in his humdrum small town cop routine: applying sobriety tests to drivers under the influence, reuniting stray pets with their owners and breaking up the occasional domestic. When the body of a young man is found near Chimney Rock, K and his old buddy Robbie Begay of the Navajo Nation police find themselves drawn into a case that challenges their collective skills set and that is as perplexing as it is disquieting and as mysterious as it is tragic.

Lacandon Dreams – The Second Milagro Mystery

A missing teenager and a failed suicide lead Southwestern K to a cabal of environmental destruction, corrupted ideals and a merciless vendetta.

Milagro, boom and bust town, between mesas and desert badlands, is ruled by good ol' boys high on guns and shale. K is caught in a dystopian nightmare where Big Energy is fêted for fracking the life out of the county, a teenage girl's mysterious vanishing is callously ignored, all the Sheriff's men are out training schoolteachers to shoot and the mighty melting pot is a witches' cauldron of intercultural discontent. Navajo cop and soul-brother Robbie Begay's anarchic investigation methods and virtual track-reading skills lead where K's principles won't let him go, while an old Lacandon woman's dreams play havoc with K's certainties and open doors to another world.

CPSIA information can be obtained
at www.ICGtesting.com
Printed in the USA
JSHW051105310822
29992JS00001B/1